Likho

Likho

A Gothic Mystery

DJ Darton

Copyright © 2024 DJ Darton
All rights reserved.
ISBN: 9798321399125

To the forgotten.

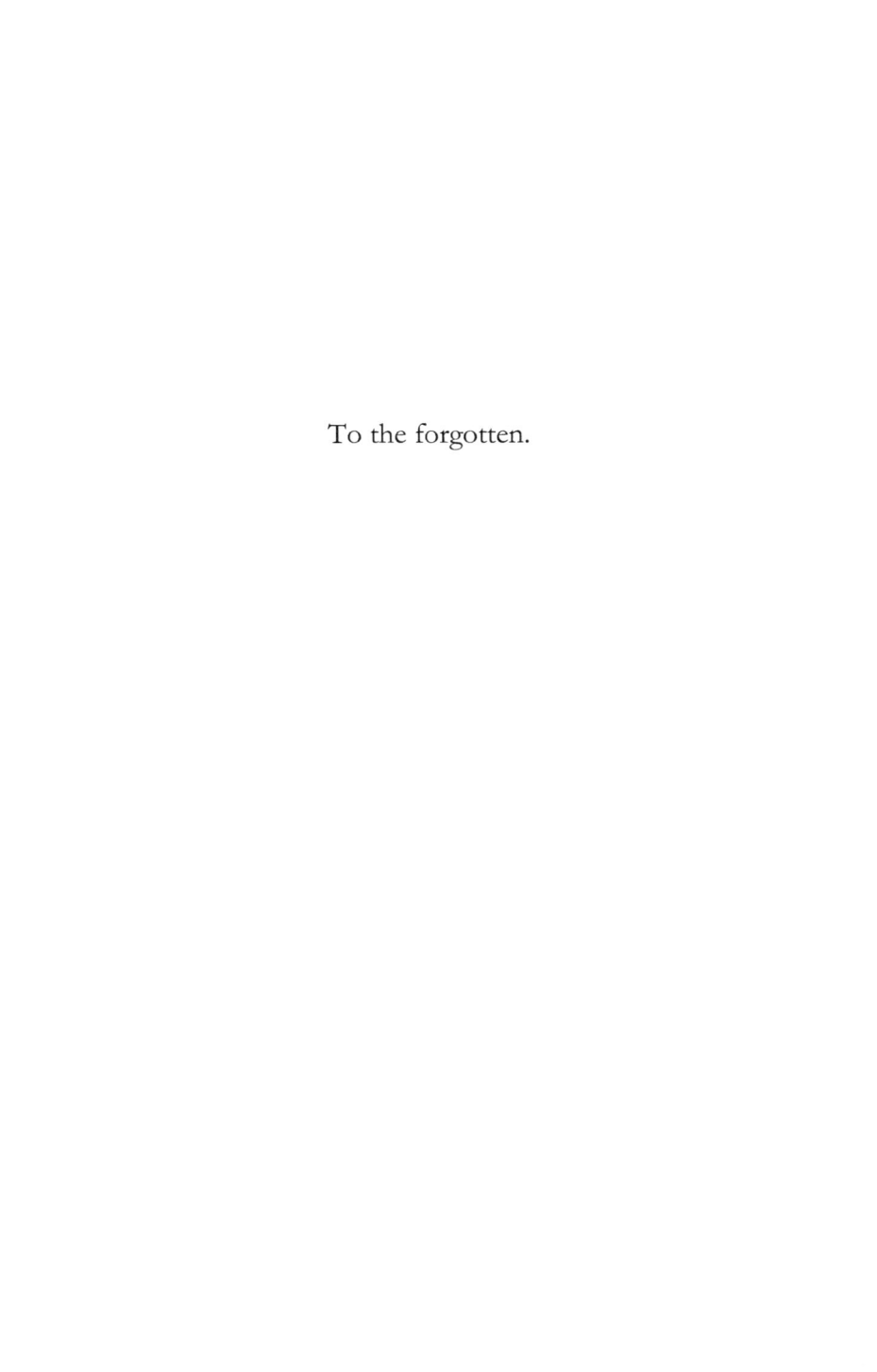

CONTENTS

	Preface	xi
1.	Au Théâtre des Ombres	15
2.	The Carpet and the Coin	39
3.	Creeping Out Of Sleep	55
4.	'Whosoever Believeth…'	83
5.	The Story of the Door	111
6.	A Mysterious Messenger	131
7.	The Stone Guest	139
8.	Der Mond	151
9.	'What Dreams May Come…'	161
10.	Subtlety and Suggestion	177
11.	Shadows, and Shadows…	197
12.	The Isle of the Dead	213
13.	Scaffold or Asylum?	225
14.	Sanctuary	241
15.	Ex Paradiso Expulsus	261
16.	'What In Me Is Dark Illumin…'	275
17.	One-Eyed Likho	299
18.	'A Sadder and a Wiser Man, He Rose…'	313

Preface

It is more than thirty years since first I saw the journal you are about to read. I was living in central Europe at the time, in a city where mediaeval streets and alleys lead you through more than fifteen hundred years of history, a city full of myths and legends where a ghost story lurks in every doorway, and a storyteller behind every door.

The manuscript came into the possession of a friend who found himself sole heir to the estate of a distant cousin of whom he knew nothing. Part of the bequest was a large apartment in the old town, and naturally curious, I was happy to go along with him when he went to have a look at it…

Having remained unoccupied for decades, the place was in a very poor state. The floors were bare, the walls damp and blackened with mould, stucco ceilings crazed with cracks, and cobwebs hung heavily in every corner. It was bare of furniture, other than in one of the larger rooms where an old threadbare armchair sat by the fireplace, and next to it, a small table on which stood a dust-covered wine bottle, a glass, and a bundle of papers which, on inspection, seemed to be the diary of a man whom we supposed to have been the last occupant. Thinking it might be of interest, we took it away with us…

The first sheets were missing, so we don't know if the author identified himself on a title page, or when he started his journal. As it is, the record begins part-way through a conversation with a neighbour, and so we must take the part of late-arriving eavesdroppers and try to catch up as best we can.

His narrative leads us through a series of strange and disturbing events, in a picture-postcard mediaeval city where dreams and nightmares crawl steadily from sleep to invade the day, and the terrors to which darkness gives existence force their way into the light. Unable to break free from the ghosts that begin to haunt him, and which conflict with a philosophy that he refuses stubbornly to abandon, can the man hold on to his sanity?

Though it has been many years since first I read his story, it has come to mind often, and I cannot help but wonder what became of the poor fellow? Did he end his days confined in an asylum somewhere, screaming at shadows? Or might he yet be sitting in a threadbare old armchair, in a decaying apartment, with only those shadows for company?

Anyway, read on, and then give some thought to this — does a man's troubled mind confine within itself the demons it invokes to terrorise him? Or might that mind become a door through which, once conjured, they are free to pass into our world?

Finally, before I leave you, would you like to know if *I* have ever seen a ghost? Well, honestly, I cannot say I have. And I cannot say I have not...

And what about you? What do *you* say?

DARTON.

"The mind is its own place, and in itself
Can make a Heav'n of Hell, a Hell of Heav'n."
 —**John Milton, Paradise Lost.**

Likho

1. Au Théâtre des Ombres

Page intentionally blank

Darton

Page intentionally blank

he leant forward and, as he moved, the threadbare chair on which he sat groaned, as if the shifting of his weight pained its old joints.

"A *photograph* of a ghost?" I responded dismissively, "I wouldn't believe it to be genuine. Such things are easily faked, and I'm not so gullible."

"No? No. I don't believe you are." The old man's colourless dry lips cracked as they stretched into a grin which exposed his crooked and rotten teeth to the yellow light of the gas lamps, releasing a wave of foul breath into the room. The stench was repellent and caused me to draw quickly away from him, a reflex action which afforded no chance to mask my disgust, and which I was certain could not have been unnoticed or misunderstood.

"Quite" I replied, "I accept no proofs other than those obtained through my own experiences, though I am not always inclined to believe what I see because even one's own eyes are capable of deceit… as, indeed, are *all* human senses."

"You shouldn't be so suspicious. Not everyone is trying to deceive you."

"You may be right, but it is no matter because I *prefer* to be deceived. I think it is flattering – it takes thought and imagination to deceive; no thought or imagination ever went into being honest…"

"No doubt that would be thought very funny in the right company…" the old man sneered. "But for all your wit, you are too much of a cynic."

"To be a *wit*, one must first *be* a cynic, I think?" Feeling pleased with myself, I paused for a response; if he *was* amused, he said nothing and left me to fill the silence. "But anyway, as you might have gathered by now, I am a

Sceptic... or so experience leads me to believe, though I have my doubts... but then, *doubt* is the only certainty."

"Well, that is your lookout, my friend."

"I don't see why?"

"Because as some clever fellow once wrote *there are more things in Heaven and Earth than are dreamt of in your philosophy...*"[1]

"Ah, well, *my* philosophy does not compass *Heaven*."

"You might want to think again about that." The old man thrust his head forward and stared hard with his eyes wide open; it is difficult to say what colour they are, though *whatever* it is, they looked badly bloodshot, and the harder he stared, the more I feared one of those pulsing capillaries would rupture.

"I see no point," replied I, "in concerning myself with a place I shall never see."

"Oh? What makes you think that?" He relaxed back into his chair and sat with his arthritic hands casually clasped before him.

"My mother told me," I said with an unnecessary but satisfying smile, "and my mother was right about all things; indeed, being right about all things was vital for her continuing good health." For the record, that is not true; it was my father who was infallible, or so he told us. My mother *did* tell me once that I would never go to Heaven; I don't recall what I had done to merit eternal damnation, but as I was about four or five years old at the time, it can't have been too serious.

"I see..." he said with a nod, his cracked old face breaking into a smile, "and did you believe her?"

"Of course. A young child believes everything it is told. It is no matter though because only good atheists go to Heaven. But enough of this... my present concerns are with this world rather than the next one... specifically our neighbours."

"Well, if you don't believe what I say, what is your theory?"

"*Theory*? I'm not sure it's worth a *theory*. I have heard voices coming from that apartment... people talking and children crying. I haven't imagined it, and I am not mad. I have heard them several times, and very clearly too. *You* tell me it must be a family of ghosts and are surprised that I don't believe you."

"Well, sir, that apartment hasn't been occupied for years... many years... *twenty*? No, forty... or *fifty*, maybe... so I can think of no other explanation."

"And yet there must be one."

"You refuse absolutely to accept there might be any possibility at all of such a thing?"

"I do not deny the *possibility*. I ask only for proof, and without proof, I deny it as a present reality. It's very simple, really – if ghosts *do* exist then someone would have proved it by now, but no one has ever done so conclusively. Man has had thousands of years to find proof, but has he? *No*, he has *not*. As it is, all evidence is anecdotal... ghosts exist only in the minds of children, the feeble-minded, and writers of fiction. The supernatural is a creation of men desperate to believe in a continuity of existence beyond death. I accept no such thing because nothing exists until it is proven to do so, and no one can say I am wrong."

"You may argue that nothing exists until it is proven, but you cannot prove that a thing does *not* exist – and you cannot dispute that..."

"I do *not* dispute it" I interrupted, "because my position as a Sceptic allows me to hold that two opposing conditions can exist at the same time, until one or other is observed and the question settled."

"Ah, then you want the best of all worlds. I see no point in any further argument."

"Well, we are in agreement there, at least..." Hoping that signalled the end of it, and anxious to get away, I took a couple of steps towards the door. "I will admit, though," I added, casting a glance around his shadowy sitting room, "that if one were seeking the perfect *mise en scène* for telling ghost stories, one would need to look no further than here. But never mind because you cannot frighten me with such things."

"I have no desire to frighten you... or to have anyone else do so." The old man shook his head and smiled, as if trying to look like a kindly grandfather expressing disapproval of a wayward child's bad but endearing behaviour; if that *was* his intention, he succeeded only in looking even more sinister.

"You would be wasting your time" I replied dismissively, finally taking my leave of him.

Stepping out on to the dimly lit landing, my only thoughts were of warming myself by the fire but, as I halted to retrieve my key, I couldn't help thinking of the old man's words: why had he felt it necessary to assure me that he had no desire to have *anyone else* frighten me? It was an odd thing to say, was it not?

The only sound to disturb the silence was made by my keys as I pulled them from a waistcoat pocket, and, strangely, I found the noise rather reassuring because I was feeling a little unsettled for some reason or other. Perhaps I am more open to suggestion than I admit? Maybe talk of ghosts bothers me after all? Now there is an idea too ridiculous to accommodate.

Likho

The lamps in the stairwell are just bright enough to enable a safe descent but do not cast any light beyond the edge of the treads, leaving the middle in darkness from top to bottom throughout the night. I say *stairwell* but that is not really what it is... actually, I am not certain what its original purpose was. It is a square and solid tower at the centre of the house, with stairs built into the walls and which climb in irregular flights to the upper floors; the absence of balustrades means one must take particular care, and a fall even from my landing would no doubt result in fatal injuries.

It is only a few paces from my neighbour's apartment to mine, so I was soon at my door where, with a shivering hand numbed by cold, I let myself in and went directly to my bedroom where the fire was still burning nicely in the hearth. Throwing off my coat, I sat down to warm myself. As blood began to circulate to the tips of my fingers and the extremities of my imagination once more, I couldn't stop my mind from wondering on to the subject of the old man... alone and confined, as I suppose him to be, in that room. And *what* a room? I've never seen anything like it in my life... it is in such a state of disrepair that, in my opinion, it should be condemned as uninhabitable. Perhaps my standards are unreasonably high, but even so, I wouldn't keep pigs in such conditions...

No doubt the place has known better days; it must once have been a fine and elegant apartment, and, perhaps, the old man a complement to it? One cannot help but wonder what events have led that home and its occupant to their present state? It is none of my business, of course, but even so, I struggle to suppress my curiosity.

On the occasions I have visited, there was no fire lit and if that is his custom then I think him unlikely to survive the winter. Indeed, it looks as if it has been a long time since the place has had the benefit of any heat at all, and with no warmth to keep the damp away, mould has invaded and discoloured every surface; where it has penetrated the plaster, it has caused it crack and in places to fall away from the rotting laths behind; some ancient arsenic-soaked green floral wallpaper has done its best to bring a little cheer, but has faded wherever sunlight has managed to reach it, blackened where it has not, and with barely a trace of its once vibrant colour, long since given up the fight.

There is a tall, narrow window which must once have let the sun in, but now the glass is so filthy that I cannot suppose much light succeeds in getting through; above it is an old brass curtain rod from which hang the remnants of some dusty old moth-eaten drapes, but other than that, the only fittings are some wall-mounted gas lamps which give off a dull yellow light and make the room and its occupant look sick with jaundice. There is neither picture nor ornament anywhere about the place and, as for furnishings, it is spartan: two unmatched chairs, a small low table and a square of threadbare carpet are the only comfort to be had...

It was with thoughts of my unfortunate neighbour that I must have dozed off in my chair by the fireplace, only waking at some unnumbered hour when the last dying embers could no longer keep the cold at bay. Feeling a little disorientated, I undressed hurriedly and climbed into bed, though as I pulled the quilt up to my chin, I sensed that the best hours of my night had passed and all that remained for me was a restless watch for the dawn...

Monday 28th

I was right. Well, mostly. Once in bed, I drifted in and out of a sleep so light that even the sound of my own

Likho

heartbeat woke me at times. The night seemed endless as hour after hour of ever-lengthening minutes pushed the prospect of sunrise further and further away until I began to worry that it might not come at all. I couldn't get comfortable, and on the few occasions when I did, I began soon to feel either too hot or so cold that I was convinced I had a fever. However beneficial my earlier sleep in the chair had been, I felt only tired and ill-humoured when the first light of the morning began to cast faint grey shadows across the room. Opening the curtains, it was a relief to see the dawn, though that relief was tempered by annoyance at its tardiness. It was like having a friend come to one's rescue who, though arriving too late to be of any help, is determined to assist all the same, even though it is plain to all that no further assistance is needed...

I bathed, dressed, and breakfasted, drifting through all those operations in a haze of drowsy resentment, and then set out for a walk in the hope of finding something to dispel my mood, and give some sense of purpose to the day. Pausing for a moment by the door of the empty apartment adjoining mine, I listened for any sounds from within, any sounds which might confirm occupancy, either by the living or the dead, but there were none so on I went, stopping again by the door of my neighbour, but all was silent there too... silent as the grave and, I thought, probably as cold as one...

Another pace or two and I was at the top of the stairs where I halted again. How different things look in the daylight? Mind you, not much daylight manages to find its way into our old tower... there are some small arched windows at the top, just below the vaulting, but other than that we have only the gas lamps to guide us, day and night. I'm certain it must be the oldest part of the building, and the rest built and rebuilt around it with splendidly organic abandon...

At each landing an arcade gives access to the apartments on that floor, and someone went to much trouble and expense to have the stone richly worked. Each pier and arch are uniquely executed... on the ground floor they are incised with simple geometric patterns, but as the masons climbed higher their imaginations took flight too, and the columns of the first-floor loggia are carved as trees, with the arches springing from leafy capitals and curving up like stone branches. On my floor, the second, the columns are entwined serpents which snake upwards to make pointed arches where, at the apex, they join with the head of a gorgon. On the upper floors an assortment of mythological beasts bear the load of the vaulting above, whilst here and there are carved various distorted human faces, some odd-looking putti, and some rather strange, winged creatures that might be angels or demons... I cannot be sure which, but it is all very well done, and I find it fascinating – and every time I look at it, I see some new feature which I have overlooked before. It is a curious place, and I would love to know its history. I shall have to make some inquiries.

Anyway, having descended from on high and with my footsteps still reverberating around the empty lobby, I stepped out on to the street only to find the world as I knew it had disappeared...

I had no doubt it *was* all out there somewhere, but it was lost in a thick fog that had formed in the night and now hung heavily in the air. The streetlamps, though barely visible, remained lit, and as far as I could see, which wasn't far at all, no one other than I had stirred out of doors. I stood for a moment to consider if it might be wiser to remain at home, but wisdom had no place in my decisions for once and so, without further ado, I pulled my collar up and sallied forth, feeling like an heroic explorer stepping boldly into the unknown. For all that, I was reassured greatly to feel the flags beneath my feet and know that at least the pavement was still there…

Wet or dry, cold or hot, however heavy the rain or deep the snow, the café owners never fail to set their tables out on the pavements – whether from habit or in hope, I don't know – but it would have been a brave man, or a fool, who chose to sit *à la terrasse* this morning, and it was likely the cold would get to him long before any waiter. As it was, with no brave men or fools to be seen, I suspected that, today, those tables represented one of Hope's lesser triumphs…

Beyond the empty chairs, condensation trickling down the windows revealed distorted watery views of interiors furnished with old panelling and hung with faded sepia photographs, large mirrors advertising cigarettes or absinthe, and of old and once fine stucco ceilings discoloured by tobacco smoke and yellow lighting. The few patrons who had found their way through the fog were stood at counters or slumped at tables with cups of coffee and glasses of brandy to sustain them against the weather should they have to venture out ever again, and though it was still early, there were a few whose glazed expressions proclaimed them to be already under the spell of *la fée verte*…

Further along the street a rather shabby café which appeared to be as much lacking in customers as it was in style caught my eye. It is just the sort of place I like, a place where no one speaks to me, where attention from the staff is negligible and customers are regarded only as a necessary inconvenience. Sitting at a table by the window, I was served some coffee by a resentful old waiter who plainly wished that one of us was dead, and I really couldn't say which, before he shuffled away muttering curses which might have made a fishwife blush. The proprietor stood behind the bar where he counted a pile of scruffy banknotes and barked orders at some unseen character whilst a cigarette burning in an ashtray next to him sent smoke drifting into his eyes, something that seemed to irritate him even more.

I sat quietly with a morning paper, one of the more scandalous types provided by the house, though I was more interested in watching the street than reading the news, if a word of it could have been called *news* – story after story about the intimate affairs of people of whom I've never heard and who have no worthy talent other than for self-publicity. I turned page after page without reading one of them, and then settled on studying the view through the window, well, as much as the fog permitted me to see. Now and then a shadowy grey figure went past, collar up, hat pulled down and scarf wrapped around its face obscuring all but the eyes; they all looked the same and each of them could have been anyone. The headlamps of a car moved cautiously up the street, the rest of the vehicle following somewhere behind, and in its wake came a man, crossing the road towards me. I noticed him particularly because he wasn't wearing a hat, his face was not masked by a scarf, and on his left arm was the vague and foggy figure of a black-clad old woman. Now, you might not think that to be of much interest and, usually, I would agree; that I recognised the man as my elderly neighbour, though, *did* make it worthy of note because, having yet to see him rise from his chair, I had supposed him confined to it by reason of age or infirmity.

Likho

Allowing curiosity to get the better of me, I settled my bill and went out on to the street, and I will admit, shamefully, that I conducted myself with rather more haste than I consider decent. Even so, in the minute that it took me get outside, my quarry had vanished. I couldn't have been more than ten paces behind him but, as hard as I looked, I could see no one. He couldn't have been too far ahead and so, thinking that he must have gone into a café or shop, I strolled along the pavement, casually glancing into each as I went; but hard as I looked, the old man was nowhere to be found. By the time I reached the end of the street, my interest had dwindled sufficiently that I resolved to forget all about it – for the time being, at least, and, turning towards the river, I walked down to the embankment.

The road was busy with traffic, though none of it was moving, and judging by the number of people crowding the pavement it looked as if those with any sense had realised that this morning, going on foot was the best of the few options available. Walking has always been my preferred means of travel, and with every vehicle at a standstill I ambled slowly between them as I crossed, enjoying a sense of superiority so rarely granted to we pedestrians, and made my enjoyment as obvious as I could. The pleasure was a short-lived one, though, ending as I reached the opposite pavement, leaving those unfortunate motorists to their wait…

The fog was even denser over the river and if it hadn't been for the sound of the water rushing over the weir further upstream, a stranger might not have known there was a river there at all. From somewhere out there came the muffled foghorn of a boat, suggesting some reckless crew had decided to chance in it the murk, and I listened intently for a few minutes expecting to hear it colliding with another vessel, or perhaps striking the bridge; no noise of such calamity reached me though, and so as some brave bargee drifted blindly towards the unseen, my mind drifted on to thoughts of other things…

With nothing much to do, and in no hurry to do it, I held my position until, after about a quarter of an hour, my feet became so numb with the cold that I was compelled to resume my walk… a walk along streets where everything was hidden from view by the fog, and where, for all I could see, I might have been the only man alive. If that *should* ever be so, I don't think I'd mind much, though some better weather would be nice…

Away from the river, in the old square, the towers of the town hall and spires of the cathedral were only a memory, erased from the skyline by the fog, hidden high above us where the faces of saints and kings must have been looking down from their niches, unable to see we sinners and subjects below, whilst grotesques and gargoyles grimaced into a misty void. Thus, my friends, if you want to admire the work of those masons whose skilled hands gave life to dead stones so many centuries ago, you'll have to come back another day…

To the south of the square, the buildings of the university which line the narrow passages were, no doubt, still there somewhere to be found by any students who cared enough to look, and I imagine the winding lanes and alleys of the old town have seen a profitable morning's work for industrious pickpockets using the fog as an innocent accessory to their crimes. A stroll through those ancient streets can be a delight on a fine day but having no wish to put myself in the way of our local *truanderie*, I turned towards home.

Likho

On arrival, I found the concierge carelessly mopping the stone floor of the outer lobby, surrounding himself with a moat of soapy water. I smiled politely at him, he nodded unsmilingly at me, and with pleasantries done I climbed the stairs whilst he went on splashing about like an infant in a bath. The sound of children laughing echoed down through the stairwell and when I looked up, I caught a glimpse of two shadows moving quickly along the wall of the landing and up the stairs to the floor above.

When I reached it a minute or so later, all was quiet, and I entered my apartment without giving them another thought. The concierge's wife had remade the fires, a task she undertook daily for a small charge, along with attending to the cleaning, laundry and other domestic chores with which a single gentleman doesn't wish to be troubled, and as I wish to be troubled by little or nothing other than my thoughts, my morning walks allow such domestic activities to be undertaken in my absence, and appear as if done by magic.

It is my custom to remain at home in the afternoons and sit by the fire with a book, casually browsing through its pages and habitually drifting into a light sleep during which I dream I am awake and reading. If you have nothing better to do, I can recommend it as a most agreeable way to pass some of the time between lunch and dinner.

By the time I went out again, the fog had turned to rain. It wasn't good, regular, pouring rain though, but that dense drizzling rain which doesn't actually fall but instead seems to hang in the air like a fine mist, blurring and scattering light like a frosted window; that rain which gets everywhere, makes everything damp and covers the flags and cobbles in a thin greasy film; that rain which seems only to come on autumn evenings and makes everyone feel nostalgic for long summer nights, and dread the long winter nights which lie ahead.

The rain had turned the paving stones into mirrors, but their unevenness distorted all that they reflected, and like a painting by one of those Impressionists, it had a melancholic charm just right for the season, suiting the evening so perfectly that I lost myself in the pleasure of it and walked much further than I had intended.

After an hour or so, I found myself at the flower market which was empty of all but a couple of stalls where a few cold and wet traders were packing up for the day, leaving only a few petals and buds crushed on the ground. I will admit it was a rather sad view to have as accompaniment to one's dinner, but it suited me as I ate mine in a small restaurant overlooking the square.

For me, eating is a necessity, not a pleasure, and it is something I prefer to do alone and undisturbed. Annoying is the maître d' or waiter who, though well-meaning, insists on trying to have some conversation about my health, his health, that of his wife or children, the weather, the state of his business, the state of *my* business, the plat du jour, or the difficulty of obtaining this or that at that or this time of the year…

I don't doubt that people think me rude. My social skills have never encompassed inconsequential conversation, and, lacking the talents of an actor, I cannot affect interest where I find none. Freely I admit this failing, but I do not apologise for it, or strive to overcome it.

By the time I finished my supper the rain had stopped, and the market was deserted. I made my way home along empty streets where the wet flagstones shone in the light of the streetlamps. Most buildings were in darkness except where a few late customers lingered over their last drinks at a bar, whilst on the floors above, the occupants preparing for bed unwittingly presented a *théâtre des ombres*, their every movement projected in a shadow dance on closed blinds…

The lobby of my building was silent, and as one who appreciates the rights of others to peace and quiet, I moved as softly as I could up the stairs. It was just past midnight, and I couldn't decide whether to call on my neighbour or not but, as I reached his door, I saw that it was ajar and, on that account, I tapped gently and went in to find him sitting in his armchair, just as I had left him, in his cold and ruined room.

"I was unsure if I should expect you this evening…" he said with a look of indifference. "It is rather late, is it not?"

"Yes, after twelve, I think, but your door was open, otherwise I wouldn't have disturbed you at this time of the night."

"It was? How strange."

"Perhaps you didn't close it when you came in earlier?"

"I haven't been out."

"A negligent visitor then?"

"That would be one explanation, yes…"

"You should ask your friends to take more care… anyone could have come in."

"Ah, I see… you think me a poor helpless old man? You think I might be murdered in my bed, so to speak?"

"Well, I think it is a possibility."

"And I think it is *not*… but it is no matter. You should not trouble yourself regarding my wellbeing."

"As you wish. I don't usually concern myself with the welfare of others."

Darton

"Yet you concern yourself with mine?"

"Not particularly... you are my neighbour, but *not* my problem."

"Lucky for me, then, that I am *not* in want of help."

"And for me, since I have none to offer."

"Then we are both fortunate, are we not? We spare each other obligation and embarrassment." The old man grinned, exposing his rotten teeth and exhaling more of his rotten breath. "But never mind that, we are in danger of serious conversation...

"God forbid." I crossed myself as I spoke, but in mockery rather than devotion.

"Ah, so you *do* believe in a god?"

"No, but if any god *would* like me to believe in him, he need only make himself known..." replied I.

"And if one should, how will you know? He might appear to be very ordinary and unremarkable."

"Well, I have never given it much thought... I hope he would be courteous enough to introduce himself. And maybe a show of his divine powers might help his cause? Nothing too extravagant, mind... just turning water into wine, something like that? But I don't think I need worry too much, do you?"

"Maybe he is already here? Maybe I am he? I *could* be."

"Oh, well, I think that would be a bitter disappointment to many of the faithful." I knew I was being rude, but the man was beginning to irritate me with his talk of gods. As far as I am concerned, gods and religion have been good only for inspiring magnificent architecture and music. "Anyway, for my part, I hope no god *ever* makes an appearance because if they do exist then we might have immortal souls and there might be no end to any of this.

Likho

Imagine going on for eternity? Up there, in Heaven with the good and the righteous, or down in Hell with the bad... and the *self*-righteous. I find neither option appealing."

"Ah, well, that is your problem..." He shrugged his bony old shoulders and then went on "but what concern *is* it that keeps you out so late tonight?"

"Oh, nothing much... or rather nothing *and* much."

"Is either of any interest?"

"I'm not sure I can say. Nothing was of much interest, and much was of such a muchness as to be nothing much of consequence at all..." I had no idea where that sentence was going, so I let it go on its way and didn't bother to follow.

"What a strange man you are... how can you occupy such an abstract world with such a closed mind?"

"There's nothing abstract about the world as I see it. It is built on logic and integrity, and my mind is not closed... I insist only on my right to reserve judgment. By the way, before I forget, did you enjoy your walk this morning?"

"*Walk?*"

"Yes, this morning."

"You saw me, then?" He didn't seem surprised.

"Yes, I saw you *then*."

"And where was I going, may I ask?"

"Isn't that for *you* to say?"

"Strange, very strange..." he nodded thoughtfully. "Why didn't you speak to me?"

"Ah, well... I was sitting in a café when I saw you pass. By the time I got outside, you were lost in the fog. I am certain it was you though. You had an old black-clad woman on your arm and passed slowly enough for me to get a good look."

"Interesting... *an old black-clad woman*... and who was that?"

"Surely that is another question best answered by you? I saw only someone dressed from head to foot in black... and I had the impression it was an old woman. I'm sure of it."

"You are sure of it? Based on nothing more than an *impression* you are *sure of it*? Is that compatible with your philosophy?"

"Of course not, but this is hardly a matter worth subjecting to philosophical deconstruction."

"No, and I suspect *that* is something only to be done when it suits you." The old man sneered, a gesture I was about to take as my cue to leave but, alas, I wasn't quick enough. "But never mind..." he went on, his sneer turning into a smile, "because you couldn't possibly have seen me this morning."

"No?"

"No. I have not been out of this apartment today. Your eyes must have deceived you."

"I can assure you they did not, sir. It *was* you."

"I have not left this apartment today or any other for many years. It is not possible for you to have seen what you think you saw... I suggest that what you saw was either a man who looks very like me, or perhaps fog and fatigue caused you to imagine you saw what you could not have seen."

"Well, then, you have an identical twin, I think."

"Ah, I must confound you there too. I have no twin."

"A *doppelgänger* then?" I laughed but only to make it clear that I wasn't serious.

Likho

"But, of course, you don't believe in such things, do you?"

"No, not in the supernatural sense. It is possible, though, that you have a double of somewhat less spectral substance."

"You know it is an ill omen to see a man's doppelgänger?"

"Really? What does it portend?" I don't know why I asked because I didn't really care.

"As I recall it foretells illness, or danger… and seeing one's own is a warning of death. It seems I must take care if, as you say, mine is walking the streets."

"If you believe such things, then *yes*, but if, as you say, you don't go out then I should think you are reasonably safe. Perhaps, though, you should have a fire lit to warm this room? There is a good chance you will freeze to death." I shivered as I spoke, even though I still had my coat on.

"Ah, but there is also a danger from fire, is there not?"

"Well, I would rather risk a fire than freeze to death, and as it is, the chances of the former are far smaller than the latter. I am surprised you can bear it."

"I don't feel it."

"Really? Well, it's too cold for me…"

"You are not compelled to stay. Your company is no matter to me. I managed well enough without it until recently, and I am certain I can do so again."

"Ah, I have the impression that you are offended?" I should tell you now that I didn't care if he was, nor had I any intention of apologising; the man is of no consequence to me.

"No" the old man replied with a shake of his head, "I am not. I mean only that you are under no obligation here. I neither invite nor refuse company... yours or anyone else's. You may go as you please or stay if you will."

"Well, it *is* getting rather late," said I, feeling suddenly uncomfortable, "and perhaps I should go. I am rather tired."

"Then I wish you a good night. I shall expect you, or not, tomorrow evening."

And so it was that I left my neighbour to his icy apartment and returned to mine where a fire in the sitting room hearth was waiting to welcome me, inviting me to pull up a chair and relax a while before bed.

With no lamps lit the only light came from the flickering flames in the fireplace which sent long shadows dancing across the floor towards the corners of the room which were out there somewhere in the darkness. All was silent except for the sound of my breathing and the crackling of the fire in the grate. It was perfect for relaxation, and for thinking... and the subject on which I found myself ruminating yet again was my neighbour...

A strange man indeed. Who is he and why does he live as he does? How did he come to it? It is only on the last two nights that he has engaged me in conversation and so I know nothing about him other than what I have written here.

Why is he lying to me about never going out? I suppose I can't expect him to trust me; he doesn't know me, so why should he? But as it is, I can suppose only that he was up to no good because, after all, innocence has no need to hide behind lies.

Perhaps he is engaged in a clandestine, adulterous romance? Maybe he is the lover of the old woman? Could he be defending the honour of his aged mistress? It is as possible as it is absurd. Wait, I have it... it must be something criminal... maybe they were on a crime spree? Running amok through the town, dashing along the fog-bound streets and committing robberies or acts of wanton violence? Less plausible, I think, than star-crossed lovers snatching a moment together under the cover of some inclement weather.

Well, whatever is behind his deception I cannot guess, so I give it up as unworthy of my attention and chastise myself severely for entertaining such stupid thoughts.

I am not a man inclined to fancy or fiction; indeed, I am incapable of suspending disbelief, and for that I have been pitied often. I cannot count the times I have been told how much richer my life could be if only I were to indulge the imaginings of others. Well, it might be true, but there is nothing I can do about it and, before you ask, I *have* tried. Anyway, I am sorry for the man who needs to enrich his own life with the fantasies of another when, if only he would try, he might find his own thoughts far more rewarding.

Outside, above the rooftops across the street, the sky was showing itself at last, and from east to west stars came slowly into focus against patches of blue-black night, whilst from somewhere overhead and out of sight, the moon sent shafts of light skipping hypnotically across the floor towards me until a cloud obscured it once more. In a moment, though, it cleared again, and another bright blue-white beam illuminated the room, and although for less than a second, it was just long enough to see someone standing in the window...

2. The Carpet and the Coin

Tuesday 29th
Shadows and imagination working together can create the most terrifying illusions, and the illusion they created last night certainly terrified me… a figure in the window, revealed in a flash of moonlight – the stuff of nightmares. All right, I agree that it isn't the most original of plot devices, but it is no less effective for that.

The image imprinted like a photograph on my retinas, and if I close my eyes, I can see it still… a dark shrouded figure about five feet tall, with long white hair and a round, white face devoid of features except for a gaping black mouth and a single eye which sparkled as it caught the light from the fire. Relief from the horror came fast on its heels, though, as the moon was obscured by another cloud, and the apparition fell back into the darkness, leaving me alone again, and shivering as a cold sweat soaked my shirt.

My heart was pounding against my ribs as if it were trying to break free, and I couldn't breathe because the air was suddenly freezing even though the fire was blazing in the hearth next to me. When at last I did manage to draw a breath, the air was so foul that it made me retch.

With trembling hands, I lit the lamp on the table beside my chair and as the wick began to glow and light the room, I saw what I hoped to see – I saw *nothing*… I saw nothing where nothing should be, and where nothing *could* have been. My visitor had been an illusion drawn from shadows by a tired mind, and that it should have taken the form of an old black-clad thing ought not be a surprise as I had been thinking of my neighbour and his companion only moments before.

"Only this and nothing more…" Now, I wondered, from what quaint and curious corner of my mind had that long-forgotten line come to disturb me?[2]

Outside, the stars and moon were lost again above a menace of clouds which had blown in on a strengthening wind, and the rain which they brought began to fall heavily, lashing hard against the window. I watched it pouring down the panes and listened to the gale whistling along the street, wondering if I would be able to sleep through such noise, and when, at last, I went to bed, though the weather didn't respect my wish for quiet, tiredness triumphed with unexpected speed.

Though I slept until dawn I did not have a restful night. A succession of strange dreams disturbed me, most of which were vague and unmemorable, although my mother appeared several times which was odd because I have hardly given her a thought since the day of her funeral ten years ago…

Now, this is not meant to be an autobiography, but I think a brief account of my life could be appropriate here. Who knows? It might be of interest to someone one day…

I was born to wealthy parents who lived sometimes at a grand house in a good part of the town, and other times at a rambling old place in the country which might once have had hopes of becoming a *chateau* but, like the family, had never risen high enough to merit a title.

My first meals were at the breast of a wet-nurse, and thereafter I was looked after by servants until sent away to school; when I left school, I went to university and after that my parents gave me a very generous allowance to travel. Everything that came from my father was sent on his behalf by the family notary, and his letters were written with all the sentiment of a court summons. In twenty-five years, I saw my parents on no more than ten occasions, and those small family reunions were always brief. My relationship with them was like that of strangers grudgingly obliged to share a compartment in a railway carriage – resentful of each other's invasive presence, we had nothing to say beyond polite greetings, and our only common interest was to get away as quickly as possible, even at the risk of giving offence.

When my father died, my mother inherited his estate, and when she died it passed to me as the only surviving member of the family; as such, I felt obliged to see her safely into the ancestral tomb, although I had not seen her since the day on which we had watched my father borne thence. I did not grieve for the loss of either, but I did regret the ten long years which had kept them apart.

There, I think that covers the most interesting points of my early life. As for the rest, well, the years since have never equalled those of that happy childhood and are not worth recounting...

Anyway, where were we? Yes, the lamentable visitations of a dead mother in the night...

The woman had made no effort to dress for the occasion, but chose, instead, to appear wearing only the shroud in which she went to the grave. Her eyes remained closed, but her mouth opened repeatedly, shouting the same word at me over and over. It was a word I didn't know – it might have been a foreign language for all I could tell, and she wouldn't stop however much I shouted at her. I tried running away but wherever I went she appeared before me, and though I wanted to sleep, I knew that the only way to escape was to wake from the dream.

Darton

I never cease to be impressed by the power of the human mind, and its ability to cause the body to act, even when in a deep sleep... so wake, I did, and was much relieved to see the daylight throwing grey shadows across the ceiling as I lay amongst a mess of bedclothes. One pillow remained on the bed, but the others were on the floor along with the quilt and blankets, and one of the sheets was twisted around my neck like a fine white linen rope. With some difficulty, I freed myself from it and then lay back on the bed feeling quite exhausted, though reluctant to sleep again lest my mother return to plague me once more.

Dreams and nightmares have never troubled me much; I set no store by them whatsoever. They are nothing more than the result of the brain throwing out the leftovers of the day, sweeping up miscellaneous ideas and filing away forgotten thoughts, ready to begin afresh in the morning. Whatever the sincerest oneiromancer might say, I do not believe that dreams relate to a single thing or event, or that they are warnings or premonitions. Consequently, although fatigued, I am not disturbed by my nightmare, though I will admit to being curious as to why my mother should have featured in it. Neither of my parents had been in the habit of calling on me when they were alive, so why one of them should do so now, I cannot imagine. Anyway, I have concluded that she was no more than a long-forgotten loose end which has now been tidied away nicely, never to come again.

The heavy rain which failed to keep me awake was still falling by the time I finished my breakfast but, undeterred by it, I set out for my morning walk. The wind had dropped sufficiently to make the use of an umbrella practical and most people were carrying one, though as they also wore hats it seemed pointless to me, and I went forth

Likho

bravely with neither; carelessly having left many behind in all manner of places, I find it less profligate to get wet, and it was in such a condition that I took refuge in a small café near the river. My first stop of the day, I sat by the window drinking coffee and watching the rain lashing the cobbles of the little street…

It is one of those short, narrow passages which connect nothing much with nowhere in particular and where you will find only its few residents, people who are lost, or those who *want* to be. You may imagine, then, that I was rather surprised to see my neighbour pass by with his companion, just as before. Today, though, he turned his head and looked directly at me.

There was no mistake. It was he. The daylight showed him better than ever I have seen him in his apartment, and I could see every detail of his old grey face, thin white hair, dull sunken eyes and rotten teeth which were on full view as he grinned broadly at me.

I wondered if, having seen me, he would come into the café, although something told me he wouldn't. Whatever that something was, it proved right, and the old man and his friend went on their way in the pouring rain, not stopping to take shelter or refreshment, and leaving me feeling both irritated and intrigued. I was as much vexed by my own curiosity as I was with my neighbour for taunting me again with another of his mysterious appearances, and though the urge to pursue him through the streets once more was hard to resist, resist it I did, ordered more coffee and resolved to think no more about it, which, as you'll gather, I have been unable to do.

It occurred to me that I was *meant* to follow him, that it was some sort of game with which I was supposed to join, though to what end I cannot imagine. Well, *not* joining with it seems to me the more interesting part to play, and if the old man wishes to indulge in games, then let us see to what lengths he will go to draw me in…

Certain that he had seen me, certain that he *knew* I'd seen him, and certain that he will again deny the possibility, I decided to make no mention of the incident. It won't do for him to get the idea that I might be interested and, besides, if I say nothing then he might just give himself away out of frustration. I shall feign a more aloof approach and draw *him* into *my* game, though I have no more idea about my game than I have about his.

The rain was easing off and so, having consumed my fill of coffee, I went on with my walk. A stroll by the river eventually led me to the fish market, north of the old town bridge. I don't much care for the produce, but the building is worthy of note. There are three open-sided pavilions with glazed roofs carried on cast-iron columns; the metalwork is splendidly intricate and decorated with fantastical sea creatures. Some of the columns are formed like entwined sea serpents; the tentacles of giant octopus and squid support the glazing bars, and the glass is etched with thousands of fish which creates quite an impression against a blue sky. It was built at great expense in the first half of the nineteenth century and is well-worth a visit, even if you have no interest in buying anything. When I arrived, it was a little before eleven; most of the stalls were closing and with the business of the day nearly done, I was able to walk unhindered amongst them for a while. There was nothing new to see, though, and so I left the bare wet marble slabs behind me, piles of crushed ice to melt into slush, and pools of fish guts and blood to be swept into the gutters for the local cats and rats to gorge themselves, if the smell doesn't put them off.

Likho

An hour later, leaving the sounds of the street outside, I entered the lobby of my building and climbed the stairs to my apartment which was as quiet as a tomb, though somewhat warmer than one thanks to the wife of the concierge who had remade the fires whilst I was out. All was clean and tidy, and my lunch laid out in the dining room as usual; she always provides me with fresh bread, cheeses and cold meats, and a bottle of good red wine which is usually the cause of a post-prandial nap. I *have* thought of omitting the wine and the nap with a view to pursuing more productive afternoons; as I write, that thought remains on my list of things to do and never likely to be accomplished…

With lunch finished I retreated to the sitting room, sat in my chair by the fire and lazily turned the pages of a book. It soon slipped from my hand and I into a light sleep where, regrettably, my mother joined me again. Appearing out of nowhere, she stood by the window, in the same place as my other visitor had appeared last night. What is it about that particular spot which makes it so favoured by wraiths?

She was the same as before except her mouth was slightly open and there was a silver coin in it. Sending our dead on their way with the fare for the ferryman was not a custom indulged in by my family, so I don't know where she came by it. It was symbolic, I suppose. Did it mean that something had drawn her back before she could cross over? If so, she'd been a long time about it…

I shouted at her to go away and leave me alone, but my command had no effect. I shouted again, rising from my chair and taking a step towards her, and then another and another so that I was standing directly before her.

Still she would not go… I grabbed her arms and started to shake her, but my action succeeded only in dislodging clouds of dust from the folds of her shroud. The air around her was cold and fast growing colder, and she was giving off a stench so foul I thought I was going to vomit. As I tightened my grip and shook her more violently, I felt her bones cracking, and, as they splintered in my hands, this thing which had the appearance of my dead mother let out a long loud scream and raised her eyelids to reveal two empty black holes…

Letting go of her, I backed away, but with my eyes fixed on her face I tripped on something behind me and fell backwards, landing in my armchair where I found myself suddenly awake once more.

Momentarily confused, I sat forward and reached with a trembling hand for the glass of wine which remained half-full on the table beside me and as I did so I noticed an odd thing… on the other side of the fireplace, towards the window, the edge of the carpet was turned back, and on the floor lay a small silver coin.

The sight of it made me shiver. I stared at it, hoping it was a trick of the light, or that perhaps I was still asleep and dreaming. Alas it was neither of those things. There *was* a coin on the floor, and I *was* awake.

"Don't be so stupid…" I said aloud to myself as I took a drink, "just a silly dream…and some sleepwalking… and I must have dropped the coin earlier."

Well, it was a good theory but for one *tiny* flaw… when I had dozed off, the book which I was browsing slipped from my hand and came to rest on my outstretched legs, and when I woke up, it was there still. That would seem to deny the possibility of my having moved from the chair, would it not? I confess I have no explanation, and though I am resolved to think no more on it, I admit to being intrigued by the mystery of the carpet and the coin…

Likho

Later.

At eight in the evening, I set forth in search of my dinner, and it was in the university quarter where I found a café in which I was sure to be a stranger. The waiter found me a table in a corner from which I was able to watch the room whilst I ate an indifferent meal, and the food being no distraction I was free to study my fellow diners, many of whom were students reading quietly for end-of-term examinations. An elderly man with a long beard and half-moon glasses was making notes on small cards; a girl by the window looked at everything but the book which lay open next to her half-eaten dinner, and nearby a young man stared at *her* rather than the volume which he held open before him; it didn't seem to me as if either had learning uppermost in their minds.

I was never much devoted to study when at school or university. The thought of failure never troubled me because I knew I would never have to depend on employment for my income. I do regret it now, but not so much as to wish myself back to those miserable years.

Having been used to solitude from infancy, I never sought the company of my classmates; consequently, they thought me to be an unfriendly, antisocial snob; my teachers, on the other hand, believed me to be an imbecile. Anyway, regardless of their differing opinions, together they took pleasure in victimising and humiliating me at every opportunity. For the most part I ignored them; they were nothing to me, their approval or otherwise was no matter, and if they had any effect on me, I never let them see it. But enough of that.

By the time the waiter brought my coffee and brandy, only the old man remained, and he soon paid for his dinner and left. I sat a while longer until the waiters began to hover, unashamedly displaying their desire for me to leave, and in what can only be described as an act of churlishness, I kept them waiting whilst I counted out the smallest coins I could find to settle the bill. Without a word I stepped into the empty dark street, the door was slammed rudely behind me, and I set off on my walk home. It was late, well after eleven o'clock, but I was in no hurry. It was cold but dry, the night was clear, and the moon was up, shining brightly in the east, though its light didn't reach down into the narrow passages along which I strolled in near darkness. Pausing occasionally to look up at the sky, I tried to identify some constellations and understand how the ancients had managed to see all those zodiacal characters in the stars. I can never make them out at all – they must have had better imaginations in those days. Or stronger wine?

When I arrived here it was past midnight, and too late to call on my neighbour, or so I thought. His open door suggested otherwise, though, and I felt almost obliged to go in. The old man was in his chair as usual.

"Good evening" he said with a wide yellow grin, "I had given you up for the night."

"Your door was open again; I thought I should tell you."

"Ah, how disappointing. I hoped it was the pleasure of my company which drew you in."

"At this hour? The only thing which draws me to it is my bed." I find no pleasure in his company at any hour of the day, but the time to say so has not yet come.

"You have had a tiring day then?"

"I wouldn't say so, no. Have you?"

"I am never tired. What keeps you out so late?"

"A leisurely supper and slow walk home, nothing more."

"What a life you lead... don't you wish there was more purpose to it?"

"My life is full of purpose," I replied rather curtly, "unlike yours, from what I have seen."

"Ah, you would be surprised. I *do* have a purpose... one which is very dear to me."

"Really? Then perhaps you shouldn't be too long about it?" That might sound a little rude, but it was a part of my strategy to be less engaging.

"Don't worry, it will be resolved *very* soon, I hope, and despite your observations I am far from idle in the matter, as you will discover for yourself."

"Your business is none of mine and I don't wish to discover anything of it. If you are trying to pique my interest, sir, you will have to do better than that... and you will have to do it on another occasion because I must go to my bed... perhaps I shall see you tomorrow."

My neighbour wished me a goodnight and I left him alone in his room, pleased with myself for managing to remain indifferent despite temptation.

Wednesday 30th

I went directly to bed; I felt very tired and was certain I would sleep, but that certainty turned out to be ill-founded, and I lay awake staring into the darkness for what seemed like hours. No sound came from anywhere, not even the usual creaking and groaning of the old building relaxing on its foundations for the night. It was *too* quiet, and as I lay in there, I began to think perhaps I had gone deaf. With no light by which to see, and no hearing, I was in a state of sensory deprivation, floating in the blackness. It was strange but not unpleasant, and as my body relaxed, at last I drifted off to sleep and into a dream where I was sinking in a dark bottomless river, and though I might have been drowning it didn't seem to matter. When I awoke, I was soaked in perspiration, shivering and feverish. All that remained of the fire was a few glowing embers in the grate, so I curled up tightly beneath the bedding and, feeling thoroughly miserable, tried to sleep again. It was impossible, though, because a thousand thoughts running through my mind kept me awake, and when at last I *did* start to doze off I was disturbed by a sense that there was someone in the room. Lying still and listening hard, I could hear children whispering and then laughing quietly as one of them lifted the quilt and climbed in next to me. A second child got in on the other side and I had to move a little to make room. I couldn't think who they were, and I certainly wasn't happy about sharing my bed with them, but I didn't have the heart to turn them out before daylight, so I lay there in silence and just listened to the sound of them breathing as they slept. Of course, I wasn't surprised to find them gone when I awoke, because they could have never been there in the first place...

Despite feeling tired and unwell, I was determined to keep to my daily routine and so set out as usual for my morning walk, but after resting in a café at the end of my street for a while, I felt as if I shouldn't go further. I thought I had recovered from my night fever, but I felt weak, and it seemed the best thing was to go home. When I arrived, I found the wife of the concierge standing in the lobby of my apartment and obviously surprised to be disturbed by my unexpected return.

"Good morning, sir" she said, looking me up and down suspiciously through narrowed eyes, "are you all

Likho

right? You don't *look* at all right, if I may say so. Here, let me take your coat…"

"Thank you, yes…" replied I, rather feebly, "I don't feel too well, I think. I shall sit by the fire for a while..."

"Oh, I haven't lit one yet…" she said as she pushed past me and dashed through the sitting room door. "Soon have that going for you sir, a good fire, yes, just what you need…" I followed her and sat down in my chair whilst she busied herself with kindling and matches, all the time muttering to herself, though it sounded more as if she was talking to someone else and I had to check more than once to make certain she was speaking to *me*. With my eyes half-closed I listened to her idle chatter until the fire was blazing nicely and she stood up to go. "All right there, all done… now you just sit there and get warm… I'll bring you some nice hot soup in a while, that's what you need sir… fire and soup, yes, just the thing when you're not feeling too well… fire and soup… yes…"

"Thank you, you are very kind…" I said with a feeble smile, whilst thinking that the only thing I wanted really was to be left in peace.

Sunlight streamed in through the window, fuelling a furnace in my head where a blacksmith was striking furiously on an anvil, and his every strike sent a bolt of pain shooting outwards, each one cracking my skull from the inside. I wanted to close the curtains, but a growing nausea pinned me to my chair, and I dared not try to move. All I could do was shut my eyes tightly and cover them with a hand to keep the light out.

I have never been prone to illness, but now these bouts of feverish insomnia have started me thinking perhaps I am suffering from something serious. It has occurred to me to consult a doctor but then, in the light of day, I think it all sounds rather trivial. It is nothing more than a general fatigue, and nothing which won't be remedied with a good night's sleep.

My self-appointed nurse reappeared at midday with the promised soup and then left me alone again. It was very good soup, as soups go, and followed by a glass of hot spiced wine, I thought I felt the better for it. When the woman returned a while later and I expressed my gratitude, it drew forth such an outpouring of self-effacing deference that it made me wish I hadn't bothered. She scuttled away still mumbling as she went, leaving me in peace once more although she came back at dusk to see to the lights, the fire, and bring me some more soup. I know I don't sound it, but I *was* grateful; she was under no obligation to me and did what she did out of kindness. It is just that I like things to be done with no more attention than is required, and she is given to fussing a bit too much. Anyway, I was pleased not to have to go out for my supper and as I dozed in my chair thoughts of employing a full-time servant drifted through my mind... a gentleman's gentleman to run my bath and lay out my clothes, to bring me letters, visiting cards or a glass of sherry on a silver salver and say *"will that be all sir?"* and *"very good sir"* as he bows out of the room. I was a little troubled, though, by the fact that my imaginary valet seemed to have two children somewhere about him, and I was certain of it because I could hear him talking to them as he closed the door...

The next time I opened my eyes, it was daylight again. I had slept all night in my chair, and I woke with my every limb stiff and immoveable. It felt as if the bones in my neck had fused making it almost impossible to raise my head from my right shoulder, and my lower back ached... no, it pulsed, or throbbed, well, I don't know what it did, but it was only just endurable compared with everything else. Slowly, painfully, I managed to get to my feet and move a pace to the mantelpiece where I leant wearily and stared at my face in the mirror. It was a face I didn't know. It was old, lined and sagging, and the eyes which stared back at me were not mine. They were cold and dead like the eyes of my old neighbour. My face was like his, or his was like mine, I don't know which, and even my hair looked like his... thin, limp, lifeless...

My fingers stretched out on the mantel shelf like the dead branches of an old white birch, and the skin was beginning to peel like papery bark; the fingernails were grey and chipped, and the knuckles all swollen, as if inflamed with arthritis. My aching shoulders slumped, and my head drooped like a dead grey flower on a forgotten grave...

The face staring back at me was *not* mine. It could not have been mine because from the corner of my left eye I could see myself fast asleep in the chair... head tilted to one side, my arms limp, with one hand clutching the edge of a blanket which was draped over my knees and trailing on the floor. It was not *me* staring back at me from the mirror. It was my old neighbour's wrinkled and leathery face, dry and cracked lips and broken yellow teeth... it was his half-open mouth which smiled out at me. It wasn't a broad and cheery smile, it wasn't a kind smile, it wasn't the smile of a friend... it was the twisted smile of the sadistic executioner, sharpening his sword as he watches a condemned man dragged to the scaffold...

I stood for what felt like an age whilst time crawled onwards, or stopped, or maybe even ran backwards; the only thing which mattered was the mirror, and the face reflected in it... a face which should have been mine but was not.

Darton

The face which belonged to *me* was sleeping soundly by the fire, whilst the face in the glass was looking in from a nightmare; one of its dead, grey hands rested on the frame, its bony fingers scratching at the gilding, digging its broken, blackened nails in and breaking off small splinters of limewood which crumbled to dust on the sill below.

3. Creeping Out Of Sleep

Thursday 1ˢᵗ
The next time I opened my eyes, it was daylight again. I had slept all night in my chair, and I woke with my every limb stiff and immoveable. It felt as if the bones in my neck had fused making it almost impossible to raise my head from my right shoulder, and my lower back ached... no, it pulsed, or throbbed, well, I don't know what it did, but it was only just endurable compared with everything else. Slowly, painfully, I managed to get to my feet and move a pace to the mantelpiece where I leant wearily and stared at myself in the mirror. The man who looked back at me looked like one who had slept all night in a chair, and I made a mental note not to do it again as I stretched my arms and legs slowly to get some blood flowing into them again. I had slept but it had not been a restful sleep, it had done me little good, and these disturbed nights are beginning to take a toll, a very visible toll on my face which, I think, is beginning to look old and tired, and not unlike that of my decrepit neighbour.

As I stood before the mirror, in contemplation of my prematurely aging appearance, a cold shiver ran down my spine, like a large venomous spider looking for the best place to bite, and I was overcome suddenly by a nauseating sensation that some frightful thing was about to happen.

Minutes went by, but no frightful thing did happen, and whatever it was that didn't happen left me feeling a little cheated which, you'll agree, was a strange and rather perverse feeling to have. Then I remembered... I had awoken after sleeping the night in my chair... I'd stood before the mirror, and where *my* reflection should have been, I had seen the face of my old neighbour, and the memory of it became so clear that even now, hours later, I am struggling still to accept that it can have been no more than another bad dream.

There was another odd thing, though, for which I can't account so easily... whilst I was staring at myself in the glass, I noticed that some of the gilding on the bottom of the frame had been scratched, and flakes of it lay on the mantel shelf beneath. Then, just as I was thinking on who might have done it, I became aware of a strange and unpleasant odour very like the stench which had accompanied the apparition of my mother... damp, musty and foul, I can only describe it as like a coarse blend of rancid vomit and the sweet scent of summer flowers. It seemed to have saturated the very fabric of the room, and the residue hung heavily on the air.

Overcome with nausea again, I ran to the window and opened the casements, desperate for some fresh air and to flush out the lingering stench, a stench which couldn't have been real but was there, nonetheless. The air was cold, but it felt good to breathe it in, and as I drew it deep into my lungs, the shock of it sent a shudder through me which shook off those lingering night terrors, like a wet dog throwing water from its coat.

Dreams, nightmares, hallucinations, or the onset of madness? Things are becoming muddled, boundaries are becoming permeable, and dreams are creeping out of sleep and into consciousness, whilst the living and dead are appearing in places they ought not to be...

Am I going mad? I begin to wonder...

Likho

Enough of this – I am *not* going mad. I have been sleeping badly and that is all, so let's have no more of it lest all these thoughts and ideas *do* drive me into insanity.

Anyway, having recovered from whatever indisposition ailed me yesterday, I went out for my morning walk, and with nothing particular in mind I ambled aimlessly about the town for a couple of hours, returning to my street just after midday. It is not quite the oldest in the town but is nevertheless very ancient, and one of the first to develop outside the ramparts towards the end of the twelfth century. The south barbican stands close by, though the adjoining walls were taken down some centuries ago and the stones reused to make the buildings which now stand in its place. Some parts remain but only where houses were built into and against it as the town outgrew its fortifications; they are easy enough to spot, should you be looking.

There is one house near the gate which is supposed to be unaltered since it was built, and if you could see it, I think you would support that supposition. The twisted old timbers of the upper floors look as if they have done their best to break free ever since they were first hammered into place… shrinking and warping but still holding together, although without a true line remaining, and it looks almost as if the posts and beams have tried to reform into the trunks and boughs of the trees from which they were cut. Beneath them, the lower storey on which they rest is rather more solid, built from stone, pierced only by narrow windows, and a small round-arched doorway through which a man of average height would struggle to pass freely.

Most of the other buildings on the street have been extended, remodelled or entirely rebuilt several times over since the first brave pioneers left the safety of the old town in search of space and clean air without… or, more probably, to escape the control of the guilds which so strictly regulated activities within. The passing of centuries has seen it ravaged by invading armies, fire, neglect and general changes in taste and fortune, and no doubt those who first walked it would find it much altered since they set out their stalls on a muddy track in the shadow of the city walls.

Like the old half-timbered house, much of mine appears to have survived from mediaeval days, though being built entirely in stone from bottom to top, it has kept its shape a little better than its neighbour.

To the city and the world, it presents a well-designed, ordered face which denies the sprawling disorder of the building behind it. At street level, the wall is solid and almost defensive in its mass, with only arrow slits to light the rooms inside; the residents on the first floor fare a little better with pairs of narrow round-arched windows. Above them, however, and beyond the reach of any marauding foreign soldiers, revolutionary mobs and jobbing burglars, I can enjoy the daylight which floods in through the high casements of my apartment, as well as the view out of them. Over my rooms on this side, there is only a low attic, and it is concealed behind a deep cavetto cornice which is finished with fine sgraffito decoration, and, in my opinion, a thing of great beauty.

The builders were not found wanting when it came to adorning the exterior, and there is no shortage of fine detail – there are bands of strapwork carved with delicate geometrical patterns in bas-relief above and below the windows, which are further framed by a jumble of foliage and mythological beasts carved in the reveals. If none of that is enough to get your attention, then maybe the faces which have been sculpted in random blocks of the stonework will excite your interest? You might, as I do, look up at them and wonder at the reason for their strange and tortured expressions, or who they might have been and why there were put there? Well, I can answer none of those questions, but it is a mystery worthy of investigation... an investigation which I should like to do, but almost certainly will not.

If your curiosity is not yet satisfied, then our doorway might stir further interest because it looks out of place where it is, and you might be forgiven for expecting to find yourself in church upon entering; its columns and carvings would be better suited to one, I think. If it has remained in situ since it was built, and if its style is true to its time, then our building, or at least a part of it, has been standing since the twelfth century. Of course, it could be a confection of stonework brought from elsewhere and assembled here the week before I arrived, but never mind that now. Step through it and you will enter a low vaulted passageway which takes you deep into the core of the house and our magnificent stairwell. On passing, the visitor will note a succession of low doors on the left which are always locked and lead I know not where, though I like to imagine a maze of secret stairs and passages, to hidden rooms full of forgotten treasures. I am sure the reality will be far more prosaic...

I have heard it said that some think the place a bit gloomy and even a little sinister; I would substitute *atmospheric* for *gloomy*, and rather than *sinister*, I would say that it is *charmingly elegiac...*

My apartment is spacious, a labyrinth of rooms, and many more than I need. There are bright and airy rooms; there are some into which the sunlight struggles to reach; and then there are those which are never quite the same from one moment to the next, where light and shadows come and go freely and unhindered, bringing such moods as they please.

My apartment is spacious, too spacious for one man to occupy on his own, but the thought of sharing my home with another is a thought I cannot entertain. My home is an inviolable sanctuary, and my privacy is the thing most dear to me. In my youth it was the one thing I was denied, and thus became the thing I wanted most...

The home of my parents was always busy with servants prowling about the place, and as a child I had no rights in anything; at boarding school I never knew a moment of solitude, and at university our accommodation was shared, and as no door had a lock to it, it wasn't until I was twenty-three that I had a room where I could shut myself in and everyone else out. To have one's privacy violated is, to *me*, worse than a physical assault, and I know whereof I speak since I was frequently a victim of violence at school; by the age of fourteen or so, most of us had been subjected to a decent number of assaults, and a number of *indecent* ones too. Maybe I have blocked the memories, but I cannot recall ever feeling troubled beyond the duration of the experience itself. It was just something we went through, and no one seemed to care... it was all *part of growing up*, or so we were led to believe... although now, of course, as I look back on those years, I realise how wrong we were to think it so. It degraded us, it bred bullies and cowards, it gnawed away at self-respect and it crushed confidence; I am not certain what is left when those things are taken away, but I know that the damage is irreparable.

But enough of that... the past is an ill-tempered sleeping dog with very sharp teeth, and best viewed at a safe distance, if at all. As for the future, well, it is like a taxi – you can't be certain that there will be one, that the driver will want to take you where you want to go, or by which route he will travel. Man is no more than a muddle of memories and plans; but memories fade, and plans come to nothing; the best he can hope for is to be remembered, and without friends or family, that is unlikely to my be fate. I should have been a philosopher…

Anyway, after passing the afternoon and early evening in my spacious apartment, which is too big for one man, in a building which is an architectural enigma, on a street which is older than it looks, I went out for supper.

A bistro on the small square behind the old town hall satisfied an inconvenient hunger, and then, to aid the digestion of an indifferent meal which lay heavily in my stomach, I extended my route home with a walk to the cathedral and on down to the river.

The sky was clear and littered with stars from end to end, and beneath them a mist was forming over the water, and a frost on the pavements. The sound of water rushing over the weir came out of the darkness upstream, whilst below me it lapped gently at the embankment wall. All along the opposite bank and up the steep paths and passages to the castle, the streetlamps were flickering through thickening fog. Most people were sleeping soundly in their beds, but here and there, a light in a window betrayed a wakeful occupant within, whilst above those restless heads rose the walls and towers of the sprawling fortress, standing black against the starlight.

I remained a while, a little hypnotised by the view, but eventually the cold got the better of me; it is not the season for evening walks, lazy sightseeing and taking the night air, so, with a shiver and some reluctance, I turned away and began to walk slowly home.

Darton

I decided I would not call on my neighbour since it was late, but on reaching the second floor, I found his door ajar as usual. Knocking quietly, I pushed it open and went in, crossed the small vestibule and entered his shabby sitting room. He was there in his chair, much as I expected him to be, except that he was dead.

I wish I could say that I was shocked or horrified by what I saw, but the truth is that I didn't feel anything at that moment, and before I could have any sort of reaction, a voice came out of nowhere, cutting through the stale, icy air…

"*He's been murdered…*" The words came in a whisper, carried on a chilling draught which sent a shiver up and down my spine and it stopped only when I realised that both words and whisper had been mine, and that made me laugh, and as I laughed, I began to take in the horror of the scene, and *that* was no laughing matter…

With his head thrown back, his throat displayed proudly the bruises left by the hands that had choked the life out of him; his bulging eyes stared with a look of surprise, and his mouth gaped wide, frozen in the act of gasping for a final breath.

Curious but cautious, I stepped closer to get a better look, though it was quite plain that the old man was beyond help. I stood still, held my breath and listened hard to hear any sound which might give away the presence of a murderer lurking somewhere about, but there was only silence, and I was certain I was alone with the corpse. It was only then that fear struck me, almost as if it had been waiting until I wasn't expecting it, and without another thought, I ran from the room, from the apartment, down the stairs and into the empty dark street…

Likho

Once outside, I stopped for a moment to get my breath back and to think about what I ought to do. The obvious and sensible thing was to go directly to the police. There was a bureau in the next street which I supposed would be open all night and so I set off at a quick pace, arriving breathless and flustered about five minutes later. I was not in the habit of hurrying anywhere and I was furious with my neighbour's murderer for causing me to do so then – if only he'd closed the door behind him, I'd have been asleep in my bed and blissfully ignorant of his crime. With that thought and no other in my head, I stepped inside to find a small empty room with some chairs along one wall and a reception counter opposite. Beyond that, two men sat at adjoining desks; one had his feet resting on a chair and appeared to be sleeping whilst the other was reading a newspaper. I waited for a moment, expecting to be noticed, but neither man paid any attention although they must have heard me come in.

"Excuse me…" I said loudly. The reading man looked around the room, looked at me, glanced around the office again, then slowly and deliberately closed and folded his paper, laid it on the table and stood up, displaying all the attitude of a man who is seriously inconvenienced. He pointed at himself and looked at me quizzically, as if seeking confirmation that it was he whom I had addressed. I nodded and he walked slowly across the room to the counter.

"Good evening" said I, a little brusquely, affording the man as much courtesy as I felt he deserved.

"What do you want? You wish to speak with me, sir?"

"I wish to speak with someone…"
"But not necessarily with me?"
"Well, I can't say… is there another?"

"No, no there isn't."

"Then it seems I must speak with *you*, if I may?"

"You may."

"Very well." I was becoming a little frustrated. "I wish to speak with someone about a murder. Now, is that possible?"

"Someone *here*?"

"Of course. I thought we had established that..."

"You expressed a wish to speak with someone, I think, but there was no mention of where... or, indeed, why."

"No? Well, then, please allow me to clarify my requirements. I wish to speak with someone here... with *you*, if you insist, and the subject of which I must speak is a murder."

"Well, just to be clear, sir, I do not *insist*, but as I am here then you may as well tell me, if you *must*. A murder, you say?"

"Yes. A murder..."

"And tell me then, who is planning this murder? Someone you know, I assume? Who is the intended victim? Are you to be the victim? When and where is it to take place?"

"What? What are you talking about?"

"Your murder, sir. It hasn't been committed yet, has it?"

"What sort of question is that?"

"A perfectly relevant one if I may say so."

"A perfectly *stupid* one, if *I* may say so?" I was beginning to wonder if I had walked into a police station or a madhouse.

Likho

"Stupid? Not at all. If the deed has not yet been done, then it might yet be prevented. Now, please, go on. Has this murder taken place or not, sir?"

"Of course it has. Why would anyone report a murder which hasn't happened?"

"Well, people *do*, you know… although usually only when they want us to intervene which, of course, not all of them do…"

"Really? Why would they report it if they didn't want it stopped?" I admit I was a little confused.

"Oh, you wouldn't believe it if I told you."

"I see… then don't bother to tell me." My patience was running out.

"No need for that attitude sir. I am only trying to help."

"Really? Help? How? I come to report a murder… a murder which *has* been done, by the way, and your reaction lacks the urgency with which you might enquire about next year's weather…"

"Well, what would you have me do, sir? If it has been committed then I presume a man is dead, in which case there is not much need for urgency, not as far as I can see."

"Then, may I ask, are you interested only if a murder is yet to be committed?"

"That is a good question sir…" he said, scratching his head and looking thoughtful. "The way I see it is that if a murder has yet to be committed then nothing has been done, and if nothing has been done, well, then there is nothing in which to be interested, is there?"

"That is sophistry. Are you interested in anything? No, don't bother… I think I can guess the answer to that one. Tell me one thing though, are you actually a policeman?"

"Well, of course I am sir. Why else would I be in a police station at this hour of the night? Really. The things people ask. Didn't I tell you? People come in here and ask the strangest questions."

"No, you didn't mention things people *ask*."

"I didn't? Oh well, never mind... I don't suppose it matters." The man shrugged indifferently.

"Now look here," I said, jabbing the counter with a forefinger, "I've had just about enough of this. Are you interested in this murder or not?"

"Honestly, sir? No, I am not. However, since you are evidently determined to make something of it, I suppose you'd better wait here whilst I fetch the inspector..."

With that he turned and walked away to his desk where he sat down and began speaking with the man who had appeared to be asleep. I couldn't hear them, but I was not assured that they were taking anything very seriously. Words were exchanged, glances at me, more conversation and even laughter until my policeman stood again and left the room. Ten minutes later he returned, resumed his seat, picked up his paper again and quickly disappeared behind its large pages as he unfolded them. Having little hope of any further assistance, I was just about to leave when the door behind me opened and a man in a smart grey double-breasted suit entered.

"Are you the gentleman with the murder?"

"Yes, yes, I am he. Who might you be?" From the way he was dressed I thought he might be selling something.

"I'm in charge sir, I'm the inspector. I think it is I to whom you need confess..."

Likho

"Confess? *Confess*? What are you talking about? Confess to *what*?"

"Why, to a murder, sir... or do you have other confessions to make?"

"I have *no* confessions to make. None. None at all..."

"You don't? But I was led to believe that you wanted..."

"*To report a murder*... to *report* one, not *admit* to one."

"Ah, I see sir. Please accept my sincerest apologies. I have been misled indeed... although, you *do* look as if you *might* have committed a murder, if I may say so..."

"Well, I *haven't*, although I might do so very soon."

"I beg your pardon sir?"

"Never mind. Do you want to hear about this murder or am I wasting my time?"

"Of course I do, sir, of course I do. Come with me, we'll go somewhere a little quieter."

I couldn't imagine a little quieter somewhere, but I followed as he led me out and along a corridor to a small windowless room. Two uncomfortable chairs were separated by an old desk. The floor was covered in dirty linoleum of indeterminate colour and the walls were shedding successive layers of green paint which blistered, flaked and peeled like a snake sloughing off its dead skin. A cheap old clock hung on one wall; it was showing the wrong time and shamelessly ticking very loudly as it did so, and the single lamp which lit the dismal room had attracted a large brown moth which fluttered around, launching frequent but futile assaults on it. We sat down on either side of the table; the inspector pulled a pipe and some tobacco from his pocket, placed them on the table and then looked at me.

"Now, sir, what's all this about a murder? Who is to be killed and when?"

"*What?*" I was beginning to regret bothering, feeling more than a little annoyed.

"Well, sir, we need to know who is to be…"

"I heard what you said. I exclaimed '*what*' in order to express disbelief rather than interrogatively or from a want of hearing. The murder has been committed already. It is finished. Over. A man is dead. His *fate* is *accompli*, if you will…"

"I see. Well, that's a different thing altogether wouldn't you say?"

"Different from what?"

"From a murder yet to be done. That is quite different. You see if…

"Yes, *yes*, I understand." I began to think the man an idiot.

"Ah, good, that's good. Now, you say that you don't wish to confess to this murder?"

"I do. I mean I do *not*... that is, I *do* say that I *do not* wish to confess to this murder."

"Why?"

"Because I did not commit it."

"Ah, yes… the best of all reasons." He picked up his pipe and stared at it for a moment, placed it back on the table and looked at me again. "Do you have a match?"

"No."

"Oh." He looked again at the pipe and nodded his head. "It is no matter. Well, sir, is there anything else?"

"*Anything else?*"

"Yes? No?"

"Well, now you mention it, *yes*, there is one small matter, though I am almost reluctant to trouble you with it."

Likho

"Oh, please go on, sir… nothing troubles us here."

"Yes, I have come to that conclusion… but never mind."

"I don't mind at all sir. Now, what more might you have to tell us?"

"Well, would you like to know where this murder took place? It seems to me that might be helpful."

"Helpful? In what way, sir?"

"Helpful, *sir*, in your enquiries…"

"What enquiries? Oh, yes, of course, I understand you… please, continue."

I explained as simply as I could for the benefit of the obtuse detective where my dead neighbour was to be found and gave a brief account of the circumstances in which I had happened upon the body. All the time I was talking and for a moment after I had finished, the man stared at his unlit pipe, occasionally reaching out and stroking it gently, as if trying to reassure the thing that he hadn't forsaken it. I was about to prompt him when he looked up and, with a very strange expression, began to speak.

"I see. Well, that is all very interesting, or it would be if it were true…"

"*If it were true*? What are…?"

"I fear, sir, that you have been deceived, or indeed that you are deceiving yourself, and *me*, with this tale."

"Deceived? Deceiving myself… what? *What*?"

"Yes sir, I think so. Is it possible you are the victim of a practical joke?"

"A practical joke? There is no joke… except for *you*."

"Me, sir?"

"You sir, I think you are a joke, you and your colleagues…"

"Oh, that's a little harsh, don't you think sir?"

"No, I do not, and I shall be saying so to your superior officer. This is absurd."

"Absurd? No sir, not at all… it is all perfectly reasonable."

"How is it so? How is this reasonable? It is the most *ridiculous*…"

"It is all remarkably simple… you know that the apartment of which you speak is unoccupied, do you not? Well, you must do if you live next to it…"

"I know no such thing. It is, or rather it *was* occupied by an elderly gentleman, my neighbour, and his murdered body occupies it still, if you would but care to go and see for yourself."

"You say so, sir, but you are mistaken. We know your street… we know *every* street, *every* building, *every* apartment, *every* occupant… it is our business to know, and that is how I can assure you that the apartment you mention has *no* occupant, and if there is no occupant then an occupant cannot have been murdered, can he?"

"That would be true if your information was correct, but it is not. The apartment is occupied by an elderly gentleman, or rather, it was, and he has been there as long as I have… well, longer, obviously, since he was there when I moved in."

"Sir, our information *is* correct. It is *always* correct; it always has been and, I dare say, always will be. We take great care to ensure our information is accurate and up to date. The apartment of which you speak is unoccupied. It has been so for many years and if I had the time to verify the details I could tell you the name of the last resident, the date he moved in, where he came from and where he is now. I do *not* have the time, however, and thus you must take my word for it."

"You don't know what you are talking about. There is a dead man in that apartment. I have seen him. He is my neighbour, and he has been murdered... *strangled*, I should say, from the look of him, and he is there as large as life, no... well, he is there for all to see who might be bothered to look."

"*Strangled*? You are a pathologist then, sir?"

"Indeed I am not."

"Then how can you be certain of the cause of death?"

"I did not say I was *certain*. I said '*strangled... from the look of him*' – nothing about being certain."

"You are familiar, then, with the look of strangled corpses? You have seen many of them?"

"No, sir, I have never seen one before..."

"Yet you claim to know how one should appear... odd, wouldn't you say? *I* would not claim to know the look of a thing I had never seen. When I discover a body, I await the opinion of an expert on the cause of death rather than take it upon myself, lacking any medical training as I do, to voice an opinion based on nothing but assumption."

"Oh, this is getting us nowhere..."

"I don't know where it is you wish to go, sir."

"I wish to go home, and I wish to be accompanied by you in order that you may see for yourself the victim of a murder."

"A victim who does not exist, despite your insistence. Our facts are not wrong, they are never wrong. Our reputation for not being wrong is unassailable and the envy of the world, if I may say so. No one lives in that apartment; you have no neighbour, and thus he cannot have been murdered, not by strangulation or any other means."

"Well, you may have an unassailable reputation for not being wrong, I don't know about that... but I, on the other hand, if *I* were to be known for a thing then it would be for being certain of my facts. My neighbour has been murdered."

"But you are not known for it, are you sir? For being certain of your facts, that is?"

"Well, now that you mention it, I am *not* known at all, and have no wish to be."

"I am sure you *are* known to *us*, sir... everyone is known to us... well, except your neighbour... *on account of his not existing.*"

"You will do nothing then? Why will you not at least send a man to have a look?"

"There is no need. I know he would find nothing... but look, I am not an unreasonable fellow, and I will indulge you if it makes you happy..."

"*Indulge* me? You mean *patronise* me...this is beyond belief..."

"The only thing beyond belief, sir, is your tale... but come, tell me about this man whom you believe to have been so brutally murdered... *strangled*, I think you said? What is the name of this unfortunate gentleman, your neighbour?"

"I don't know. He has never told me his name... I suppose that must seem strange? It certainly seems rather odd to me now that I think about it."

"No, sir, it doesn't seem strange at all. Why should it? How could you know his name? After all, he doesn't exist. Never mind that though, please go on..."

"Is there any point?"

Likho

"None at all but go on anyway."

"No, I will waste no more of your time, or mine…"

"Time is not ours to squander or save, sir. Now, tell me, how do you know this gentleman, your neighbour?"

"I don't know him. I have called on him on several evenings after returning from my supper."

"He invited you to call on him?"

"No. He did not. I found the door to his apartment open when I passed… I went in to enquire if he was aware of it. That was the case on several nights, and we happened to engage in conversation…"

"Every night?"

"No, not consecutive nights."

"The subjects of your conversations, sir?"

"Oh, various subjects," said I, and with a dismissive shake of my head added "and none of them relevant, I'm sure."

"Well, that is not for you to say, but never mind for the present. Now, sir, did your neighbour call on you?"

"No, he did not."

"Then you saw him only in his home?"

"Ah, no, not quite. I saw him twice in the street."

"Oh? Which street? Yours?"

"No, but others nearby."

"The names of those other streets?"

"I couldn't say, I pay little attention to such things unless they are a specific subject of interest at the time."

"You spoke with your neighbour when you saw him in the street?"

"No. On both occasions I saw him through the window of a café… he passed by outside, and I was sitting inside, with a good view of the street… though whilst the window might have allowed an exchange of views, the glass prevented any exchange of words..."

"I see." The inspector nodded, and a slight look of exasperation appeared on his face.

"Good."

"It is? What is good?"

"That you see."

"Ah. Actually, I don't, but never mind. Now, what more can you tell me? Your neighbour... has he friends? Other visitors?"

"How should I know?"

"It's your story, sir... so if you don't know, well, then..."

"When I was in his apartment, I never saw another person. He never spoke of friends or acquaintances, or of much at all, now I think of it, well, nothing relating to his own circumstances."

"You know little about him then... not even his name. Well, I can't say I am surprised since you are the only person who has seen this man..."

"Ah, no, no... there was the woman with him... she must be friend or family..."

"Then he did have a visitor?"

"No, she was with him in the street... she was holding his arm, I think. I saw her with him twice."

"Can you describe her? Do you know where she might be found?"

"No, I know nothing of her, and I cannot describe her except that she was an old woman dressed in black."

"Well, describe her face... your saw her face, did you not?"

"Alas, I did not. I'm not even sure she had one."

"Really? Oh well, not to worry."

Likho

"No?"

"It's an inconsequential detail, isn't it? We have no means of finding her, so it doesn't matter if she has a face or not, does it?"

"No, I suppose not, though it might matter to her? Ah, but what about the concierge? He and his wife must surely know the man... come and speak with them. They will tell you."

"Ah yes," he said, adding thoughtfully "I had forgotten him and his poor wife... what a terrible tragedy..."

"Forgotten him? What's so terrible about forgetting someone? I suppose it might cause offence to some people, but it's hardly a tragedy."

"That wasn't what I meant. I was referring to their children."

"They have no children."

"No, they do not. They did, but now they do not."

"Really? What became of them?"

"You don't know?"

"Well, no, obviously not... why would I ask if I knew? I am not in the habit of enquiring after facts I know already. Where is the point in that?"

"No point at all. Nevertheless, I am surprised that you *don't* know..."

"A man can only ever be surprised by what he knows, and never by what he does not."

"No doubt there is logic in that statement... and it might even be funny?" The inspector stroked his moustache, a feature I hadn't noticed until that moment, and the thought occurred to me that he had grown it during our conversation.

"Thank you. But what of the children who once were but are no longer? What happened?"

"They were drowned in a bath, sir, both of them... a boy and girl... the boy was eleven or twelve, the girl eight, I think."

"*Two children?*" Suddenly I felt rather uneasy. "What happened? An accident?"

"No, it was no accident. It was murder..."

"*Murder?* What happened? Who did it?"

"It was a long time ago. I was a young *gendarme* at the time and had just been posted here... it was a terrible shock, such things were unheard of... well, you must know that yourself? Anyway, it was their father who found them in one of the apartments. They had both been held under the water... held by their throats and drowned. Poor things..."

"Who did it?"

"Oh, yes... well, of course, it was the people who lived in the apartment. An old man and his wife..."

"They were arrested, I suppose? Why did they do it?"

"Ah, well, no... they vanished before the bodies were discovered. They were never found, not a trace of them, and so we have never known their motive for the... well, you know. No one could understand why anyone would do such a thing and, of course, only they could tell."

"I see. Well, now you have told me I wish perhaps you hadn't. But how can two people disappear without a trace?"

"I do not know, but disappear they did, almost as if they had never existed... indeed, there was a theory at the time that they *had* never existed."

"Why?"

Likho

"Well, sir, it's strange, but neither parent of those unfortunate children could ever recall the names of the old couple or give other than the vaguest of descriptions. Of course, that made *them* suspects in the opinions of some, but they couldn't have committed the crime as they could attest to their movements all that day, and there were many reliable witnesses to support them. It remains a mystery to this day. I *am* surprised you haven't heard about it. It was something of a *cause célèbre* at the time."

"What a dreadful thing to suffer… to find your children dead like that, the poor man."

"Indeed. It disturbed his mind greatly… and he spent quite a time in hospital, if you get my meaning?"

"*Hospital?* Oh, yes, I see. How long ago was he released?"

"Released?"

"Discharged, allowed to go home?"

"He wasn't. He killed himself… drowned himself in a bath, as I recall… died just like his children… not sure how he did it though, never heard of anyone drowning himself in a bath. Anyway, all very sad."

"No, no, that can't be right. I have seen him."

"I doubt that sir."

"I tell you I have seen him… I saw him recently; he was mopping the floor in the lobby."

"No doubt you saw someone, sir… maybe a cleaner, but not the concierge, most assuredly *not* the concierge. If you do not believe me then ask his widow…"

"His widow? You mean his *wife?* I shall do just that," I replied, standing up to leave. "I am not imagining dead people, or people who do not exist."

"If you say so, sir. Perhaps you might ask her tomorrow when she brings your lunch."

"What are you... how do you know that?" I sat down again.

"We know everything, sir. How do you think we manage our work?"

"What do you mean? What are you? Some sort of intelligence service? Spies?"

"I wouldn't put it quite like that, but we like to keep ourselves informed."

"*This is outrageous,*" I exclaimed, my outrage unrestrained, "*absolutely outrageous.* I've never heard anything so... well..."

"*Outrageous*, sir?"

"Exactly. How can... I mean, don't we have *rights*? Don't I have the right to privacy?"

"You might think so, sir, you might think so... but *rights* are a luxury which a civilised society can ill afford," the inspector said, looking thoughtful, "you see, *rights* are invariably used to cover *wrongs*; they are a privilege habitually misused and so must be withheld for the common good, because people *without* rights dare do no wrongs..."

"That, sir, is a paralogism, plain and simple," said I, adding "though it may very well be true, which is rather troubling... but never mind – what possible use can such trivial details about my life be to anyone?"

"In my experience, sir, a thing which seems trivial today can be crucial tomorrow."

"And to gather all this potentially vital intelligence you have a network of spies, I suppose? Perhaps we are *all* informants?"

"Perhaps you are."

"Oh no, not I. Most assuredly not." I wagged a finger in his face to emphasise my point.

Likho

"Well, sir, your presence here would suggest otherwise." The inspector sat back in his chair and looked incredibly pleased with himself, as if he just ensnared a suspect.

"I do not see how; I haven't told you anything."

"Ah, but the things people *don't* tell us are just as interesting as the things they *do*…"

"And what" I said, interrupting him rather rudely, "have I not told you that is so interesting? And what do you infer from it?"

"Now that *would* be telling, sir…" He winked at me and then began to laugh.

"I've had enough of this nonsense," I said, "although, there is *one* more thing before I go… tell me, if you will, inspector… in which apartment were those children killed? Was it mine?"

"Well, your apartment is on the second floor is it not? Your *neighbour*, according to your story, lives, or rather *lived* across the landing, at the top of the stairs…"

"That is correct."

"Yes, that's what I thought. Well, it was the apartment next door to you… the apartment between yours and your imaginary neighbour's."

I was silent for a moment and admit to having been rather unnerved by that information. The police inspector smiled at me, nodding his head and trying to appear what I took for sympathetic. I sat back in my seat and drummed my fingers on the table.

"That apartment… it is unoccupied, I suppose?"

"You are right sir; no one has lived there from that day to this. People don't care to live in places where… well, you know…"

Darton

"Yes, my neighbour insisted it was empty... the elderly gentleman who doesn't live in the empty apartment beyond, at the top of the stairs; that same elderly gentleman who you say cannot have been murdered..." With a shake of my head, I stood up.

"Is that all? You are going?"

"There seems little point in staying. I have reported a murder, and you don't believe me. You do not intend to investigate and so there is nothing further to be said. I shall go home."

"*Investigate*, sir? To what end, other than for me to go out now on a freezing cold night to see an empty apartment? No, sir, it would be waste of my time..."

"What? Do I hear you right? You consider investigating a murder to be a waste of time?"

"In this case, I do, sir, yes. It doesn't merit our attention, especially considering that it cannot have happened."

"I have never heard anything so unbelievably stupid in my life. What do you do if not investigate crime, if that is not a silly question?"

"It *is* a silly question. As a citizen of this town, you must be familiar with our mission statement?"

"Be so kind as to refresh my memory."

"Of course. It's very easy... '*Working together in the pursuit of justice.*' You see? No mention of crime, or of investigating anything."

"Yes, but what about the *pursuit of justice*?" I was determined not to let it go.

"Oh, well, that's easy," he replied with a grin, "because, as we all know, there is no such thing as justice... and therefore no point pursuing it."

Likho

"That applies to this conversation too… Ah, but wait a moment, what about the murder of the children… you investigated that?"

"No, there was nothing to investigate. The occupiers of the apartment were culpable, but they had vanished without trace and that was the end of the matter" the inspector said proudly.

"Well, sir" said I, moving to the door, "it is quite plain that I have made a mistake in coming here, so I shall bid you… oh, just a minute… perhaps could you tell me what I should do about the corpse of my neighbour? It seems a little heartless to leave him where he is."

"Quite so." The inspector laughed and then went on "perhaps you might ask the concierge to take care of it?"

"I am obliged, thank you. Good night. I shall trouble you no further."

"Good night, sir…" said he, all too cheerfully, "and mind how you go." I'd say he was feeling rather pleased with himself.

Leaving him alone in that grimy room I walked down the passageway, through the deserted lobby and out into the fresh night air. There was a short flight of steps leading down to the pavement and, as I stepped cautiously on each frost-covered tread, I had the oddest idea that they had not been there when I'd arrived…

It was well after midnight, maybe as late as two, or even three o'clock, although I couldn't say it mattered much what the time was. The street was empty and silent. The moon was up somewhere behind me and shining much more brightly than the streetlamps which stood like a guard of honour, lining my route home.

The windows of the concierge's rooms were in darkness and the lobby silent. I closed the outer door as quietly as possible, crossed to the stairs and climbed slowly to the second floor. I hadn't a clue what to do about the old man's body other than to pull his apartment door shut and then worry about it in the morning. I would tell the concierge and leave it to him to do as he thought proper; I didn't believe *he* was dead any more than I believed my neighbour to be non-existent. Actually, I wasn't sure what I believed... the police inspector had been very confident with his facts, and what reason had he to misinform me?

When I reached the old man's door it was shut firmly. I pushed at it, but it didn't give. The concierge must have been up already and so, with that taken care of, I let myself into my apartment and went to bed. I wasn't the least bit tired, but that was where I wanted to be – it was where I was *meant* to be... not discovering bodies, reporting murders, or out in the dead of night taking the salute from a parade of lampposts...

4. 'WHOSOEVER BELIEVETH...'[3]

Friday 2nd
My dead neighbour remained with me through the night, only departing when the first light of the day drove him off into the shadows…

Despite my best efforts to put him from my mind, every time I closed my eyes and tried to sleep, I saw him in his chair… eyes bulging, tongue hanging out, his throat crushed and blackened with finger marks. Then, as the hours passed, I had the same vision of him with my eyes open, and after a while I wasn't sure whether my eyes were open or not, or if I were asleep or not; then I thought I might be *dreaming* I was *awake*, and when I got out of my bed at dawn, I thought it possible I was dreaming that too.

My grip on reality was further loosened when I went to run my bath, only to find it already full. Having no recollection of filling it and supposing that I *must* be dreaming still, I jumped in…

The water was freezing. Cold as it was, though, its effect wasn't instantaneous and my reaction delayed momentarily because I was still wearing my night clothes, dressing gown and slippers; but the shock, when it came, restored me quickly to my senses. Cursing aloud, I leapt from the bath, slipped and ended face down on the wet floor where I lay still to wait for the pain of fractured bones to set in. A moment or two later, realising the only thing to suffer any injury was my dignity, I got to my feet, pulled my wet things off, wrapped myself in a warm dry robe and sat down on a chair in the corner of the room.

There was no doubting that I was awake, but if I wasn't dreaming then who had filled the bath? And when? Well, the solution with the fewest assumptions is the one that suggests I did it, and that I must have been sleepwalking. There can be no other conclusion, *and* it answers the question as to whether I slept, which was a nice, if unexpected bonus.

I pulled the plug and watched the water drain away. After a couple of minutes, only a few drops remained, trickling like tears down the white enamel; but, whilst the bath had emptied, my head had filled with drowned children…

With my mind much disturbed, I was anxious to be outside where I might find something to distract me from such thoughts. Forgetting breakfast, I dressed hurriedly and went downstairs. Passing my neighbour's door reminded me that I had to speak with the concierge concerning the possibility of a corpse in need of attention, but when five minutes of knocking loudly at his door brought no response, I tired of waiting and went out, leaving the matter unresolved, and firm in my resolve that it be my problem no longer.

After a cup of strong, sweet coffee which I took standing at a nearby bar, I felt sufficiently reinvigorated to continue my morning walk and, thinking I'd like to put some distance between me and the scene of the crime, assuming there had been one, I crossed the river and walked along to the old abbey, a place where solitude is almost guaranteed at this time of the year.

The monastery estates are spread out below the castle hill, encroaching on the lower southern slopes where,

Likho

for centuries, the monks have cultivated fruit trees, harvested honey from beehives, and grapes from vineyards which have kept their wine presses busy year after year for as long as anyone can remember. Above those bountiful acres, though, the ground is too steep and remains thickly wooded right up to the old ramparts.

The mediaeval abbey church was built on the lower ground, near the river, and so a frequent victim of its floodwaters; but, in the first days of the seventeenth century, it was abandoned and a new one built nearby on slightly higher ground where the faithful can be assured of dry feet all year round as they stand, lost in its baroque vastness, awestruck by sacred relics and humbled before its mighty gilded altarpiece. The focal point of all this splendour is the statue of a child to which countless miracles have been attributed over the years, and who has been seen to weep real tears, though I have yet to see him weep for me.

The old abbey stands as a soulful ruin; its crumbling cloister is still a sanctuary for those seeking it, whilst for those less inclined to solitude, the adjoining gardens by the river are popular on summer evenings.

Behind and a little way up the hill, the library and its adjoining scriptorium stand well above the highest of all possible floods and separated from the main buildings they are safe from the spread of fire too. Every twenty years, for one day, we, the people, are allowed to walk through the vast gallery and though we cannot browse through the books, we can at least enjoy the spectacular frescoes on the ceilings, from which watchful gods and putti make sure we don't dare touch anything. I'm not certain how many volumes line its walls, but there must be tens of thousands, and amongst them are many priceless ancient books, all safe from the ravages of sunlight and greasy fingers. The monks still produce intricately illuminated pages, though I imagine that these days it is done for profit rather than piety.

As well as their artistic talents, those industrious brothers are famous for the produce of their brewhouse, winery and distillery. They brew a particularly good beer, and for *good*, you should probably read *strong*, very strong, and along with a passable white wine, they distil a pear brandy which is not for those of a weak disposition. There is a popular opinion that the monks are a silent order, but my suspicion is that a state of perpetual inebriation has rendered them incapable of speech. Anyway, tempted though I was to fortify *my* spirit with some of theirs, I avoided the bar of the abbey *auberge* and went instead for a stroll through the old cemetery, and if you are wondering why I should want to be in such a melancholic place, I can say only that it suited my mood.

Although it was cold, I wanted to sit for a while and share in some of the peace which those in their graves were enjoying, although not quite so eternally. The chest tomb of a long-dead abbot or prior served me as a bench and though it seemed disrespectful, it provided a good resting place for both of us, and I hoped that the old boy would be as charitable in death as I trust he was in life. There was an inscription on the stone, but centuries of rain and frost had worked hard to erase it, leaving its occupant nameless. I wondered what I might find were I to lift the slab? His empty skull grinning at me, happy to see the light of day once again?

All around lay the graves of long-dead brothers, their headstones encrusted with lichen, all forgotten and neglected, some leaning, and others toppled by the unstoppable tree roots which are pushing up the ground and forcing old dry bones from the world below into the sunlight above.

A mind more suggestible than mine might imagine, on a dark night, a voice whispering from beneath…

"Remember me? I was brother so-and-so…"

"Yes, brother," comes a reply, *"I remember you… it's I, brother…"*

His voice is joined by another, and then another, all free from the constraints of monastic rule to indulge in idle chatter for all eternity, with the gossip of the cloister carried away on the wind…

When it became too cold to remain sitting, I bade a silent farewell to the dead and walked back through the ruins of the old abbey church, along the nave and out by the south transept door.

Sunlight flooded through the broken vaults and the few remaining ribs cast shadows on the ground where grass now replaces flagstones, and where the sound of chanting monks was once heard, now the only music is made by the wind whistling through the ruins. The massive piers which once bore the weight of the roof now support only wild roses and honeysuckle which have grown up around them, and where incense used to fill the air, now the scent of flowers hangs upon it on long summer evenings. Little by little, nature is strengthening its hold on the old building, imperceptibly weakening it, and one day, one day many thousands of years from now, it will have reduced it to dust. It might survive for a while in the memories of those to come, but when there is no one left to remember, it will be as if it were never here…

As I reached the cloister I thought about my old neighbour. Where would he end up? With no one to care, his only memorial will be a name in a cemetery ledger, where it will be soon forgotten. I feel no pity for him. I didn't like him. Besides, he was an old man, and his days were numbered; his murderer has done only what nature was taking too long to do...

Leaving the monastery behind, I walked back to the bridge and crossed over to the old town, to my street, my apartment, and my lunch. There was still no answer from the concierge, though his wife had evidently been up to discharge her usual duties for me. My neighbour's door was as firmly closed as ever it had been and so for the second time that day, I tried to forget all about him, which, of course, I couldn't. Whatever I did, wherever I did it, he was in my mind. He sat with me as I ate; he spent the afternoon in my sitting room, and later, when I went out for supper, he joined me for that too. It would be fair to say that he was beginning to irritate me which, I think you'll agree, is a difficult thing for a dead man to do.

Luckily, that growing sense of irritation lasted only until I returned home because when I got here, I found the old man's door ajar and a light coming from within. Thinking it must be the concierge I went directly in and was just about to speak when I saw my neighbour sitting in his chair as usual, very much alive and certainly looking as well as ever he had. I stopped in the doorway, mouth wide open and eyes staring in disbelief at him. He stared back for a moment and then broke the silence with what I can only describe as an ill-judged attempt to be funny...

"What's the matter? You look as if you've seen a ghost."

"I...well...I thought...no, wait..." Whilst words didn't quite fail me, they didn't exactly come rushing to help, and the few that did made no attempt to work together. Overcoming the shock, with racing heart and trembling from head to foot, I managed to croak a sentence "I thought you were dead."

"I beg your pardon?" The old man frowned inquisitorially.

"*Dead.* You were dead."

"Yes, that's what I thought you said."

"The last time I saw you, you were dead…" I peered hard at him, not sure if I was seeing things; I wanted to touch him, just to check he was real and living, but the thought of physical contact with the old man was utterly repellent and made me feel sick.

"Really? And when was that, may I ask?"

"Last night… about midnight, I'm not certain. Time doesn't seem to have been following the normal rules over the last couple of days."

"Curious," the old man said with a nod of his head. "You are quite sure? I ask only because I don't *appear* to be dead at present… I think you'll agree?"

"I am sure, yes. You were dead. Very dead. There, in that chair, sitting just where you are now…" I pointed a shaking finger at him, "but you are right, you do seem to be alive."

"I see. In this chair… last night?"

"Last night… well, I suppose it might have been the previous night… or perhaps it's tonight, or tomorrow." A casual shrug gave some emphasis to my uncertainty.

"You seem a little confused and a little upset too, if I may say so?"

"A little tired, that is all… I am not sleeping well. Things are a little muddled. I am sorry… but surely you can see that this is all rather strange?"

Darton

"Well, as *you* can see, I am here now, and as for being dead last night, or the night before, well, it would seem unlikely, wouldn't you say?"

"Yes, it would... it was all very real at the time though. You were sitting there... in that chair... and you had been killed..."

"I had?"

"You had. Strangled. You were as dead as any corpse I have ever seen."

"You must have been dreaming."

"There's no other explanation. A strange thing for me to dream though... mind you, if it was a dream then at least I didn't go to the police to report your murder. That was all a bit odd too, now I come to think of it."

"Oh? You went to the police?"

"Well, yes, at least I think I did... isn't it the thing to do when one discovers a murdered neighbour? I certainly thought so. I spoke to a nice fellow, an inspector – not that he looked like one – he was dressed in a very smart suit and looked more like a salesman than a detective. I'm sure I was there, the memory of it is very vivid. Perhaps I should go back and ask them?"

"Perhaps you should."

"They would think me rather stupid... and they didn't believe me anyway, so perhaps it doesn't matter? Perhaps I should forget all about it?"

"Perhaps you should do that too." The old man stared into space, unblinking, and nothing in his expression gave any clue to what was in his mind; then, he snapped out of his trance, focussed his eyes on me and asked, "*why* didn't they believe you?"

"Well, *that* is a strange tale indeed," said I, "are you sitting comfortably? Good, then I'll begin...

Likho

"The most significant obstacle concerned your existence and the fact that, well, that it is *doubtful*... well, I *say* doubtful... what he *actually* said was that you *don't* exist at all, and that this apartment is unoccupied and has been so for years..."

"Really?"

"Oh yes," I affirmed, "he was most insistent on that, and consequently refused to send anyone to investigate your death. He said I must have imagined you."

"Well, that was very unhelpful."

"Yes, I thought so too. I argued the point, but he wasn't having any of it. He told me the concierge doesn't exist either. It seems I have been imagining him too because he has been dead for ages... committed suicide in the asylum... drowned himself in his bath. I didn't know a man could do that... I think the inspector said that too. Apparently, it all happened after his children were murdered – the concierge's children, *not* the inspector's, obviously – murdered... drowned in their bath by the old couple in the apartment between this one and mine."

"It seems he knows much, this inspector of yours..."

"Well, he *doesn't* know you. I'm not sure whether that is a good or bad thing. I suppose you should take care not to be murdered though, because he will not lift a finger to find your killer..."

"Lucky for the man who does away with me then, although *I* should hardly care. But never mind, I don't expect to be murdered again."

"*Again?*"

"Well, have I not been murdered already? You saw my corpse."

"I did, and I have seen the ghost of the concierge too, downstairs mopping the lobby floor…"

"But you don't believe in such things?"

"No, I do not. The inspector is wrong about the concierge and quite plainly wrong about you as well…" I paused for a moment before asking cautiously "although… is he right about the murder of the children?"

"Ah, yes, that… well, it was a long time ago."

"Yes, thirty years? Were you here?"

"Then and long before."

"The story of the murders is true then? I didn't dream that?"

"Your dreams may be strange, but the facts in the matter are true, more or less."

"They were drowned in the bath next door?"

"Yes."

"Did you know them? I suppose you must have done. The children, and the couple next door?"

"*Must* I?"

"Yes, of course you must have, if you were living here at the time…"

"You are making assumptions again about what I know. You should not." The old man wagged a finger at me as if I were a naughty child. "I didn't *know* the children. I saw them from time to time, but I didn't *know* them. I don't care for children; they are a nuisance."

"What were their names?"

"I don't recall. Perhaps I never knew their names. I had no reason to know them. Is this an interrogation?"

"What of the old couple? Your neighbours?"

"I didn't know them either… and, actually, I thought the old man lived alone, I don't recall ever having the idea that he was married. Of course, I could be wrong…

at the time everyone was certain that he had a wife living with him and with whom he drowned the children."

"What was his name?"

"Ah, now that is a good question..."

"Does it merit a good answer?"

"Perhaps, but I'm afraid you'll have to seek it elsewhere."

"Everyone in this seems to be anonymous... a mystery indeed. You didn't know him well then?"

"I don't remember ever having a conversation with him."

"And you never saw the woman?"

"No... well, I might have seen *a* woman, but who she was I cannot say."

"Then he *might* have had a wife? What did she look like?"

"What is this? Why all these questions? Are you working for the police now?"

"No, of course not... at least, not as far as I know. I am interested in the case; that is all. How could anyone *not* be interested? I thought only that if you were here at the time, you might have something to tell."

"I have as much to tell now as then..."

"Well, what of the woman you saw? What can you tell me of her?"

"Not much. I saw her only two or three times. She was old, very old... I thought she was an old widow because she was always dressed in black. I certainly never thought she was his wife. Oh, there was *one* thing, though – I think she had only one eye..."

I shuddered as my neighbour described the old woman, and it was a reaction which the old man did not miss. He said nothing though, and merely studied me with undisguised suspicion. After a moment of uncomfortable silence, I recovered my thoughts.

"You are certain she didn't live here, next door?"

"I am certain of nothing regarding that woman, or any former neighbours, other than what I've already told you. If you wish to know more then you will have to ask her yourself."

"What? Is she still alive?"

"Probably not. But even dead, she can say more than I am able. I *can* say one thing though…" With an elbow on the arm of his chair he leaned towards me like an old woman about to deliver news of a scandal. "It is my opinion that a thin and frail old woman such as I saw could not have drowned healthy young children in a bath… I doubt she had the strength even to turn on a tap."

"You think that the man acted alone then?"

"No, I don't think that either. He was too old, a weak old man, much as I am… it is hard to see how he could have managed it."

"Then you think them both innocent?"

"Ah, who is truly innocent? I will say only that I was surprised anyone could think the man physically capable of the crime of which he was accused."

"Then who do you suppose did it?"

"Well, I wish I could tell you."

"If the old man and his alleged accomplice were so obviously incapable then why were they presumed guilty?"

"There were no other suspects… except for the parents, but they couldn't have done it, they didn't have an opportunity, or any reason to do it, not as far as I understood. The fact that the old man next door disappeared so promptly did his defence no favours, but I didn't think that was sufficient reason to convict him."

Likho

"I find it hard to believe that these people could have vanished quite so completely. Someone must have known where they were."

"Believe it or not as you choose, but that is how it was. Speculate as much as you like, you will get no nearer to the facts than you are now. Perhaps the old man threw himself in the river? Perhaps, plagued by guilt and shame he drowned himself? Just imagine the scene... *a dark and stormy night, an icy wind blows through the streets, the bent and broken figure of an old man – a child-killer pursued by a mob, jumps to his death from the old town bridge, to be swept away in the swirling waters below.*

"Or perhaps he grew a beard, changed his name and lives in the next street? Or maybe I am he? You wouldn't know if I were."

"Ah, but someone would..." replied I, confidently, "the concierge and his wife would surely know you?"

"Not necessarily, they were unable to recall anything about the old man, not even his name, which is odd considering that they must have known him for some time."

"Ah, yes, the inspector told me that. So, *are* you he? Are you the murderer of two children? No one would think of looking for you next door to the scene of the crime... well, not if my experience of our police is anything to judge by."

"That is an interesting theory, and as good as any other. Perhaps you should share it with your inspector?"

"I don't think I have much credibility with him. Oh, I can see it now... I walk in there and tell him that a murderer whom he has sought for thirty years has been living right under his nose all the time and that it is none other than my non-existent neighbour whom I claimed had himself been murdered only the day before, and who now, by the way, has been miraculously restored to life. How long do you think it will be before I am dragged away to the asylum?"

"Yes, that is a distinct possibility. Anyway, amusing as it is to irritate our local police, I don't think we want to stir them up too much. We don't want our peaceful home swarming with detectives, do we? We don't want them re-opening old cases and poking around in corners... who knows what they mind find?"

"Don't we? For all *I* care, they can poke about as much as they like; I have no old cases to open, or *re-open*. But I shouldn't worry too much, the inspector didn't seem interested in poking around anywhere... and as far as it concerns you, well, he's unlikely to call upon a man who doesn't exist, is he?

"Anyway, I'm rather tired and I think it is time I went... with your murder on my mind, I slept badly last night – if it *was* last night? Assuming no further attempts are made on your life, perhaps I shall speak with you tomorrow evening?"

"I'll look forward to it. Come as late as you like." With that he smiled and raised his right hand in a gesture of farewell, though with his twisted arthritic fingers it looked more like a parody of a papal blessing.

I left him alone in his room, returned to my apartment and went directly to my bed. The moon was up, shining brightly and throwing its light across the floor where shadows cast by wind-driven clouds marched past in a stately parade. My head sank into the pillows, and I into a deep and untroubled sleep.

Saturday 3rd

I slept until nine and awoke feeling better than I have for days, after a long and dreamless sleep. I am not much in favour of dreamless sleep; it seems to me that it is time wasted, time during which the unconscious mind ought to be unravelling unresolved problems and working through them in dreams and nightmares in readiness for a new day. But let us continue...

After a leisurely breakfast I set out on my morning walk. The air was cold and fresh; breathing it deep into my lungs felt good and made me feel a little light-headed as a rush of oxygen flooded my brain. All the confusion of the last few days was gone, my thoughts were clear, and as I watched fruit sellers in the market square from the comfort of a café, I decided to call on the police inspector again. It was a loose end which needed to be dealt, and then I could forget about the whole thing.

The police station looked just as it had done before, all exactly as I remembered... the outer room and its counter with the office beyond, and even the two men sitting at their desks just as they had been before – one quietly reading a paper and the other seemingly asleep, his feet resting on a chair. The man who appeared to be sleeping stood up and came over to the reception desk.

"Good morning, sir. How may I help you?" He was polite but with a subtle hint of annoyance from which I inferred that my presence was an irritation.

Unsure whether this was my *first* or *second* visit, feeling a little anxious but unconcerned, I smiled and replied confidently to his question.

"I was here the day before yesterday, late in the evening. I spoke with your colleague over there, and with an inspector. May I speak with either of them now please?"

"Wait a moment." He turned, walked back to his desk and said something to the other man who peered at me over his newspaper. Standing up and shrugging at his colleague, he strolled across to the counter, placed his paper on it and looked directly at me.

"You wanted to speak with me sir?"

"Yes. You were here the evening before last?"

"I was."

"I came in quite late; you and that gentleman were at your desks. I spoke with you here... you recall our conversation?"

"No sir, I do not."

"You remember me though?"

"No sir, I do not."

"Are you sure? I *was* here; I spoke with you about a murder. You remember? You must do?"

"No sir, I do not. Perhaps you were in a different station?"

"I assure you I spoke with you, and it was here at this very desk. Surely you cannot have forgotten? I came to report a murder... the murder of my neighbour."

"That is not something I would forget," he said, tapping his head with a finger, "but *you*, on the other hand, I do *not* remember..."

"Then how do you explain it?"

"We are the police sir; it isn't for us to explain things."

"Well, what about the inspector to whom I spoke? Perhaps I could have a word with him?"

"Wait here." Off went the policeman, back to his desk where he spoke briefly with his colleague before leaving the room. It was an odd situation... if these men didn't know me and I had not been to report the murder of my neighbour, well, then that was good – it meant I hadn't made a fool of myself after all, though it *did* mean that I was *about* to do so...

Likho

Five minutes later, the inspector appeared in his smart double-breasted suit; he looked to me just as he had before and looked *at* me without any sign of recognition.

"Good morning, sir. I understand you wish to see me?"

"Yes, I do… though I *should* say that I wish to see you *again* as this is not our first meeting."

"I think you are mistaken, sir. We have not met; I am sure of it. I never forget a face."

"The evening before last? I came to report a murder… a murder which you assured me could not have happened… you remember?"

"Sir, not only do I never forget a face, but neither do I forget a *case*. You reported no such murder on the evening before last."

"I didn't? Are you quite certain?"

"Never more so, sir."

"Right," said I with a nod, "well, it is good that you are certain, but it does leave me in a rather odd position…"

"A position which is no concern of mine, I am pleased to say," the inspector said as he pulled a watch from his waistcoat pocket – a gesture I interpreted as meaning my time was up and our conversation at an end. It was not a satisfactory end, and I as far as I was concerned there were some significant questions remaining unanswered, but it was plain that this was not the man to answer them, and so, confident there was nothing more to be had from him, I gave up my cause.

"Well, inspector, it seems I must accept your assurance that I didn't come here the night before last… and as for the murder, well, I spoke to the victim last night and he was definitely of the opinion that it had not happened either…"

"Then I should take his word for it, sir."

"Yes, I might just do that. Good day, sir."

With that, I stepped towards the door and, without looking back, out into the street. The freezing air hurt my ears and as I walked home it felt as if someone behind kept pinching them with sharp fingernails, as if trying to compel me to turn around.

On entering the lobby of my building, I encountered the concierge. Surrounded by a pool of soapy water, he was leaning heavily on a mop whilst lazily contemplating the wet floor and looking for all the world as if he'd forgotten what he was supposed to be doing. Hearing the door close he looked up and nodded at me; I took that to be a greeting of sorts.

"Good morning" said I in response. Then, as I mounted the first stair, I had an odd thought. "Tell me," I asked, "are you a ghost?"

"How should I know?" His reply came with an expression of puzzlement, and I wasn't sure whether that look was prompted by the absurdity of my question or his own lack of certainty. Smiling, I went on my way, leaving the man to consider his condition.

As I sat in my dining room and picked at a plate of cold meats, my thoughts drifted back to the murder of my neighbour. I am not convinced it was a dream, but if so, then I think it was the most extraordinarily *real* dream anyone can have had. When did it begin? Had I slept through an entire day and dreamt every detail of it? It seems unlikely. Maybe I am dreaming now? Maybe my whole life has been one long dream? If that is the case, then none of this matters. If not, well, then I think something might be awry in my relationship to reality, or at least the popular perception of it.

Likho

Whatever the status of my old neighbour, whatever the state of my mind, there is still the mystery of the murdered children. Why does it trouble me? It didn't happen in my apartment; I didn't know the victims or the suspects; it has absolutely nothing to do with me. Why, therefore, should I care?

It must be the irresistible draw of the mystery.

Well, I am no detective, and nor have I ever wished to be, but my interest has been piqued and I fear I shall not enjoy another night's rest until I have done my best to establish the facts... though hopefully without this journal reading any more like a cheap novella.

And so, *the game's afoot*, as I recall someone saying...[4] though I'm not sure what game is being played, or in which team I am playing, though whichever it is, I suspect it is losing at present.

What, then is the state of play? Well, to begin with, we have a vague account of events from the police inspector, corroborated by my old neighbour. The obvious thing would be to speak with the concierge or his wife. How does one go about it though? It isn't the sort of thing one can bring up in any of the minimal exchanges which pass for conversation between us. If I knew them better it might be easier, but as things are it would be an unacceptable affront to ask about what must remain a difficult subject for them. At best it would be insensitive of me, and at worst, cruel; I hope I am neither of those things.

I must leave the parents out of it, at least for now. That leaves the police and the old man across the passage; the former no doubt think me quite mad, and the latter insists he has no more to tell. Where to go next then? I have an idea...

Evening.

My afternoon has been spent amongst old newspapers.

It had occurred to me that the murder of two children must have been something of a sensation at the time; such a crime could not have gone unreported, at least in the local press, and the so the archives of the old town library should be worth a visit. A helpful assistant found the local papers from the period and left me alone to browse through the yellowing pages of crime reports, but not having a date for the event meant having many through which to sift. Hard as I tried to resist, I found myself frequently distracted as some article or other caught my eye, and when not distracted I found myself dozing off in the overheated room where stale air and silence conspired against all efforts to remain awake and alert.

In the end, I found nothing. But how could such a thing have gone unreported? Maybe if the victims had been of a better social class, the papers would have been full of it, but it seems the children of the poor are not worth an inch of newsprint, even when horribly murdered...

Having made no progress and feeling frustrated, I crossed the street to a café where, seated at a table by the window, I ordered some wine; the warm dry air in the library had left me feeling dehydrated and in need of a drink. As I filled my glass, I began to run through the facts... facts of which there are few, and of which none are verifiable. What *do* I know? Two children were murdered, the only suspect disappeared without trace, and grief drove the victims' father, our concierge, to commit suicide... though he is quite plainly not dead, and as that part of the story is so wildly inaccurate, then maybe all of it is untrue?

Likho

Who is dead and who's alive? Who has fled and who has died, by murder or by suicide? It is all a veritable muddle... and quite a poetic one too.

The thing which troubles me the most in this business is the means by which I first came to know of it, and that disturbs me far more than knowledge of the event itself. There is no logic to it and however hard I try I can make no sense of it. But for all that, I am certain of one thing: the key to the mystery is my old neighbour, although as to the nature of his involvement, I have no idea. To be sure of a thing without sound evidence goes against my rules and does not sit well with me at all; nevertheless, I *am* sure of it, and you may make of that what you will.

On the walk home I realised I am in serious danger of becoming obsessed, a new and very unwelcome condition for me, and a little worrying. The sensible thing, the *best* thing to do would be to forget about all of it before men begin to doubt my sanity; and why shouldn't they? After all, I am having doubts of my own...

The lobby was empty and quiet when I entered but as I climbed the stairs in the feeble light of the flickering lamps, the sound of laughter came from above, though it was silenced by the sudden sharp crack of a door slamming shut which the walls passed playfully from one to another, prolonging it unnaturally until it died away at last in the dark recesses of the lobby below. When I reached the second floor I paused outside my old neighbour's door; it was closed so I put my ear to it but could hear nothing from within. Moving on, I stopped outside the apartment next to mine; again, I listened but heard nothing. Beyond my door was silence too, though in my home I have come to think of it as peace and quiet; *silence* is beginning to sound sinister.

Darton

Ten minutes later, I was here in my study, seated at my desk, a glass of wine in one hand and a pen in the other. I like to keep a journal, though for my amusement only and not as an historical record to be studied centuries from now; if, though, that should happen then I trust the learnéd curious yet to come will appreciate my work, and I shall expect extra marks for style and quality of writing...

Setting one's thoughts and ideas down on paper and ordering them amongst the events of the day sometimes serves no useful purpose other than as an occupation for idle hands; there are times, however, when a wayward mind needs to be brought back under control and when that is so, it can prove to be an indispensable aid in identifying where and why it went astray.

Anyway, I think I have managed to make some sense of the little from which any sense can be made, and I have set aside the parts which make no sense lest some sort of sense maybe made of them on another day; and now, exhausted by all of that, I am going out for supper...

Later.

As I passed between the towers at the far end of the old town bridge and into the small square beyond, a church bell chimed the hour, and though I counted *nine*, I had an idea that I might have missed the first strike, momentarily distracted as I was by an empty stomach.

My intended destination – a place where empty stomachs are always welcome – was an old building on the right which adjoins the south tower and against which it sits like a slightly nervous child clinging to its mother, hoping not to be noticed. I think it was built in the twelfth century, and has changed little since – at least, not on the outside, where its walls give little away as to the activity within, although its original purpose would have been well known as a bridge chapel, a place to pray or give thanks for safe passage across the river. It has been a long time, though, since it satisfied any spiritual needs, and now it is a restaurant – a place for sustaining the body rather than the soul – and that, if you ask me, is far more useful.

Inside, the original ground floor has not kept up with the level of the street and now it is reached through a door which must once have been an upper window, and from which an old stone stairway gives access for those brave enough to descend its narrow and uneven treads, and though I understand the food is worth the risk, my chief interest is in the building.

I was lucky enough to get a seat at a small table in a corner from where I was able to study my fellow diners whilst I ate. They were of all ages, some alone, some in pairs, some in small groups, some eating, others drinking and all chattering away to anyone who would listen about whatever mattered most at that moment.

As for me, well, my curiosity was piqued by a couple sitting at the table next to mine, eating their dinner in a cheerless silence, exchanging infrequent looks but no words. At first, I thought I recognised them, but then was sure I did not. They looked respectable but otherwise unremarkable, and it was only their lack of conversation which sustained my attention because I could not help but wonder at the cause of it. Perhaps they were happy in silence? Or maybe it was one of those awkward post-argument silences? Or perhaps the argument was yet to come, and this was the prelude? But, alas, my observations were soon ended by the waiter as he brought their bill, and with it the realisation that I shall never know the why or wherefore, or the what next. They, on the other hand, will never know how annoyed I am with them for introducing another unwanted mystery into my world...

I sat for a while with a glass of brandy, observing the room as it emptied of patrons whilst waiters busied themselves clearing tables, no doubt looking forward to getting to their beds; anxious not to delay them, I finished my drink, settled my bill and left them to it.

Outside, it was cold, but not so cold that a brief stop on the bridge was out of the question. I always find views from bridges inspiring, but the view from the old bridge on a clear starry night is, in my opinion, the most beautiful in the world as I know it, and most assuredly never to be rushed. Leaning on the parapet, I watched the water as it moved slowly beneath, its black rippling surface torturing reflections of the city lights as it went... stretching and squeezing them as if trying to extract a confession. It won't be long, though, until winter brings them some relief, trapping the water beneath thick ice and deep snow, and the only things to play across it will be skating children.

I can't say how long I remained there; I think I might have slipped into a mild state of hypnosis, but eventually the cold air brought me back to life, and I resumed my walk home.

Late evening is my favourite part of the day when, strolling slowly through the empty silent streets, I find a sense of contentment which I don't experience at any other time, with no one to spoil the solitude or intrude on my thoughts. It was with that in mind that I decided that I would not call on my neighbour; whatever the topic of conversation he manages always to unsettle me somehow, and I didn't want my mind clouded again with, well, with I don't know what...

Likho

You won't be surprised to hear that my good intentions counted for nought because when I reached the old man's door about twenty minutes later it was open as usual, and I was irresistibly drawn in. There he was in his chair. Does he ever move from it?

"Good evening" he said with a grin, "I thought you weren't coming."

"Really? Why? Did I say I wouldn't?"

"No, but it's rather late and I thought perhaps you had decided not to call this evening."

"Ah, well I did consider it on my walk back just now."

"But you changed your mind… well, few of us are constant in our decisions. Indeed, it is good to be flexible in one's plans, and always ready to accommodate the unexpected."

"I try not to make plans" I said with a shrug, trying to look indifferent, "especially if they involve other people – it is in the nature of man to resist falling in with the plans of others... we invariably attempt to thwart them somehow in an effort to assert our liberty and free will… though mostly, I suspect, we do it for devilment. But never mind that… I am not staying long. It is late, as you say, and I have had a busy day."

"Oh yes, how did it go with your police inspector?"

"Did I say I was going to see him?"

"No, but I had a feeling you would. *You did*, I suppose?"

"Yes, I did. At least I *think* I did, because it's quite possible that it has been no more than another strange dream."

"What did he have to say?"

"Not much. He said that he did not know me and that I had never called on them to report anything. Actually, I think I might have caused him some confusion."

"Oh." The old man frowned.

"That troubles you?"

"Not I, but have you considered that you might have stirred his interest in you?"

"You think he might turn up here in search of a deranged man who may or may not know something about a murder? Well, I suppose it's possible, but it doesn't concern me much. Why should I be bothered? I'm sure he'll be satisfied to see that it was all a misunderstanding when he finds you alive and well. I imagine that should clear it all up nicely."

"If you think so..." The old man looked a little stern and began to shake his head slowly at me. "It would have been better for you if you had not spoken with him though, particularly about *me*... and it would be better if he did *not* come here."

"I see no reason why he should not call on me if he wishes. However, *you* are not obliged to admit him, *you* may do as *you* please, as shall *I*. And for now, I bid you good night, sir. It is late and I am tired."

I left him alone in his dingy room. He said nothing as I went, giving the clear impression he was annoyed with me, and I couldn't have cared less. There was something menacing though, perhaps *threatening*, in his words and manner that set my mind wandering again. Damn that man... he has done the very thing I had planned to avoid tonight, and once more he has managed to set my thoughts on a course I don't wish to follow. Lying in my bed, tired as I was, my mind would not shut down. Why does that old man not want the police here? Twice now he has mentioned it. Have I touched on something in an earlier conversation? Could he really be the same old man who vanished after drowning the children? I hadn't been serious at the time, but I begin to think there might be something in it. Does that make him dangerous? Certainly not to me. What possible harm can that feeble old man do to *me*?

5. The Story of the Door[5]

Tuesday 6th

My neighbour's door has been closed to me for the last two nights. I suppose the old man is making a point about something, and *I* have decided to make a point of not caring. I am sure he knows more than he is letting on about those murders but if he chooses not to tell then I can do little about it. Anyway, pursuing the matter can only be a waste of time. If the police were satisfied as to the identity of the criminals twenty years ago, then who am I to argue? And if it *was* the mysterious old couple in the empty apartment then they must be long dead and well beyond the reach of justice in this world… not that I believe there is another.

I think the best thing to do is forget the whole affair, though that will be hard since I must pass the door to the crime scene every day, knowing what happened on the other side of it, and I find myself stopping to stare at it every time I go by…

It is an unremarkable panelled door, just like mine, made of good solid oak with good solid brass fittings which are kept highly polished – a task I imagine to be a difficult one for the concierge or his wife to discharge? But I digress… there is nothing at all unusual about it… it is an ordinary door, just like mine, and just the same as that of my old neighbour. Of course, it isn't *quite* the same, because *this* door was an accessory to murder… it opened to welcome those children in, stood shut whilst they were killed, and then opened again only to allow a killer to escape.

Since then, it has been closed and locked, and whenever I look at it, I cannot help but wonder if it is keeping something in, or something out...

It has never been my habit to anthropomorphise doors, and you will be reassured to know that I have reprimanded myself very seriously for having such a stupid idea. There's something about it though... as if it retains some memory. Do inanimate objects have memories? There I go again. No, of course they don't... except for the memories imposed on them by us. But still, there is something about that door...

But it is *only* a door... an ordinary, unremarkable door, just like mine, and one to which I am determined to pay no more attention lest it drives me mad. The problem has worsened though, because now every door I see makes me think about our mystery, and doors are difficult things to avoid, unless one lives in a field. Much as I try, I cannot get it out of my mind and I'm certain I shall have no peace until I find out the truth, or at least get as close to it as I can.

The consumption of a bottle of wine after dinner prompted an idea... the people who lived in my apartment before me might know something. I know nothing about them, so my old neighbour might be a good place to start, though I do not intend to explain my interest, at least not to begin with. Of course, this means having to speak to him, and much as I dislike his company, it seems I have no choice.

Wednesday 7th

Now, some might think it a strange coincidence, but it just so happened that I found my neighbour at home to visitors last night. His door was open, so I tapped on it as usual and went in.

Likho

"Well, good evening," he said with half a smile. "I had given you up for dead."

"Why?" I thought his remark to be a stupid one but didn't say so.

"Because I haven't seen you for three days."

"Ah, well your door was closed. I don't disturb you unless your door is open. If it is closed, then I assume you are not receiving callers."

"Very perceptive of you. If only others were so respectful of one's privacy."

"You have other visitors?"

"Oh, you'd be surprised." The old man grinned, exposing his broken yellow teeth.

"I don't much care to be surprised… indeed, does anyone actually like surprises?"

"I couldn't say. I suppose it depends on the nature of the surprise."

"Well, I don't like them, whatever their nature, unless I know what they are and when to expect them."

"Then they are not…"

"Quite." I couldn't be bothered to wait for him to finish his sentence; from the way it began I suspected it would be a waste of good hearing. I had more important things to think about and to that end had concocted a small fiction which I was anxious to reveal. "Never mind that though. I am glad to find you at home because I have something to ask."

"Really?" Another yellow-toothed grin made me shiver slightly; there was something distinctly unpleasant about that mouth.

"Yes, really. It concerns my apartment and specifically the previous occupant thereof…"

"Intriguing… go on."

"*Intriguing?* I wouldn't say that... at least, *not yet*, but never mind... I have received a letter from someone who wishes to be put in contact with that gentleman, and he hopes that I might have a forwarding address. Alas, I don't. I know nothing at all about him and I was wondering if you did?"

"Were you?"

"I was. Indeed, I *am*."

"And who is the *someone* from whom you have received this letter? May I see it?" He looked at me with suspicion.

"I don't have it with me... and I can't remember the name. I have a bad memory for names, besides which it doesn't particularly matter does it?"

"It might do. But never mind, perhaps you will bring it next time you call?"

"Perhaps I will, though I don't see how it matters to you."

"Neither do I until I see it. Anyway, what is it you want to know?"

"If you have a forwarding address?"

"Why would I?"

"Well, I thought you might have been on friendly terms with him."

"*Them*." He grinned again. "Them. *Him* was *them*."

"Right. So, were you?"

"Were I what?" He was beginning to annoy me.

"Were you on friendly terms with them? *Them*, the people who lived in my apartment?"

"No, I wasn't. They were only there for two weeks..."

"Two weeks? Are you sure?"

"Absolutely certain. Two weeks, that was all."

Likho

"Why did they stay such a short time?"

"How should I know?" The old man shook his head.

"You didn't ask them?"

"Why should I? It was, and *is,* none of my business. I didn't speak to either of them in all that time. I had no cause."

"You saw them though?"

"Yes, briefly…" The old man looked thoughtful for a moment. "They looked like a normal couple, a smart respectable couple. He was immaculately dressed in a well-tailored suit, shoes polished like mirrors… not a hair on his head out of place, and his face so clean-shaven that no whisker with hopes of a long life would dare show itself. As for her, well, she too was well-dressed in expensive clothes, hair nicely done… tasteful jewellery… you could tell they were people of quality."

"Ah, you had a good look then?"

"It would seem so, wouldn't it?"

"Was there anything else memorable about them?"

"About him, no. She, on the other hand, well, she was thin and very pale, she seemed nervous, a bit shaky… I noticed her hands trembled constantly… and do you know what I think?"

"I can't begin to imagine… do go on."

"Well, I would say she was afraid of something. Perhaps she was afraid of her husband? Maybe he beat her? Maybe he was cruel? I don't know, but she was troubled… a frightened little creature, I'd say. And that, my friend, is as much as I can tell you about your predecessors. Where they went, and *why*, I cannot say. Why are you so interested?"

"I am naturally curious, as you should know by now, and it is a mystery, is it not? These people buy an apartment, live in it for two weeks, disappear without explanation, and then years later they sell it. Why wait?"

"Perhaps they expected to return? I don't know; I can't even begin to guess." The old man sat back and closed his eyes for a moment.

"Well, I do not intend to guess. I intend to find out. There are too many mysteries about this place, and this is one that might be easy to solve."

"Just how do you intend to do that, may I ask?"

"I don't know, but I shall think about it."

"Do as you please" said he with an air of nonchalance I did not believe to be sincere.

"Oh, you may be assured that I shall..." I replied, turning to the door as I spoke.

Leaving my old neighbour without ceremony, I came to my apartment... to these rooms so strangely and hurriedly deserted by the previous occupants...

In my sitting room the fire was blazing nicely, and I sat in my chair by the hearth to warm myself; after fifteen minutes in my neighbour's freezing room my hands and feet were in need of some heat.

Outside, the wind whistled down the street, bringing the first snow of the season We shall have no other weather now for the next four months... each day it will snow, or it will not; it will be windy, or it will not, and it will be very, very cold. That doesn't trouble me, though, because I am much in favour of certainty.

Forgetting about the onset of winter, I sat and stared into the flames... they were rather hypnotic as they danced about and raced up the chimney, drawn by the wind as it blew across the roofs. As the fire roared and cracked, I thought about the couple who lived here before me... and those thoughts had the undesirable effect of causing my imagination to kick open its stable door, jump the fence and run away with itself across the endless rich and fertile lands which lay before it…

My aged neighbour said the woman was frightened… but frightened of what? Did she fear her husband? Perhaps he'd murdered her? Had anyone seen them leave? It was quite possible that he had done away with the woman and then disappeared into the night. It seems to be the thing to do around here. Maybe his dead wife is walled up somewhere in my apartment? Or rotting away beneath the floorboards? Or her dismembered corpse buried in the cellar? With numberless grisly theories in mind, I am determined to get to the bottom of this new mystery.

The only thing to do is to find them, and hopefully not under the floor of my sitting room. The agent who acted for the sale of the apartment must know where they are, and I have decided to visit him in the morning.

Thursday 8th

I drifted off to sleep in my chair, a lapse I regretted later.

The gale blew all night, both outside in the street where it brought snow, and inside, in my head where it brought visions of residents past, present and imagined…

The first visitor was my mother. With her mouldy shroud twisted about her, she stood by the window and muttered some words which I could just about hear but not understand. Then, in the shadows, came the old woman with the long white hair and the thin featureless face; her single eye flashed red and yellow in the firelight as she swayed gently from side to side, drifting in and out of focus, and just as I began to wonder if she were there at all, my neighbour arrived. The old man stepped out of the mirror above the mantelpiece, jumped down on to the floor where he landed without a sound, and moved to the window, taking up his place alongside the one-eyed shade who began, somehow, to laugh. This drew protests from my mother who turned on her and started to scream unintelligible curses, though she failed to silence the laughter which, if anything, became even more demented.

I watched in silence, more curious than disturbed up until now, and almost keen to see what would happen next. I didn't have to wait though, because my attention was drawn suddenly by the sound of the door slamming shut. I turned to see a couple who, even though we had never met, I knew had to be the previous occupants of the apartment. They were just as my neighbour had described them, but I was certain, too, that I'd seen them somewhere before. The woman was screaming in terror, her face wet with tears, her eyes red from crying, and though it seems unkind to say so, she looked a mess, with her hair and clothing in such disarray that she might have crawled out of a ditch. She stared at me but then saw something which sent her into such a fit of hysteria I thought she would drop down dead from fright...

I looked to my left, to the fireplace, and I saw what she saw. A cloud of steam was emerging from the hearth, making the fire hiss and spit as it partially smothered the flames. It didn't spread into the room but instead halted a few feet from me where it began to divide; almost imperceptible to begin with, it quickened as it formed two columns which reached down to the floor, like tornados descending from a storm. As we watched, the steam started to condense... it started to form into bodies. I sat in my chair and stared, fascinated, as the watery apparitions of two children took shape before the fireplace, sparkling in the light like a blue sea on a summer day...

Their faces were not properly formed and seemed to change continuously, so I cannot describe them other than to say one was taller than the other. At first, they looked at me, laughing and whispering to each other, though I couldn't understand what they were saying, and then they turned and pointed at the woman by the door; she stood petrified, staring, wide-eyed and incapable of reaction, whilst her husband appeared to be oblivious to her distress. His face was as sharp as his suit, and his expression blank with just a hint of annoyance, or so I thought, as if being summoned to appear in my nightmare was all a dreadful inconvenience to him. Then, to my surprise, he began to speak to me, and though there was no sound, I had the idea that he was angry. It was then that I realised where I had seen them before... I had been seated next to them in the restaurant across the river, and they were the intriguing pair who had sat in sulky silence. I think my subconscious, struggling to give form to the required characters, must have found them sitting idly in a cell full of discarded memories and put them to use in my dream.

Despite the confusion, I had managed to think of a hundred questions for him, but just as I was about to speak, my old neighbour stepped forward and, foaming at the mouth, he started to shout at me...

His bulging eyes looked as if they were about to explode from their sockets, but his rage was silenced by the roar of a gale which blew up suddenly from somewhere behind me, and the force of it carried the sound of his voice away as it threw him back against the window. It grew in strength, whipping up the floor into waves which rose and fell, making me feel seasick, and as the wind strengthened, the swell increased until it rolled up into one enormous wave which swept up all before it and crashed through the wall, demolishing it like a tsunami hitting a sandcastle, before disappearing into the black emptiness beyond. As the storm passed, the only sounds were the screams of the drowning, somewhere out there in the night.

I don't know what happened next. I must have fallen asleep, and when I awoke, I was in my bed. I had no idea of the time and, as I lay staring up into the darkness, I thought I could hear the whispering of those children again. It could not have been, of course, because they existed only in a dream, and I am certain I was awake. It was only the wind outside...

When I was a boy, I would wake every morning and look forward to bedtime. Bed was my refuge, and sleep was my friend... a friend who always brought good dreams, and freedom from a miserable world. Now, though, I begin to fear that he might be turning against me.

Meanwhile, daylight arrived unnoticed, and so I think I must have dozed off after all, despite my fears. Awake as my mind was, my body struggled to stir, and though weighed down by lethargy, my limbs twitched uncontrollably as if they were over-tired and didn't know what to do with themselves. I closed my eyes and tried to relax, but hard as I tried to empty my mind, my night visitors kept creeping in to fill the void. Eventually it seemed that the only thing to do was to get up and go out, and with that decision made I surrendered control and, like an automaton, dressed and went out without another conscious thought.

Outside, the icy freezing wind on my face was just what I needed to bring me back to my senses, and minutes later I was in a local café where I sat by the window, drank strong coffee, and watched people go by.

Likho

Nothing remained of the night's snowfall except some small drifts in shadowy corners, but the cloud-covered sky looked ready to try again at any moment. The weather was not going to distract me from my mission though, and I felt more determined than ever to visit the property agent.

Finishing my drink, I paid my bill and set off down the street, and at the end of it I boarded a tram which carried me through the centre of town to the corn exchange where I alighted. The office of the agent is in the legal quarter, a mediaeval maze of narrow alleys beyond the old bourse, and it took me a few minutes to recall just which of those old passages I was after, though, as it happened, I found it quite by chance in a matter of minutes.

The man I needed was there and remembered me well, though I'm not sure why… I don't think I'm especially memorable. I explained the purpose of my visit; he listened attentively, nodding his head constantly until I finished my speech when he began shaking it slowly instead, whilst stroking his chin in the manner of a great philosopher about to divest himself of a revolutionary thought.

"Alas, we are not able to help you sir. We can supply no information as to the present whereabouts of those people. We remember them well, of course, but we are unable to say where they went." The man was just as pretentious as I remember him, and wearing the same dark grey frock coat, the same cheap cologne, and his slick macassar-oiled hair shining like the plumage of a courting raven. Everything about him is oily, including his attitude; he is the sort of person whom you can never decide whether to laugh at or punch.

"You had an address until recently though?" I do not give in easily.

"Well, no doubt we did sir. Indeed, we must have had a means of facilitating such communications as were necessary, yes, or at the very least some route by which to direct them. We cannot disclose such information though… it is confidential, and the law prevents us revealing such things, even if we *wished* to."

"Ah, I understand. You do not *wish* to assist me."

"I did not say *that* sir…"

"Actually, I think you *did*, sir." It might have been more politic not to antagonise him, but I couldn't help it.

"Well, *sir*, it is no matter, as are my wishes in the case because we are bound by the law…" He paused a moment to continue his ascent of the moral high ground and then, from atop it, went on "after all, you would not want us to discuss confidential details relating to *your* affairs with strangers."

"I do not have affairs with strangers." Mocking the careless structure of his sentence was too irresistible, especially after he'd braved such a climb to deliver it; anyway, whilst he descended in silence, I used the opportunity to continue. "Do you know why they took such a long time to sell the apartment after they moved out?"

"Why would we? Perhaps they intended to return one day, after all it is a very fine property. You would have to ask them, wouldn't you?"

"Well, I should very much like to. Did they make the original purchase through your agency?"

"We would have to check our files, which, of course, remain confidential. How would that information help you?"

"It wouldn't. I am curious to know as much as I can about them. Did they ever say why their stay in the apartment was so brief?"

Likho

"Why would they? And even if they did, it would be no more *our* business than it is *yours*, sir." The man grinned, presumably pleased with his response, though I couldn't think why he should be; he lacked the wit and intelligence to say anything clever or amusing, and he compensated for that deficiency with rudeness, doubtless unaware of the difference. "Maybe they found the place unsuitable after all? Strange really, since it is such a splendid property, and in such a good area, indeed a very much sought-after area, if I… *we*… may say so?"

"Right, so other than permitting yourself an accidental moment of self-indulgent speculation, there is nothing more you feel able to tell me?"

"No, nothing."

"You met them, I presume? What were they like? It cannot be a breach of confidentiality to describe someone."

"Indeed, you might think so. They seemed perfectly normal to us, though the woman was a rather nervous type, a bit jumpy, if you know what I mean? Her husband always spoke for her which I… well no matter…" In danger of giving himself over to gossip, my oleaginous informant stopped, recovered himself and retreated behind his façade of pompous superiority. "But, of course, I am sure you understand that it is against our policy to discuss clients?"

"It is a shame because I need to contact them. Do you think they are still living here somewhere? Is it possible I could trace them through the city directory?"

"If they are here still then yes, I suppose it might be possible."

"Of course, I would need to know their names… unfortunately I have no record of them."

"Weren't they written in the contract? As the vendors of the property, they must be named in the contract. It is the law, you know. Can't you find it there?"

"No. The transaction was done through a third party... an unnamed trustee, if I recall correctly."

"Really? Well, I wouldn't know about that sort of thing."

"No, of course not. Is there really nothing you can tell me which might help? Perhaps, if you know where they are, you could ask them to contact me..."

"We could not possibly presume to do any such thing sir. We have our reputation to maintain."

"You have a reputation? Yes, I imagine you do..."

"*Sir?*"

"Never mind. Well, I have one last idea... perhaps you could forward a note to them? A letter from me..."

"Well, that might be possible. Of course, we cannot guarantee they will reply. If they should choose not to do so, then there is nothing more *we* can do."

"In that, sir, you do not exceed my expectations," said I; my unwilling helper seemed to be unsure whether or not I was being sarcastic. "Anyway, as that seems to be the only option open to me, I shall go home and write a letter... might I find you here at this time tomorrow?"

"You might."

"Until tomorrow then..." With my fists firmly clenched in my pockets, I left the man to himself, both pleased and disappointed for having denied him the punch he so richly deserved.

Outside, the temperature had dropped, and it had started to snow; it wasn't too heavy, but it is not unknown for a blizzard to blow in suddenly and bring the town to a standstill, and as I didn't want to have to go all the way

Likho

home on foot, I walked quickly back to the tram stop and joined the queue. After a lengthy wait I managed to board one, crowded as it was, and I endured my journey wedged in amongst a crush of chattering women who were all weighed down by shopping bags bursting with enough provisions to withstand a very long siege.

By the time we reached the end of my street the snow was falling heavily, and the pavements were alive with people, all dashing in one direction or another, heads down into the wind, and consequently crashing into each other at every step. When, at last, I got indoors, my coat was covered with thick slush, though it began to melt away very quickly as I climbed the stairs, leaving a trail of water droplets behind me.

Afternoon.

My lunch was laid out ready for me, and though I felt hungry, I couldn't be bothered eating much of it…

I couldn't be bothered to do much else either and have spent the afternoon in my sitting room not bothering to do any of it and feeling very disappointed with myself. Everything is dark and colourless, and such light as makes it to my windows doesn't have the energy left to get through them. It is all rather gloomy; even with the lamps lit, it doesn't fell much cheerier, and it isn't doing much for my mood. No reward feels worth the effort, and there seems to be no point in anything.

Is it *really* worth bothering the former occupants, assuming they can be contacted? What do I want them to tell me? What might they know? Will they tell me? And what good might it do me anyway? Perhaps I should forget the whole thing? Before my hand finished committing those thoughts to this page, a voice in my head told me that I will *not* forget it, and however hard I try, it will gnaw at the foundations of my sanity until my questions are answered, or at least, *asked*.

Why did they leave so quickly? People don't leave their homes after only two weeks without a very good reason. What was theirs? You have to agree that it is all very intriguing, is it not?

Here I am, living in this ancient house with centuries of history locked up in it – and a history of murders and strange disappearances at that. Perhaps it is time to start *unlocking* some of it?

Sitting at my desk with pen and ink, and a glass of wine to fortify me, I have written the promised letter, the text of which is reproduced here...

Sir,

I write this in the hope that you can assist me in a small matter which, I believe, concerns us both.

You will see from the address above that I live in a property previously owned, and occupied briefly, by you. I am told that you lived here for only two weeks before vacating the apartment, which then remained empty for several years until now.

In my brief time here, I have become aware of certain facts, or perhaps I should say 'stories' regarding a former resident, some children and the concierge. Perhaps you heard of them too? If you did, then I am certain you will appreciate my interest.

I understand from the old gentleman who lives opposite my apartment that he was not acquainted with you, though he claims to have seen you; he is a singularly odd fellow, and I suspect him to be neither honest nor honourable. Was he known to you?

Then there is the matter of the adjoining apartment: was it occupied during your time? I am told it has not been so for many years but, having heard sounds from within I suspect otherwise.

Likho

There are many more questions I should like ask, and on that account, I wonder if it might be possible for us to meet? Please let me know if you are able; I am available at your convenience.

I remain &c,

Evening.

Leaving the sealed letter on my desk, I went out for supper. It wasn't late but the streets were deserted, and nothing moved except the heavy snow which fell softly around me.

Some restaurants had closed early for want of business, but I found one near the cathedral where I was welcomed like a long-lost friend by a very bored waiter glad for the sight of a customer; I hadn't been there before as far as I could recall so there was no other reason for such an enthusiastic greeting. I was worried he might be over-familiar and attempt some conversation, but my fears disappeared along with him to the kitchen, where they remained for most of the evening.

I picked my way through a ragoût, drank my way through a bottle of wine, watched the snow falling outside, and I wondered what I might be getting myself into. Actually, I am not getting myself into anything… it is my imagination at the head of this strange expedition, and the question I *should* be asking is why I am allowing myself to be led by it, because I have never done so before.

Friday 9th

I convinced myself to deliver my letter to the agent. Asking favours of people makes me feel very uncomfortable, and having to ask one of such an odious man causes me much discomfort indeed; I have no choice, though, if I am to proceed with my investigation, and now

Darton

I must acclimatize, albeit temporarily, to my new position – that of being in his debt.

"What would you like us to do, sir, in the unlikely event that there should be a reply to this… well, to *this*?" He held the envelope at arm's length and between the tips of a finger and thumb as if it were some soiled undergarments, and to complete that impression, his face assumed an expression of disgust.

"Well, perhaps you could send it on to my address?" It seemed obvious to me.

"Oh, no, we couldn't do that, sir. We are far too busy. And then there would be the cost of the postage…"

"I dare say I could defray any expenses in that respect."

"Alas no, sir… the paperwork would be too much trouble for such a small amount."

"Paperwork? For the price of a stamp?"

"Accounts must be kept in order sir, or who knows where we should all end up…"

"Well then," said I, determined not to give up, "perhaps I could provide you with an envelope, stamped, and addressed to me, into which you could insert any reply and then dispatch by means of the postal service? Would that do? I think it might…"

"Oh, no, sir, that would be against the law." The loathsome man smiled and squinted at me in a manner so condescending that I nearly lost my temper. I drew a deep breath and paused a moment.

"Against the law?" I rolled my eyes to the ceiling as I spoke. "What law, dare I ask?"

"It is against the law to conceal communications… it is treasonable, or something like that… it is probably a *capital* offence."

Likho

"*A capital offence*? Seems a bit harsh, just for forwarding a letter. I don't understand how that can be a treasonable?"

"Well, it's not for us to understand the law is it, sir? We have only to obey it."

"Yes, that is one way to look at it…" I must admit that I was running out of ideas. "Perhaps," I mused, "we might avoid such minor upset as may be caused by your execution if you were to hold any reply for me to collect? I could call in next week? Would that be legal?"

"We don't offer a *poste restante* service…" he replied coldly, staring unblinkingly at me as he spoke, "but I suppose we could keep a letter for a few days."

"I appreciate you making such a helpful exception… I shall be indebted." I felt obliged to shake his hand, revolting as the gesture was, and with that done I went out into the snow with an uncomfortable feeling that I have just pushed open a door which would be better left closed.

As I waited for the tram, I amused myself with the thought of that self-righteous fool under sentence of death for posting a letter, dragged screaming to the scaffold, his cries finally silenced by the swift drop of the blade…

6. A Mysterious Messenger

*Monday 12*th

The snow has been falling so heavily that I have had no choice but to remain indoors for the last three days. This morning, though, I could bear to be confined no longer and resolved to go out in defiance of the weather…

Dressed in my warmest coat, shrouded in scarves and wearing a pair of thick gloves which made my hands almost useless, I stepped out on to the street where I found myself alone in a silent white world unspoilt by the presence of man, and which I was about to spoil. Momentarily entranced by such a picturesque scene, it seemed a shame to be the one to ruin it… but then again, someone must, so I set forth along the pavement, my boots punching through the deep, crisp and even snow to leave a trail of fresh prints behind me.

With no sign of life anywhere, I walked cautiously along the empty streets in hope of finding an open café, and though most were closed and in darkness, I found one in the square by the old south gate where a sullen waiter greeted me with all the resentment he could muster, presumably much vexed at having his idleness interrupted. He ushered me to a table by the window where I sat for an hour or so, staring out of it in the hope of seeing something interesting. My hopes were unrealised though, so when at last I felt sufficiently fortified with hot coffee and brandy, and having tired of vexing waiters, I settled my bill and left, retracing my lonely trail of footsteps in the thick snow. If I had been lost, I should have had no trouble finding my way...

Thirty minutes later, feeling cold but rather more alive than I had done earlier, I arrived home to find the wife of the concierge standing in the lobby and looking a little confused; she stepped forward and, without ceremony, handed me an envelope.

"This was delivered for you sir." I took it from her and looked at it. It bore my name, but no address, and the words "*By hand*" were written in place of a stamp.

"Thank you... who brought it?"

"I don't know sir, well, that is to say I *did* see the boy, but I don't know him."

"A *boy*?" I don't know why I thought that strange.

"Yes, sir. Is it important?"

"No, I shouldn't think so." As I smiled and shook my head, another thought crossed my mind. "*When* was it delivered?"

"Oh, not five minutes ago sir... I was just going to take it upstairs when I heard you coming in."

"Five minutes? I saw no one in the street... are you sure it wasn't earlier?"

"*Very* sure. It was no more than five minutes ago." From her tone it was clear that I had given offence.

"If you say so, of course... well, thank you for your trouble." I smiled warmly in an effort to redeem myself.

"It's no trouble sir, *no* trouble at all." With that, she turned and walked away, and I set off up the stairs.

There was nothing to be gained by arguing with the woman, but I was certain she could not have been telling the truth...

You see, on my return home, I had had a clear view of the street for about ten minutes as I walked slowly along it, and in that time, I saw no one approach or leave our door. Had someone done so at the time she said, I would have seen him – I would have been *sure* of seeing him. Of course, she *might* have had the time wrong, and I am always willing to forgive a wrong where none was intended, but even if she *were* wrong, it would not account for the means by which our mysterious messenger had come and gone… a means which allowed him to leave no mark in the snow. The only footprints present are those left by me, which is strange, wouldn't you agree? Maybe the boy had wings? But whatever he had, it is a question which will have to wait, because the item which he delivered is more deserving of our attention at present.

I was surprised to find the envelope contained a letter from the former owner of my apartment. I don't know why it had never occurred to me to expect a direct reply… it's not as if he wouldn't know where I lived. Anyway, he wrote as follows…

Sir,

I am in receipt of your letter, though I confess I'd rather not be. I had hoped that, being free of the property you mention, I should never hear of it again; it was a cause of considerable inconvenience to me for a long time.

I am not sure I can help as it has been a while since we lived there. We were unacquainted with the other residents; we were not familiar with any old gentleman and understood that both neighbouring apartments had remained unoccupied for many years. I can say nothing of the concierge; I don't believe I met him, although his wife was as pleasant as anyone might wish.

I was aware that something was supposed to have occurred in the building many years previously though made no enquiries in the matter, supposing it to be little more than gossip.

Darton

As for our departure, well, I can say only that shortly after we moved in, my wife began to think the place unsuitable. I recall that she found it rather gloomy; she was in poor health at that time, so we considered it best to make other arrangements.

It was my intention to dispose of the property as quickly as possible but despite placing it with several agents I was unable to find a buyer, the inconvenience of which I have mentioned.

Now, I must warn you, sir, that I will not have my wife upset by any reminder of that place, or the nightmares which she suffered, and which have very recently resumed.

A meeting is out of the question since there is nothing more I can tell you. I should have preferred not to reply to your letter and do so without any sense of obligation; as far as I am concerned, this matter is at an end.

Perhaps, sir, I may offer a piece of advice? If, like my wife, you find the apartment 'unsuitable', then you might consider following our example? That is all I feel able to say.

I remain &c.

How curious? He manages to say nothing and much at the same time...

I cannot help but wonder if one of his wife's nightmares brought her back here on the night she appeared in mine?

What about his final remark? '*That is all I feel able to say.*' Well, what he is able to say is interesting in a pragmatic way, but I have a feeling that the real story is hiding somewhere in what he is *unable* to say. If his intention is to discourage, he has failed; his words only incite me to investigate further.

As I stare at his letter, the words blur and merge into black stripes on the page, and as they drift in and out of focus, they form strange images... train carriages moving slowly from right to left… a line of animals in a circus parade… a city skyline panorama… and then a row of faces – the face of my old neighbour repeating over and over, each one with a more hateful expression…

Tuesday 13th

Later, when I went out, the letter went with me; I was far from done with it.

A restaurant in the small square behind the opera house was my choice for supper. Being a regular haunt of musicians from the theatre, it is not unusual to spot one at his dinner with a sheet of music set before him and a fork in hand, to eat or conduct with as required, *al dente ma non troppo…*

Well, I might have been without a sheet of music, but I did have my letter; I took it casually from my pocket, acting for all the world as if I had forgotten it was there, placed it on the table, and read it as if I were seeing it for the first time.

I read it over and over, studying every sentence, every phrase, every word, comma and stop. I deconstructed the composition with forensic deliberation, picking apart every note, every tone, and every subtle transition between. I imagined every possible interpretation as if I were learning it for the stage…

The letter is undated and bears no return address, and whilst its author assures me that he remains my most respectful servant, he has left it unsigned. The paper is of the best quality and of a decent size, the writing neat, consistent and in black ink; each stroke of the pen is carefully angled, and each loop generous, though not so much as to be extravagant. This is, I think, the writing of a man who cares much about details… a man who makes sure the heels of his shoes are clean and is never without a crisp clean white handkerchief; this is a man with religious devotion to cleanliness, politeness and punctuality. I imagine him capable of tremendous self-restraint, a man who is inscrutable in all respects... essential qualities for one who is, perhaps, devious and scheming, an obsessive, or a psychopath, one who regularly terrorises his wife for incorrectly setting the table or serving his wine at the wrong temperature, a man who must be always in control of all things. But, of course, I am no graphologist, and I could be wrong in my every assumption...

Pushing my half-eaten dinner aside and pouring another glass of wine, I re-read my correspondent's final sentence. What had his wife found unsuitable? *'Unsuitable'*? Why the emphasis? Had I said *I* found it so? No, I had not. Does he suppose I will get his meaning without further explanation? What does he mean? *'Unsuitable'*?

It was then that it struck me just how ridiculous I am being. This thinking is out of character, and my imagination is in danger of running out of control. This must stop now, before I am driven mad. I cannot deny that some strange things have happened recently – or, at least, *seemingly* strange things; but for all that, there are certain to be logical explanations, and the obsessive pursuit of logic is *not* the reaction of a sane man.

Rather astounded by the might of my intellect, I finished my wine, settled the bill and started for home, feeling incredibly pleased with myself and satisfied that the matter was at an end.

Outside, it was freezing, and as the frozen snow crunched under my feet, my only wish was to be sitting by the fire with a full glass and an empty head, and thinking of nothing at all...

Likho

The lobby and the stairwell were cold – *so* cold that my breath condensed into thick white clouds. The icy air felt heavy – *so* heavy that it deadened the sound of my steps on the stairs and silenced the hiss of the gas lights.

Relieved to find my old neighbour's door shut, I reached the warmth of my own apartment at last, where a fire blazed in every hearth, and lamps lit every room with friendly and reassuring light. Then, finally liberated from coat and boots, I stretched out in my chair by the fire, a glass of brandy at hand and my mind emptied of all thoughts.

Now, with my brain disengaged and idling quietly, and a little anaesthetised by warmth and alcohol, I should have drifted into a light sleep. The fact is, though, that I did not. I remained awake and alert, and so when the sound of laughter disturbed me, I knew I wasn't dreaming…

At first, I thought it must have been coming from somewhere below in the street because, well, where else could it be? It lasted only a minute or two and then all was quiet once more, but as I relaxed back in my chair and before I could put the disturbance from my mind, it began again. This time, though, directly I heard it, I knew it was much closer. It was not outside my window, but outside my sitting room, in the passage beyond.

Setting my glass on the table, I sat forward, remaining motionless and silent. Then, without thinking, I stood and walked slowly across the room. The sound of laughter grew louder. It was the laughter of children… children playing some game, or perhaps sharing a joke? But how could they be in my apartment? I opened the door…

There was no one there. I could hear them even more clearly, but I could *see* no one. They had to be hiding somewhere close by, though there was no obvious place for even the smallest of children to conceal themselves.

Darton

"Who's there?" I spoke calmly and quietly; I didn't want to frighten them away. On the contrary, I wanted to see them, to know who they were, in which apartment they lived, and how they had come to be in mine. "Who is it? I can hear you... who is there? I know you are there... where are you hiding? It's all right, I'm not angry..."

For a moment, all was silent. Then the laughter resumed, and it sounded close – *so* close that I could feel it moving through the air around me. All at once I started to feel nervous, and, as my failing courage compelled me to take a step backwards, I noticed that the floor was wet, and on the surface of the parquet were the reflections of two young faces.

7. THE STONE GUEST[6]

The reflections faded to nothing, the laughter stopped, and all was silent in the small lobby.

Had they been only in my imagination, then? You think so, I'm certain; and why shouldn't you? Why should you believe me? I heard children laughing and I saw a reflection of their faces, but you have only my word for it.

Perhaps it was no more than a trick of the light? And the laughter? No more than the contented sighs of a tired old building resting on its tired old foundations…That is my conclusion; a rational man who doesn't admit the supernatural cannot conclude otherwise. I heard sounds which I am yet willing to swear were the sounds of children laughing, though I saw no children. Of course, things can be heard but not seen… I can hear the wind without seeing it; I can hear the traffic around the corner without seeing it. If I tell you I hear children but do not see them, you might believe me because it is possible, but when I tell you I see reflections of faces when there are none to be reflected, you do not believe me, and why should you? If I persist in my assertion then you might think I am mad, and why shouldn't you? But, perhaps, have *some* pity for the solitary witness to an unbelievable event?

After staring into emptiness for a minute or so I stepped back into my sitting room and closed the door. My hands were trembling a little and try as I did to suppress it, I had to acknowledge what I supposed to be fear. Fear of what, though? Madness, I think… though, I wonder, *is* madness to be feared?

Darton

Sitting again by the fire I thought of the strange things which had happened since I had moved into the apartment. There was the appearance of the old woman; there were the nightmares and visitations from my mother; there was my old neighbour, his murder and resurrection; visits to the police which may or may not have happened; the mysterious departure of the previous occupants; and now there is this business with laughing children and reflections on a wet floor. Is it all in my head? There is no one to say it isn't...

Anyway, now I have written my account of what I saw and heard, or rather, what I *believe* I saw and heard, and it seems no more plausible. I doubt my senses, my judgment, and my sanity...

What is real? What is not? I am finding it hard to know when I am asleep and when awake because sometimes I think I dream I am awake, and at other times I think I am awake when perhaps I am not...

Thus it was with a disturbed mind that I went to bed where, in darkness and silence, insomnia allowed a thousand thoughts to run amok through my mind. Every possibility and then every combination of every possibility pushed its way through the muddle, weaving an impossible knot at the centre of which was surely the cause of all my confusion. I drifted in and out of sleep, never being in one state or the other for very long but always certain that I didn't know in which I was. So great was my frustration at times that I wanted to scream, and I think I might have done once or twice, or at least dreamed that I did. I thought I could hear those children again but who can say if I dreamed that too? I remember the room growing very cold, and I think that was when I heard their voices whispering somewhere above me, as if they were on the ceiling. I thought I felt a drop of water splash on my face… and then the quilt was pulled back, leaving me shivering in my nightshirt. Before I had time to react, there was a movement beside the bed, and a child climbed in next to me. The other one whispered something, replaced the bedclothes, and then, I think, quietly left the room. It was still icy cold, and the chill felt as if it came from my left, where the child was sleeping, breathing softly and doubtless dreaming of happy times past and happier times yet to come…

Wednesday 14th

When daylight came finally to relieve us of the night, I awoke to find the sheets soaking. Sitting up and throwing back the bedding I saw that next to me, on the left, the bed was wet. My first thought was the obvious one, though I was not in the habit of bedwetting, and there was no discolouration or odour to suggest that I was responsible. It was water, nothing more. But how had it got there if it wasn't I? A soaking wet child perhaps? Except, of course, it couldn't have been, could it? It would have been far less disturbing if I *had* wet the bed… and I confess that I was feeling more than usually disturbed by this strange turn of events.

Feeling somewhat distracted, I spent an hour or so wandering from room to room… rooms I use and rooms I don't, half-expecting to find something, or someone… a couple of children living quietly in a corner who dare come out only at night when I sleep. It is a stupid idea, but it is preferable to ridiculous ghost stories, and I would welcome the presence of two real children hiding in an old armoire, even if they are in my home uninvited. I should treat them very kindly as I show them to the door…

After a wasted day, in an attempt to keep to a normal routine, I went out for supper. With no destination in mind, I walked up a street until I reached the square in front of the parliament building, and I sat down on a snowy bench to gather my thoughts. A statue stared down at me from atop its plinth... a long-dead king clad in ancient armour, a regal cloak and with a golden crown on his head to confirm his status should anyone doubt it. Now, which of our long-dead princes this man is, I cannot say; I think they all look the same, though no doubt each has some unique attribute which enables identification by learnéd historians or obsessive tourists... the beard or hair, the pose, some armorial device, there is usually something to give them away. The inscription, if there is one, was obscured by thick snow which had stuck to the side of the base; I couldn't be bothered to investigate and after ten minutes I left the nameless monarch alone, pausing for a moment for a last look at him as a thought crossed my mind... *"O statua gentilissima del gran' commendatore..."*[7] Wouldn't it be amusing to invite him to supper? But then, recalling how that story ends, I decided it would not be amusing at all, and the last thing I need is a *stone guest* banging at my door in the middle of the night.

Across the square and down a narrow street, a quiet restaurant looked as if it would satisfy my very undemanding needs, so in I went and settled at a table by the window. As I took off my coat, I discovered I had the letter from my mysterious predecessor in a pocket; I must have picked it up without realising, perhaps thinking to read it again, and so whilst I waited for my meal, I did just that. Straight away, I found my eye drawn to the last sentence – the one about following his example and moving out of the apartment, and I wish I could say that I had no such thought, but with all that has been going on recently, it is a thought which has come to mind. After all, I have been in

Likho

residence for six weeks, so I have outlasted them by a month and have nothing to prove. It is not a competition, though, and even if it were, I would hope to last at least a year... anything less might look capricious.

If she was having the same experiences as I, then I begin to understand how a nervous and perhaps suggestible woman suffering poor health might have felt two weeks to be more than enough. I, though, am *not* of a nervous disposition, and nor am I suggestible or in poor health, so I have no excuse; I must stay.

Must I? I can do as please; I am accountable to no one.

After supper and a slow walk home, I found my neighbour's door open. I had no wish to speak with him, but then again, I wanted to boast of my success in tracking down the former occupants of my apartment.

"I have received a reply from your former neighbour" I announced, holding the letter in my hand.

"Really? Which one?"

"You know very well. The couple from my apartment."

"I am surprised." The old man didn't *look* surprised. "I didn't think anyone would know where to find him."

"Well, I still have a little faith in this world."

"Yes, well, you are more *of* this world than I... at least for the time being."

"And then what? Sit in a chair all day and night waiting to die?"

"Something like that, yes."

"Not I..."

"Oh, you will be surprised."

"No, I shall not. Anyway, don't you want to know what your erstwhile neighbour has to say? Aren't you a bit curious?"

"Not particularly, no. Should I be? Does he say something bad or unpleasant about me?"

"No. He says little about you. He says he never saw or met you. Actually, he says that this apartment was unoccupied when he was here… this, and the one next door."

"And what do you make of that?"

"I must conclude that one of you is not honest."

"I see. Then which of us do you accuse?"

"I make no accusation; I merely state what is obvious…"

"You *want* to accuse *me* though, do you not?"

"I don't want to accuse anyone of anything. I will say only that I don't know what reason, if any, *he* has for being dishonest."

"And *me*? Might I have one?"

"I expect so, but it is no matter for now."

"I see."

"Good."

"What else does our friend have to say?"

"I thought you weren't interested"?

"I have changed my mind."

"Too bad." I shook my head and turned to go but paused, put the letter in my pocket just a little too theatrically, and added "He did suggest I should move out of the apartment…"

"Did he? I wonder why…"

"You don't know?"

"I wasn't here…. at least that's what he says, and you believe him rather than me, I think."

Likho

"But you *have* lied though, haven't you? You told me that you saw them. You described them both to me… quite detailed descriptions, as I recall."

"Ah, but I never spoke with them. How should I know why he says what he does?"

"I couldn't say, but I'm certain that you *do* know. There is something odd going on here, some game. You should know that I am not one for games… I wish only for a quiet life free from noise and annoyance, but it seems there are people here who don't respect my rights. Well, sir, enough is enough… I have had *more* than enough, it is time for it to stop, and for a start you may tell those children I am not fooled… or scared, or amused or whatever it is they hope to achieve..."

"Children? What children? Not *them* again…" The old man sat forward, shaking his head slowly; I had the impression that he was troubled. "Are you certain? Have you seen them? I had hoped we were rid of them."

"What do you mean? Who are they? You know them?"

"Them? No, I do not."

"I don't believe you."

"Believe me or not as you please…"

"I *don't* believe you. I am a patient man, but this has gone far enough, so when you see them next you may tell them to stop their stupid games, or they will regret it."

"Oh, I doubt that." The old man laughed.

"You doubt *what*? And why is it so amusing?"

"It is your ingenuousness… your ingenuousness is *so amusing*. As for those children, well, if they are who I think they are, those children will do as they please, and certainly not as you or I wish. They will try to drive you out I expect, just as… well, anyway, do as you think best."

Darton

"You give yourself away, I think... whom did they drive out? It is obvious that you know who they are. Why must we have all this mystery?" I was getting tired with the old man and his attempts to draw me into his game, whatever it was.

"I can't say, I can tell you no more." He looked thoughtful for a moment. "Maybe you *will* leave... maybe you *should*." He spoke those last three words almost in a whisper, and then looked nervously about the room as if he feared having been overheard. Odd, thought I, *very* odd...

Anyway, in answer to that, I wished him a good night and left him alone in his cold and squalid room.

Feeling very tired, I went directly to bed, and I must have drifted off to sleep quickly because I have no memory of lying awake. How long I had slept and what hour it was when I was awoken by the knocking at my door, I cannot say, except that it was still dark. For a few minutes I lay there trying to think who could be calling at that time, whatever it was, and while I lay there trying to guess his identity, my visitor knocked louder and more aggressively. By the time I had got up, put on a robe and walked the few steps to the lobby the banging was so loud that the dead in their graves must have been thinking it was time to rise again.

"All right, all right... wait a moment," I shouted angrily. "Who is it?" There was no reply, and the hammering continued until I opened the door. At first I couldn't see anything but as my eyes adjusted to the darkness I saw a tall white figure standing outside and though he looked a bit familiar I couldn't think how I knew him. It occurred to me that he was very much like the statue I had seen earlier outside parliament... he certainly had a stony look about him, and he was wearing a crown. Slowly and silently he bowed his head a little and then extended his right hand to

Likho

me. As I moved to take it, a line from a play suddenly came to mind... "*How cold and hard his mighty fist of stone!*"[8] My hand dropped to my side, and I took a step back, overwhelmed with a horrible feeling of déjà vu.

Just as I was wondering what was going on, I noticed that behind my stone guest stood another statue, and after him another waited quietly in line. Beyond the third stood a fourth, a fifth, sixth and seventh... a queue of statues on the landing and down the stairs, disappearing into the darkness of the lobby below.

Standing as still and silent as my line of visitors and uncertain if I was imagining things, it occurred to me that I should say something, ridiculous as the thought of speaking to a statue was, but just as I was about to open my mouth, my old neighbour appeared. He must have been hiding beside the door, waiting for his moment to surprise me... and surprise me he did as he stood before me with a stupid smirk on his stupid old face.

"Ah, we have woken you... so sorry." He didn't look very sorry as he stood there grinning unremorsefully at me. "But never mind that, you have some visitors... these, well... these *gentlemen* have come to see you..." He stepped aside and made a sweeping gesture with his right arm to indicate the tall white figure and his friends. "They have come for supper."

"What?" As I spoke, an idea came to mind... "Ah, just a minute, this is a *dream* isn't it? Yes, good, very good... highly imaginative... but that's where you've gone wrong you see? It's too... *too incredible* to be anything but a dream."

"Well, I wouldn't know about that," the old man said with a dismissive toss of his head, "nothing to do with me, I just go where I'm told..."

"Told by whom?"

"Oh, I don't know... does it matter?

"I don't suppose so," I replied. "What did you say these men want?"

"Supper. They have come for supper." He stood by my door, still grinning stupidly, placed by some unknown weaver of dreams who was apparently having much fun at my expense. It did cross my mind to spoil their fun by going back to bed, but if it was a dream, how could I stop them coming with me? A little frustrated, I decided that since I was up, I might as well go along with it.

"*Supper?*" I exclaimed, "it's the middle of the night..."

"Yes, did we disturb you?"

"It's the middle of the night and I was asleep... *of course you disturbed me*. Supper? What supper? What are you talking about man?"

"It's really very easy. These gentlemen have come for supper. I cannot express it any more clearly... or simply."

"I didn't ask them to come to supper."

"I know you didn't, and they are much offended by your lack of consideration, if I may say so. You should think yourself lucky that they have come at all..."

"Well, I wish they hadn't bothered... who are they anyway? I don't know them."

"Yes, you do. You met this gentleman earlier this evening." He pointed to the first statue.

"I did?"

"You did, in the square outside the parliament house."

"Ah, no, there you are mistaken. I did not *meet* him, or he me. I admit that I *saw* him, but as for *meeting*, no. Anyway, I rather thought he was a prince, or king? He

Likho

appears to be playing the role of a mere *commendatore* in this act."[9]

"He isn't, and I suggest you show some respect... this is no theatrical performance, I can assure you." The old man wagged a finger at me.

"I don't think I shall. He is uninvited, unexpected and unwelcome... he and his fellow statues. I suggest they go back where they belong before they are missed... and you can go with them since you are not welcome here either. Supper indeed... whatever next?"

"Well, a drink, at least? You can't turn them out on a night such as this... not without a brandy to keep out the cold. You must ask them in..."

"Oh, must I? A drink to keep out the cold? They are *statues*, for god's sake. Gentlemen all, I bid you good night." Slamming the door against them, I stood leaning against it for a moment, laughing quietly. It was a mildly amusing dream compared to the nightmares I'd been having, and I did feel a bit sorry for those poor things having to stand outside all day and night, all year in all weather. Perhaps I should have them in after all? I could give them all some schnapps or something to warm them a little... what harm could it do, as long as they wiped the snow from their feet and promised not to scratch anything with their swords. I opened the door again.

"All right, you can come..." There was no one there... not a statue to be seen in the dim flickering light from the gas lamps which hissed disapprovingly at me, the villain of the piece in this cheap melodrama. "Oh, well, never mind. I may as well go back to bed." Closing the door against my own words as they echoed down through the house, I walked back to my bedroom, climbed back into bed and pulled the quilt up over my head.

Darton

As I drifted off to sleep, I couldn't help but wonder where they had gone, and hard as I tried to convince myself that it was not my problem, I was certain that, somehow, it would become so…

8. Der Mond[10]

Wednesday 14th
When next I awoke it was morning, and my room was flooded with daylight. I didn't remember opening the curtains and was sure they were closed when I went to bed, but it wasn't important. I felt rested and better than I had for weeks so what did it matter if I'd closed the curtains or not, or opened them during the night? Perhaps I did it when I got up to answer the door? Hadn't that been a dream though? I had answered the door to find a queue of statues, together with my old neighbour, and they had all come for supper. That *was* a dream, wasn't it? Statues don't call on people in the dead of night, at least not outside the opera.

    Nevertheless, it troubled me all morning, especially since everywhere I went there were statues… statues in places where, usually, there were none. There was one on the stairs which wished me a good morning as I went by; another in the downstairs lobby was mopping the floor, whilst one outside on the street was leaning casually against a lamp standard and smoking a cigarette. That one greeted me politely too, as did the one who brought me some coffee when I sat at a table on the pavement outside a café, basking in the glorious summer sunshine.

    "You see, they're very friendly. I can't understand why you wouldn't invite them in." I looked up to see my old neighbour had joined me, having appeared from nowhere to sit next to me at the table where he was happily filling two glasses with red wine.

Darton

"It was the middle of the night. I am not in the habit of opening my door to parties of statues at that hour... or any other time, come to think of it. Were they *terribly* angry?"

"No, not *angry*... they were upset, a bit offended. You were extremely rude. They came from all over the city, and most of them are not too good when it comes to walking..."

"Well, I might not have minded so much if I'd known they were coming."

"You *should* have known; you *should* have expected them."

"Why? I didn't invite them."

"I know, but you thought about it and, as the saying goes, *it's the thought that counts.*"

"Ah, I didn't think of it like that."

"You should be careful how you *do* think... that is how these misunderstandings come about. Wine?"

"Isn't it a bit early?"

"Nonsense, it's nearly midnight."

"Midnight? It can't be. The sun is up... look, there, bright as ever. It must be *midday*, not midnight."

"That's not the sun. That's the *moon*."

"Really? Are you sure? It's very bright... certainly as bright as the sun."

"Brighter, I'd say, much brighter. Apparently, they've installed new lighting on it... all gas now, I think... anyway, it's a big improvement."

"What did they use before?" I asked.

"Oh, an old fellow with an oil lamp or a candle, something like that. It'll be much better now though, more reliable... and it's all automated, you see, so it'll be a full moon every night instead of just once a month."

"Why couldn't it be full all the time before?"

Likho

"Too much for one man to manage, I expect. Probably took him a whole month to walk around it. You'd have to ask him."

"Well, I *suppose* it's a good thing... but what will happen to the old boy and his lamp? Do you think he'll find another job?"

"I doubt it. Not much call for moon-lighters these days."

"Perhaps there is a new moon somewhere else that he could go to?"

"Unlikely... I've heard that they're all being modernised – *new* moons are being phased out... all being replaced with full ones."

"Is that a joke?" Well, I wasn't sure.

"Ah... no... at least it wasn't meant to be. Is it funny?"

"Well, I imagine there's a possibility. Never mind. Anyway, it's a pity for the man on the moon.... surely there must be something he could do?"

"No. He's redundant. It's a shame, but you can't stand in the way of progress, can you?"

"No, I suppose not. Still, I feel sorry for the fellow. I wonder what he'll do…"

"Oh, don't concern yourself with him. He'll probably be happy to spend more time in his garden…'

"Garden? They have gardens on the moon?"

"Well, I can't say they do, but can you say they don't?"

"No, I cannot. But, even if they do, I feel sorry for him."

"Yes, so you have said. But why? Why be sorry for someone you don't know? Someone for whose fate you are not responsible?"

Darton

"Do we owe him nothing? Do we not have a *collective* responsibility towards him? We have all enjoyed his moonlight for centuries, and it *must* have been arduous work... we shouldn't abandon him now just because we don't need him any more... it doesn't seem right."

"Doesn't seem right?" My old neighbour shook his head and then looked up at the moon. "There *are* things which don't seem right which are *not* right, and some things which don't *seem* right but *are* right... and then there are those things which seem right, but which are not, whilst some things seem right and *are* just so... but which of those applies in this case, I cannot say. One must be in possession of all the facts in the matter to make such a judgment, and *we* are not... or at least, that's how it seems to me."

"Well, *that* is not an argument to be, well, to be *argued against*..." replied I, "or is it?" The conversation was becoming stranger and stranger, and I began to wonder if I'd unwittingly stepped through a looking-glass earlier.

"All arguments are to be argued; that is why they are called *arguments*. If we do not dispute a point – *even one which we believe to be true* – then how can we be sure of anything? *The man who questions nothing may as well be in his grave...*"

"Oh, yes," I said, "now *that*, I like... the man who questions nothing is doomed, whilst the man who questions everything lives on... and, therefore, the man who never stops asking questions never dies... and thus we have the key to immortality. My, we *are* clever today..."

"I think your logic is a little forced, but," said the old man as he raised his glass, "let's drink to your eternal existence."

"And to yours..."

"Ah, no, no... too late for that... *I* died years ago."

"Oh, I'm sorry to hear that."

Likho

"No, you're not."

"No. No, I'm not, you are right," said I with a smile, "nor sorry to admit it. But that aside, if you *are* dead, what are you doing here?"

"*I've* been wondering about that." The old man seemed genuinely confused.

"Well, are you certain that you are?"

"Are *what*?"

"Dead."

"Now you mention it, no, I'm not certain at all. This is a *very* odd conversation... have I been sent into another one of your weird dreams?"

"No, this isn't a dream. At least, it's not one of mine. I suppose it could be yours though? Last night, you invaded my dream with your statue friends... and now, in return, I have a starring role in yours?"

"*Was* that a dream? I don't have dreams... I wonder why? What does it mean? *Not having dreams...*" He looked as if he were trying desperately to remember something, screwing up his ancient face so tightly that flakes of skin fell from it, exposing more desiccated flesh beneath. "Maybe it means I *am* dead?"

"If you *are*," I observed, "you don't seem to be very upset about it. If I were to discover I were dead, I'd want to know the reason why..."

"I wouldn't bother... there's no right of appeal... well, not in *my* experience."

"Interesting. And what *is* your experience?"

"Well, that's just it – I can't remember. Not clearly. It's like a series of old fogged photographs with faces out of focus... there's a story, but I can't tell it – it *is* my story, but I can't tell it, and I have a notion that I am not *allowed to tell it*... well, not yet..."

Darton

This old man whom I had disliked from the moment I met him, my ancient neighbour for whom I felt such disgust and loathing, looked, for once, vulnerable and deserving of help... and, most of all, desperately in need of a friend. It cannot be me, though, because I cannot act a role I've never learned. I know the feelings I should have, but I have no idea how express them. I know the words, but not how to say them, not how to be *sincere*... and if one cannot speak with sincerity, then one should not speak at all – insincerity is more insulting than silence...

"What about you?" The old man's question brought my wandering mind back under control.

"What about me? *I'm* not dead. And if I keep on asking questions, I'm here forever... the statues and me; we're here for all time."

"Then you'd better be nicer to them. You'll be in need of friends."

"No, I won't. I've never had any; I don't want any... especially not statues."

The statue at the next table had been listening to our conversation, and a tear rolled down his cold marble face as he stood up to leave. Hanging his head, dragging his feet and sobbing noisily, he walked slowly away, and I feel obliged to say, in the opinion of *this* critic, over-playing his part a little.

"Oh dear," my old neighbour shook his head, "you've upset them now."

"What do I care? They're not exactly great company... not great for conversation."

"Oh dear, oh dear, you will give serious offence with remarks like that."

"I don't care."

Likho

"I think you will before long, in fact quite soon, by the look of it..." He pointed to a line of statues on the street, hundreds of them... each with sword drawn, each moving slowly towards us. Actually, rather than *us*, I should say *me,* because when I looked back to speak to the old man, he had vanished, leaving me alone to face the stone army.

Fear and panic struck simultaneously, and both shouted at me to flee. I got up and started to run. I ran fast to begin with and then so fast that my feet left the ground. With the sound of soldiers marching behind me I flew along the street whilst spears and arrows sped past, some missing only by a hairsbreadth. I had to slow down to turn a corner and it was that which allowed my pursuers to catch up and their missiles to make their target. An arrow hit me below the left shoulder; another struck me in the neck, another in the lower back... I think they must have bounced off because they didn't seem to cause any injury. Then I made the mistake of stopping to look back...

Several kings and knights had gained on me, and one was close enough to jab me with the point of his poleaxe. Spurred on by his attack, I raced onwards to down the street, only to find a phalanx of stone warriors lining my path and leaving me no choice but to pass between them. As I went by, they struck me with their swords all about my body. A heavy blow to the head nearly knocked me over, another blade passed straight through from front to back and emerged somewhere between my shoulders. I hadn't far to go but by the time I reached the door of my building I must have been cut to ribbons. I could feel the air rushing through gaping wounds in my head and chest, and although I couldn't see it, I was sure my right arm had been sliced through, whilst my left leg had gone below the knee and the rest of it was hanging loosely, attached perhaps by only a strand of sinew. I didn't dare look back again but was sure I must have left a trail of blood which would make me easy to follow and hiding pointless.

At last, reaching home, I found the concierge standing in the middle of the lobby leaning lazily on his mop and surrounded by a pool of blood-tinged soapy water. He was staring ponderously at some statues which were standing on the steps like a guard of honour, and as I entered, he turned to me, shook his head, and then just shrugged his shoulders, as if to say all hope was lost. I could hear the scraping and grinding of stone spurs and armour on the pavement outside and realized there was nothing for it but an assault on the stairs and so, in fear for my life, I made a dash headlong upwards, attacked on every tread by swords and daggers which were thrust into my left side by assailants intent on cutting me to pieces... a poniard was pushed into my head, another two lodged firmly in my arm and a sword ran me through below the sternum. Despite the violence, and even as those blows rained down on me, I was aware that none of the injuries they inflicted had caused me any pain, but then I think perhaps I was too concerned with surviving the day to notice.

Anyway, having survived the climb, I arrived at the second floor – relieved to see my apartment door, and furious to see my old neighbour leaning against it whilst casually inspecting his broken old fingernails.

"Ah, there you are." He pushed the door open and gestured with an arm for me to enter. "We've been waiting hours. Where have you been?"

"Hours? You were with me only minutes ago at the café. When you saw the statues approaching you disappeared and left me to face them on my own. Look what they have done to me..." I walked into the lobby of my apartment and took off my coat which had been cut to shreds by swords, although the absence of any blood suggested my own injuries had been less serious than I'd imagined. Indeed, I did appear to be unharmed, unlike my poor overcoat which was now good for nothing. I waved its remains furiously at the old man. "Look at this... *look*" I shouted, "it's ruined. This is your fault..."

"Well, you were warned. I did tell you not to upset them."

"Oh, for heaven's sake man... these people really need to learn how to cope with rejection. They can't carry on like that, it's not acceptable. What am I to do now? How can I go out now I no longer have my coat? I must have my coat..."

"Can't you buy a new one?"

"No. I must have *this* one, *this* coat... *my* coat..." I felt as if I were about to cry as I held the shredded garment to me like a child with a comfort blanket.

"Well, you can't," the old man said angrily, "so stop behaving like a baby."

"Oh, shut up, you stupid old man... you are to blame for all of this. Look at me..." I shouted, "I was nearly killed out there. You vanished and left me to be slaughtered by your friends... And what are you doing *here*? You seem to be everywhere these days. I thought you never went out? Oh, and who, by the way, is *we*?"

"Shall I answer those in order?"

"Do as you like."

"Then I shan't answer at all." The old man shook his head petulantly and then turned away.

"Now who's being childish? If you are going to be like that then I suggest you leave... go, and take your statue friends with you..."

"They're not my..."

"Take *them* away, take *yourself* away, and *don't* come back. Now, if you will excuse me, I have things to do..." I pushed the old man out of the door and slammed it shut after him; if he had any doubt as to my feelings, that should have quashed them once and for all. Well, I hope so...

I went to my bedroom, dropped on to the bed and lay there staring at the ceiling. Silence and tranquillity returned once more to my home, and I fell into a deep, peaceful sleep, untroubled by dreams or nightmares and in which I remained for the rest of the night.

9. 'What Dreams May Come…'[11]

Thursday 15th
To my initial surprise I was wearing my night clothes when I awoke, and then when I saw my coat over the back of a chair and showing no sign of violence, I was confused as well as surprised. I took the few steps across the floor to where that poor garment lay and picked it up. I ran my fingers over it, I turned it over and over, inspecting every inch of it for damage but nothing suggested that it had been slashed and cut to pieces by an army of sword-wielding statues. I put it back on the chair and stared at it. How it might have been so seamlessly repaired during the night? Of course, the reality of the situation dawned on me, albeit rather slowly… it had all been another dream, or rather, it all been one dream. I had gone to bed and dreamed of the stone visitors, returning to my bed, the morning, the café, the pursuit through the streets and the attack by the statues. All so obvious when you think about it… it couldn't have been real because if it had been, well, then I'd be dead. As it is, I am, quite plainly, *not* dead – *ergo*, it was all just another dream… at least, I *think* it was – it *did* all seem very real at the time, and actually, it does still.

It's always nice to wake from a nightmare to discover that that is all it was… no murders committed, no injuries suffered, in fact no harm done at all, except perhaps for a few disturbing memories. The trouble begins when you are no longer able easily to say whether you are awake or asleep and that is the point which I think I have reached. It has happened a few times now and is becoming more than a little unsettling. As I stood looking at my coat it occurred to me that this could still be part of the dream, and I was tempted to look out into the stairwell to see if there were any statues waiting for me. After a few moments I surrendered nervously to that temptation and was reassured on opening the door to discover there were none. I confess that I felt rather silly, too, but no one saw me, so it is no matter.

Standing before the bathroom mirror a little while later, I wondered how one might establish if one *is* awake. How can a man prove if he is awake or dreaming? Seeing a path to madness stretching ahead, I think perhaps I should consult a doctor before it gets any worse.

I bathed and dressed and by ten o'clock I was sitting in a café enjoying some coffee and the view of a busy street through the window. I had encountered nothing unusual at all on the way, and seen no statues mopping floors, working as waiters, or hanging about on the streets. I was thus confident that I was awake, and the day was real, though I did seek the opinion of another on my way when I spotted a newspaper vendor on the street – one of those rare strangers who can be engaged in casual conversation without looking as if one might be a touch deranged. I stopped to buy a paper and sought to put an end to my confusion once and for all…

"This will seem like an odd question," said I, "and you might think me mad, but *am I awake*?"

"I *might* think you are mad sir, but I think also that you are awake," the man replied helpfully, "at least you certainly appear to me to be awake."

"Thank you. And you are certain *you* are awake?"

"Oh, *yes*, sir, though I wish it were otherwise…" said he with a friendly smile.

Likho

"Yes, quite so... then you don't think there's a chance that you could be dreaming?"

"Well, sir... do you dream of being a newspaper seller?"

"No... no I don't."

"No," said he, with a shake of his head, "and neither do *I*."

"Quite," I said, laughing, "then we are agreed that neither of us is dreaming."

"We are, sir... though if you should find that you *are* then perhaps you might do me the favour of dreaming up some warmer weather?"

With an obliging smile, I left the man to his business and strolled away down the street, and as I went, it crossed my mind that the conversation with the paper seller had been very like the sort of silly exchanges I've been having in my dreams...

As I drank my coffee, I thought again about consulting a doctor. Our family physician had retired and besides which he was an old fool who had never quite got over the idea that bloodletting was not the panacea it was once believed to be. A waiter obliged me with a copy of the city directory which listed many fine and grand sounding medical practitioners with double-barrelled names, each one followed with a list of his qualifications and specialities. A few had taken quarter-page display advertisements, and some inventive copywriters had imaginatively elaborated on the services offered; one in particular caught my eye in which it was claimed "*...all disorders of the digestif system are guaranteed to be remedied.*" Another promised revolutionary treatments for "*aneurysms, arrhythmia, coronary disease, hypertension and other affairs of the heart.*" As I had no problem with after-dinner drinks and no troublesome romances to upset me I continued to scour the pages, eventually settling on a psychiatric consultant who claimed to specialize in sleep disorders.

Leaving the café, I crossed the street and set off in the direction of the university. Half an hour later I was climbing the stairs of a very imposing building in which my chosen specialist resided. Admitted to an outer room I found a secretary dozing at her desk, and I was unsure if that was a good advertisement for her employer's services. Disturbed by my arrival, she sat upright and grabbed some papers from the desk in an attempt to appear alert and busy, and although I was not fooled, I said nothing other than to enquire about seeing the doctor.

A woman of instantly forgettable appearance, she made up for that with a very over-inflated opinion of herself, and though she was seated, she managed somehow to talk down to me. It was plain that she enjoys her role as gatekeeper, is well-schooled in the use of her chief weapon, *condescension*, and her work in repelling those she thinks undesirable.

"*Monsieur le professeur* has a very select client list, and an exceedingly long list of those who wish to be clients. However, should sir meet with the approval of *Herr doktor*, then it might be possible to add his name... *sir's* name, that is... well, *yours*, in fact, to it." The woman spoke slowly when using foreign words, studiedly pronouncing each with the accent appropriate to its language; I couldn't decide whether it was endearing or annoying, and so settled on *absurdly pretentious* instead.

"I see," I replied with as much politeness as I could manage, suppressing a sudden desire to be rude, "and may I ask just how select is *monsieur's* client list? Who, or indeed *what*, must one be in order to be considered worthy of a place?"

"Well, let us see if you qualify…" She looked me up and down, as if she was hoping for a clue in my appearance and then, presumably no wiser, she pulled a sheet of paper from a drawer and studied it for a moment. "Now, let's see…" she began, "*obviously* not a member of a royal family… not even *incognito*…"

"Oh dear," I interrupted, "it seems I am *démasqué, madame…*"

"Flippancy will not serve you well here, sir," she hissed, "and *interrupting* will serve you less well than *flippancy*." Feigning contrition, I stood silent before her. "Now, where were we? *Nobility*. Do you hold a title?"

"My father aspired to such honour all of his life but, sadly, his hopes were never to be realised."

The gatekeeper stared at me over her spectacles, unsure if I were daring to be flippant again, and then continued in a tone so patronising it must have taken her years to perfect…

"Well, I have no doubt that must have been a cause of much disappointment to his family…" said she, "particularly to his poor wife."

"His poor wife, my mother, is dead, *madame*… and so beyond all disappointment."

"At least in *this* world, sir." She nodded and shook her head at the same time, as if she couldn't decide whether she agreed with herself or not; I, meanwhile, was tempted to ask if she knew something that I did not. "But let us continue… now, do you hold a government post? A minister? Any rank would suffice…"

"Alas no, I am not connected with the government... well, other than through its tax collectors... so I suppose I could claim to be its employer, if that helps?"

"It does not, and you are being flippant again, I think. Now, please, we are running out of options... do you hold office in any religious organization?"

"Any particular sect?"

"No sir, we don't discriminate... as long as it's one of the more established religions."

"How established?"

"Well," replied she, thoughtfully, "preferably before about 1450."

"I see, and, may I say, I approve... there were more than enough religions by then, and all that new thinking since then has caused nothing but trouble..."

"No religious office then?" She shrugged her shoulders in what I took for a combination of frustration and no longer caring.

"No."

"Well, sir, I think that's it... oh, wait, how about *freemason*? Surely you must be..."

"Ah, no. Sorry, I fear I must disappoint you again, I am pleased to say."

"You should not be pleased to say such a thing sir. Some of the best clients of *monsieur le professeur* are fre..." She left the word incomplete, realising she was speaking a little too carelessly, put down her lists and folded her hands on the desk. "Sir, do you hold any position, title or rank which might be considered worthy of note?"

"No, I do not, and I have never found it to be a disadvantage before today." It was time to play her at her own game, I thought. "I have never aspired to high office, and no royal or aristocratic titles have descended from the crown of my family tree… indeed, the only thing I inherited from my father was his fortune. Still, a man must do his best with what he is given." The expression on the woman's face changed, as I thought it might. "Anyway, it is clear to me that the interest of *monsieur le docteur* is social status, not sickness, so I shall bid you good day *madam*e." I turned to leave.

"Ah, well, just a moment sir. It is possible that *monsieur le professeur* could accommodate a *preliminary* consultation…" She stood up. "Wait here, if you please, and I will find out." She disappeared through a door and left me alone to wonder what sort of man this professor is, though whatever *he* is, his secretary is plainly a very accomplished snob and a social climber. Just as I was thinking of going, the woman came back. *Monsieur* was able to spare some time and would see me right away, if that was convenient? She led me through the door and into his office where the great man sat at an enormous desk, peering inquisitively at me over his precariously perched *pince-nez* which stuck to the end of his nose in proud defiance of gravity as if announcing to the world that the laws of physics did not apply here.

Introductions over, he asked how I thought he might help me.

"I don't know how you might help me. How you might help is for you to decide is it not? Surely, I tell you my problem and then you think how you might help me?"

"It is not always so, but no matter. What is it that brings you here?"

I related a history of recent events to the wise-looking old gent and he appeared attentive enough, though whether to me or not was hard to say; actually, he had a distant look on his face and might have been thinking about his next holiday. At length I finished my tale of nightmares and confusion and sat back in the chair to await the judgment of *monsieur le professeur*.

"A most interesting case," he pronounced at last, "most interesting indeed, though not an uncommon one."

"You will think me a pedant, no doubt, but if it is not an uncommon thing then it is unlikely to be most interesting, is it?"

"Ah, yes, you are right."

"Well, which is it... most interesting or common?"

"Neither, both, one or the other... does it matter?"

"Are you asking me?"

"Do you have an opinion on the subject that you wish to share? Would you *like* to be asked?"

"I wasn't sure if your question was rhetorical. Anyway, the issue, sir, is surely not dependent upon my likes but your curiosity? It is irrelevant whether I'd like to be asked. Men may ask what they please, and I may answer as *I* please."

"I see, I think... so how do you answer?"

"Actually, I'm not sure... what was the question?"

"I can't remember. Never mind." The erudite doctor shrugged and relaxed back into his chair; I, meanwhile, was beginning to think him rather amusing.

"It *didn't* matter then. You have answered your own question, I think." I smiled whilst trying not to look too smug.

"Yes, I think I might have done. Do you like questions?"

"Asking or answering them?"

"Either."

"If a question needs asking then I feel free to ask it."

"What about answering?"

Likho

"That depends on who is asking... and if the matter is any business of his."

"I see. It is one rule for you and another for others?"

"No. I respect a man's right to privacy, and I expect my right to privacy to be respected. Before I ask a question, I think about whether it needs to be asked and, if so, is it any concern of mine."

"Idle curiosity never gets the better of you then?"

"I hope not, but none of us is perfect."

"Yet you strive to be?" The doctor sat forward and pointed a finger at me.

"No, sir, I do not. I try only to be good... or at least not to cause trouble to others... and that is something I find seldom reciprocated, by the way."

"Does that make you angry?"

"No, no... it used to disappoint me... actually, people have been the only source of disappointment in my life. Anyway, I care no longer."

"Why?"

"Because I have as little involvement with others as I can, so it is not my problem."

"Do you think then that you have failed somehow?"

"Certainly not. Why should I? It has never been my mission to make the world a better place."

"What *is* your mission then?"

"I don't believe I have one... but if I *did*, it would be not to make the world a *worse* place."

"Very noble." The man nodded, smiling condescendingly at the same time. "And very pointless."

"Pointless? Yes, I'm sure you're right."

"How does that make you feel?" His question was as patronizing as his expression.

"It causes me no feeling at all, neither good nor ill. Is that right or wrong?"

"No, and yes."

"That is not helpful."

"It is not intended to be."

"I see." I thought for a moment and then added "actually, I don't see at all. Aren't you supposed to be helping me?"

"No. I don't help anyone. I show people how to help themselves…"

"Oh, so this is self-help course?"

"I think so, yes, and you were on it before you came here… it is what brought you here because you have come to an impasse. So why do you not ask me?"

"Ask you what?"

"Well, I presume that you want to know how to overcome your situation?"

"Do we not take that as read?" I had formed the impression that *monsieur* preferred to shun the direct route in favour of a more circuitous path to his end, and I was growing a little tired of following him. "Do you think we could come to the point?"

"Very well, if you wish. You would like to be able to know if you are dreaming or conscious… you want to know if you are asleep or awake, do you not?"

"Awake? Do you think I don't know if I am awake?"

"That is precisely what I think. Do you think you are awake? Or are you asleep in your bed and dreaming?"

"I believe I am awake."

"And this is not a dream? This is real?"

"Yes."

"You are sure?"

"Quite sure, yes."

Likho

"How? What is it that makes you so certain?"

"That's a good question. Well, it doesn't feel like a dream."

"But your dreams don't feel like dreams at the time, do they?"

"No."

"Quite. In general, no one knows they are dreaming, not until they awake from the dream, assuming that the awakening is real and not false…"

"What do you mean?"

"Well sometimes a dream can be within a dream, or just a single episode which is a part of much longer dream… you understand? In the first one you dream you have awoken but it is a *false* awakening… you are still asleep and dreaming. It is possible for a man to have multiple false awakenings. It seems that you might have experienced this?"

"Ah, I see what you mean, yes. That makes sense."

"Good. Of course, you can sometimes be aware of dreaming, but it is not so common... it is known as a *lucid* dream, and false awakenings often follow lucid dreams. In those situations, the dreamer may not be able to tell if he is dreaming or not. You might dream you are awake; you might dream you are in bed and unable to sleep… you get up and read a book or have a drink, you do unremarkable things, and all of that conspires to confuse your brain even further. Reality and unreality become muddled. Do you recognize any of these scenarios?"

"Yes, possibly… yes, I do."

"If we take your dream about the statues, for example, you might have had two false awakenings… the first when you got up to answer the door in the night, the second when you thought you were waking up in the morning. After the first you had an idea that it was a dream... it was a *lucid* dream, do you see? Following the second awakening everything seemed normal at first but then became more and more unreal, but however odd it became, you thought all must be real because you were certain you were awake. Again, do you see?"

"Yes, I understand... it's all *very* simple..."

"*Simple?*" He seemed genuinely indignant as he stared hard at me over his glasses. "Far from it my dear fellow, far from it. The subject is vast and complex... the world's greatest thinkers have argued about it for thousands of years. We are... how do you say? Only *zcratching at ze zurfaces, ja?*"

"If you say so." I don't know why he said those words in a foreign accent; maybe he did it just for added gravitas? I didn't bother to ask. It did occur to me, though, that perhaps I *was* still dreaming. "Is it possible, do you think, that I might have had a *third* false awakening... and none of this is real..."

"It is possible, I suppose, yes. Perhaps you *are* dreaming now?"

"Well, if I am, then you are part of my dream. Are you in the habit of making appearances in the dreams of strangers?"

"I don't know..." he replied with a shrug and a shake of his head. "I could know if I were in your dream only if it were *my* dream, and *your* dream was happening within it."

"Right..." I had to think for second to avoid confusing things even further, "then we could be in *your* dream now?"

"Interesting" he said with a nod, "except that I don't think I am dreaming."

Likho

"No? I didn't think I was either, but now I'm not so sure. Maybe you exist only in my dream?"

"I am flattered by the suggestion – at least. I *think* I am… but I am certain that I have a corporeal existence independent of your dreams…

"Of course," he said, "we could both be in someone else's dream. Have you thought of that? Maybe we are no more than the creations of another man's subconscious? Perhaps that is where we exist… and all our thoughts and actions, and all that we experience, are inventions of his mind? Just think of it… he might have dreamt the whole of our lives, those of our ancestors, and the whole history of mankind… and what has felt like a lifetime to you and me has filled only a few seconds in his dream.

"In dreams, as I'm sure you know, time does not behave itself in the same way as we experience it when awake… it can quicken and slow, go forwards and back, it can stop and start, it can tie itself in knots… and it can even cease to exist altogether… because in a dream everything is subject only to the whims of the dreamer's subconscious, and not to any natural laws.

"We might consider, perhaps, that the creation of the universe, of each galaxy and star… of our little planet and everything on it, is all a man's dream, and what we think has taken an eternity has taken perhaps less than an hour… and when he wakes, as he surely must, it will all end, and we will exist no longer. Who knows? We might have just minutes left to us before we exist only in the *memory* of a dream… perhaps no more than the merest fragment of a memory which will slip, inexorably and irretrievably into a darkness which has no end. Imagine it… it will not be that we exist *no longer*, but that we have *never* existed…" *Monsieur le professeur* sat back in his chair and looked very pleased indeed, as if he had delivered himself of the ultimate and indisputable theory of all things.

"Then nothing we do in our lives would have any consequence? I could murder you now, and it wouldn't matter..." I mused, looking about the room as if considering it a serious possibility, "there would be no consequence for *me*, at least..."

"Well, there *might* be..." he interrupted, "because our sleeping man might dream of your arrest, trial and execution, and *that* could shorten your existence by decades... although, of course, in his *dream* time it might be only a fraction of a second."

"I accept the possibility, but if I don't exist then at least the execution will be painless..."

"Even if the blade causes no physical suffering, you should allow that our dreamer might wish, for his pleasure, that you *do* suffer – think of the fear which could afflict you in the hours before? Execution, when it comes, might be quick and painless, but the days or weeks whilst you *await* its coming must surely be excruciating torture?"

"Oh, *monsieur*," replied I, "we might sit here and speculate on these things for the rest of time, or such time as our imaginary creator *allows* us, but it will not change the fact that, *here and now,* your conclusion is that *we don't matter, that I don't matter, and that my life is of no value*... It doesn't do much for my self-esteem, does it?"

"You mentioned no trouble with low self-esteem. Do you have low self-esteem?"

"Not presently, but if you continue telling me that I don't exist then I can see it being a possibility."

"Would it matter if you didn't exist?"

"Not to anyone else..." I replied, quickly adding "and I can see how that might lead us down another path, and it is one I do not intend to travel today, if it be all the same to you? Or even if it be not…"

"Indeed, indeed," the man said, tapping his desk with a forefinger whilst scribbling a note on the paper before him. "We shall return to that subject, no doubt, on another day…"

"*No, we shall not*" thought I.

"…but *meanwhile*, can you not see that whether asleep or awake… dream or reality, unconscious, subconscious or sentient – it *doesn't* matter. Have you come to any harm? Have you caused harm to others? No, you have not… so it doesn't matter, does it? *That is the root of your problem*… you have an idea that it is important to know whether you are dreaming or not. Can you see now that it is *not*?"

"Yes… and no. You speak of *harm*… you say I have come to no harm? But *I* think I have… I think it has been *psychologically* harmful…"

"Well, we can talk about that next time… we have made a good start but there is much, much work still to do, and our time is up for today… my secretary will arrange another appointment…"

"Oh, I don't think I shall be requiring one, thank you."

"No? That would be a shame… I have enjoyed our conversation, and I think it would be most beneficial, perhaps even for *you*. Are you sure?"

"Quite sure. You have given me much to think about already, and I shouldn't like to trespass further on your valuable time."

"Oh, we have no trespassers here, sir, only paying guests. Anyway, it is up to you…" *Monsieur le professeur* took my hand and shook it firmly, so firmly, in fact, that the pain in my crushed fingers confirmed I was very definitely awake. "My secretary will send your account, and when you receive that you'll hope you're dreaming…"

10. Subtlety and Suggestion

The freezing wind which burned my face was a welcome relief after an hour in the rarefied and stuffy atmosphere of the doctor's consulting rooms. That said, it was an interesting conversation, although I'm sure I could have been offered the same advice and opinions by a stranger in a bar; of course, a stranger in a bar probably wouldn't have the backing of some august medical association but, on the subject in question, I don't think that would make his contribution any less valid than the unfounded hypotheses of *monsieur le professeur*.

The weather had driven everyone off the streets, and I passed no one all the way to my door. Walking along the deserted pavements, I did think it a little odd because the snow wasn't the worst we've ever seen, the wind wasn't the strongest or the most biting and, for a winter's day in our dear old town, well, it's not the worst we've had.

This confusion of dreams and reality has started to affect my appetite, and the sight of my lunch laid out in the dining room made me feel a bit sick. I couldn't think of eating anything, though the idea of a glass of wine wasn't quite so nauseating and with that thought, I picked up the open bottle on the table and went to my sitting room where my armchair waited patiently to welcome me home. Presented with such an invitation, I don't think there is a man alive who would have preferred to be elsewhere at that moment…

Stretched out in the chair, sluggishly scanning the pages of a book and judging it unworthy of my full attention, my gaze drifted to the window; the snow was falling more heavily, menaced by a strengthening wind, and I was glad to be where I was.

It wasn't long before the wine did its usual job of sending me off to sleep for an hour or so, performing its duty like the reliable servant it has become, and it was mid-afternoon when I awoke, disturbed by a knock at the outer door. Now, as you know, I am not accustomed to visitors and so my curiosity was piqued by a desire to know who dared to trespass at my threshold. I confess it was a disappointment to find only the wife of the concierge standing there holding what appeared to be a letter and which she thrust at me with some urgency.

"The boy is waiting for a reply, sir, if there is to be one." She indicated with a movement of her head that the messenger in question was somewhere below. Opening the envelope, I found a single sheet of paper on which the following lines were written...

Sir,

I believe you have certain questions concerning your apartment? I can meet you presently if you wish. The bearer of this note will bring you to me directly, if you will trust him to do so.

It was unsigned, and all the more mysterious for it. Things are becoming odder by the hour today, and I was too intrigued to refuse this offer.

"Thank you. Please ask the boy to wait and say I will go with him..."

The woman nodded then scuttled away to carry out her instruction before I could complete my sentence, and I went in to get my coat. I should have been suspicious of such a strange invitation but how could I not go? With all my concerns quickly crushed by curiosity, I set forth without another thought...

Likho

My guide was waiting patiently outside on the pavement... a boy of about twelve years, he put me in mind of a nineteenth century street urchin as he stood there in his scruffy clothes with his dirty face and unkempt hair. I did wonder if he'd been dressed like that for the occasion... but why would anyone do that? It was cold and the poor lad must have been feeling it, though he didn't seem to be troubled, and it crossed my mind that I might be dreaming again. The snow had stopped falling but it lay thick on the ground and I noticed some idle hands had been making snowmen near our door... two crudely fashioned figures stood by the steps, one a little larger than the other; each had stones for eyes and carrots for noses, but neither had been given a mouth – and I can't help wondering if I am *supposed* to think that is somehow significant?

My attention having wandered momentarily, the boy tugged at my arm to regain it.

"You come?" He spoke with a strange accent which I couldn't quite place, and, unable to decide if he was from a foreign land or a different time, the latter of those possibilities seemed to be an appropriate choice...

"Yes," replied I, "where are we going?"

"I go, you follow." With that he set off along the street and I had to walk quickly to catch him up. I wanted to know whom I was going to meet. "*Is lady*" was his cryptic answer, and he declined to speak further until we reached a café in the square by the old east gate. I walked after him with some unease as he led me from the first room to another and then into a third where he stopped, pointed to a woman seated by a window, and then turned to go.

"Wait," I said, "is that the person whom I am to meet?"

"Yes sir, that is lady."

Darton

I pulled a banknote from my wallet to reward him for his trouble; he took it, nodded gratefully and scampered away, doubtless anxious to spend his earnings as unwisely as boys of his age like to do. I, on the other hand, remained where I was for a moment so that I could observe the stranger at whose invitation I had come so recklessly...

Well, with all the strange things which have been happening recently, it should come as no surprise that I recognized my *lady* instantly – it was the woman from the restaurant... you might recall the couple who had intrigued and infuriated me with their silence? It *was* a surprise though, and an alarming one at that...

A shiver ran down my spine, although barely had it passed before the idea that this was just another dream came to mind again – the narrative, the characters and the *mise en scène* were all just right, though it did occur to me that perhaps it was a little *too* just right, and someone is going to a lot of trouble to sow doubt and confusion.

Anyway, whether dreaming or awake, having come thus far, I thought I might as well go along with it.

She was looking out of the window and didn't see me approach.

"Excuse me, madam, I believe you expect me?"

She turned her head slowly, looked me up and down and then spoke with a voice so quiet I strained to hear at first.

"You are the gentleman who wrote to my husband?"

She was thin and pale – a look that put me in mind of those consumptive courtesans of the nineteenth century *demi-monde*, and the minimal effort with which she made such minimal movements as she found necessary only reinforced that impression.

Likho

"If your husband is the former resident of my apartment then yes, I did... though he said that you knew nothing of my letter and that he didn't propose to trouble you about it. I assume he changed his mind?"

"No, no he has not changed his mind. He didn't tell me, but he was careless enough to leave it in the pocket of a coat where I found it."

"I see, and then *you* spoke to *him* about it?"

"No, I didn't." She paused for a moment to summon a waiter, lighting a cigarette at the same time. "Wine? Or something else?"

"Wine will do very nicely... red, preferably." I took my coat off and sat down. "May I ask why?"

"Why what?"

"Why did you not speak to your husband?"

"Ah, well, he worries too much. He thinks I am not well enough to be reminded about... about, well, I think you *know* what..."

"I confess I'm not sure *what* I know..." I said, "because everything is rather muddled at present... and that is to put it mildly. But forgive my rudeness... are you well? Your husband *did* imply that you were in poor health, and that you had been for some years."

"I am well enough, though I admit I did get a fright when I saw your letter... it upset me a bit, but the more I thought about it, the more certain I became that I should meet you, though I will not come to that... that *place*... I have no good memories of it and no wish to see it again. But don't concern yourself; I am quite well enough *here*..." she assured me, but then adding "although one thing troubles me... I'm not sure what... you look vaguely familiar? Have we met before? I'm certain we haven't."

Darton

"Ah, you are quite right... we have *not* met. It's possible that I look familiar, though... you see, quite recently, I was seated at a table next to you in a restaurant. You were with a man whom I supposed to be your husband. I can never remember the name of the place but it's the old building at the far end of the bridge, beneath the castle hill. You know it? I think it used to be a chapel..."

"Oh, yes... I know it well. We go there often. It's convenient for our... well, never mind."

"Your home? Don't worry, I don't wish to know anything which doesn't concern me. Where you live is not my affair."

"But where you live is *mine*, I'm afraid to say..." She took a sip of wine, lit another cigarette and then sat back again. "You mentioned in your letter certain *stories*? What did my husband say?"

"Only that he knew no details of any."

"I see. Well, I infer that you were talking of the murder of the children. Am I right?"

"Yes, and the suicide of their father too. Is it nothing more than a story? I'm not sure my sources are reliable."

"Well, what *are* your sources?"

"A police inspector... and the old man in the neighbouring apartment. Your husband and the police inspector say that the old man doesn't exist. I, on the other hand, say that he *does*. They say that the apartment is unoccupied... whereas I say it *is*. Do you see where a man might begin to doubt what he hears and sees?"

"Yes, I do." She paused for a minute and looked out across the small square, almost as if she thought to see someone... an angry husband, perhaps, come to drag her home and away from some imagined act of infidelity?

Likho

"Do you expect someone?" I couldn't resist it. "I ask only because you seem a little distracted."

"Expect someone? No, no... I am expecting no one. I'm sorry; you were talking of a neighbour?"

"Yes, the old man in the apartment at the top of the stairs. You knew him?"

"Ah, no. I'm afraid not. I thought the other apartments on that floor were empty, just as my husband did."

"I see," I said, not really believing her. "Well, he never goes out, so it's possible you might not have seen him, especially if you were only there for two weeks... you would have seen him only in his rooms..."

"Well, as I say, I did not know him."

"You are lucky... he is a most unpleasant fellow. I wish I had never met him... there is something wrong, something bad about him, something... well, I don't know what..."

"Then, perhaps, you should avoid him? Perhaps, for your own good, you should not visit him?"

"That is an odd remark, if I may say so? What prompts you to make it?"

"I wish I could say." The woman looked vague and shrugged her shoulders.

"Do you mean that you do not know, or that you are prevented from *saying* what you know? I am sorry to be a pedant, but people speak so ambiguously sometimes... often artlessly, and now and then with just a little *too much* art."

"Well, in this case I believe I speak artlessly... and you are quite right to seek clarification. This business is one where subtlety and suggestion will only make matters worse... in my opinion, that is... so let us speak plainly..."

"I agree, and I am pleased not to have offended you on the point. I like clarity, not confusion."

"Offending me is the least of your problems. Tell me about the old man."

"There's not much to tell... he's a very old fellow, I don't know how old... over eighty, I should say... I'm no good at guessing these things. He sits all day in his chair and claims never to go out, although I have twice seen him in the street... though when I mentioned it, he lied... he said it couldn't possibly have been him... and *then* there was the old woman, but I didn't get a good look at her... some skeletal black-clad old dowager, though he denied that too. But no matter because for all his denials, I know it was he... I would swear to it on my life."

"I wouldn't do that if I were you, sir... not under the circumstances."

"What circumstances?"

"Well, I said we should speak plainly, so I shall..." She lit another cigarette and poured some more wine. "That building has ghosts, and I do not believe them to be in any way benevolent. It has something to do with the murder of those children... I say that because I believe *them* to be the ghosts. As for their father, I know nothing of his part... but perhaps, if he committed suicide, then he, too, might be tied to the place? I have heard that is what happens to murder victims and suicides... their spirits remain, bound to tell their story over and over until injustices are undone and some sort of universal balance is restored? Your old man... he could be one of them too? I don't know..."

I had listened politely, resisting all urges to laugh, and when she finished speaking I took a sip of wine, set the glass on the table, and after a pause, I spoke.

"You *believe* that?"

Likho

"I do."

"You will forgive me, I'm sure, but may I ask why?"

"Well, I think you know already... but I am happy to explain if it will help you? During the short time I lived at the apartment in which you now have the misfortune to reside, I experienced several things for which I can give no account. I heard people when and where there were none – *when and where there could have been none* – and I can see from the look in your eyes that *you* have heard them too, so don't insult me by denying it..."

She was right, of course. However brief it had been, she had seen it... that flash of understanding which passes between people who have shared some experience and which can't be hidden or denied, however hard we try. Our brains may force our tongues to lie, but our eyes will always betray us.

I said nothing, and she went on.

"There were the voices of children. I heard them in our rooms... I heard them very clearly and know that they were there with me... and *you* have heard them too, I am certain of it..." I opened my mouth to speak but she held her hand up to stop me. "Please, *wait*; there is more, if you will permit me? The noises were not confined to the apartment... they followed me up and down the stairs, as if they were running around me like a dog herding sheep... and as for the neighbouring apartment... the one where I believe those children were... well, anyway, there were the most terrible sounds... shouting, crying, screaming... all coming from inside, even though everyone insisted the place was unoccupied."

I watched the woman as she spoke, as she recalled to mind what she had experienced, and as she raised a cigarette to her mouth her hand trembled so violently that she dropped it to the floor. Her face, pale to begin with, looked almost grey, and her eyes widened as she went on, staring and unblinking with a look of fear such as... well, such as she'd had when she appeared in my dream. Whether real or not, whatever she had experienced seemed to have caused a deep and lasting terror, and I was convinced that this reaction to her memories was no act.

I sat a moment, picked up my glass and thought about what to say. Although I have experienced the same things, I do not believe them to be anything supernatural... I *cannot* think them to be so – my philosophy will not allow it... so as some fellow once said, *'here I stand, I can do no other...'*

"You are absolutely certain that there is no explanation for any of it?"

"Quite certain." She managed to light another cigarette but stared at me coldly whilst she did it. "There is one more thing of which I am *absolutely certain*..."

"Do go on."

"Must I say it again? I know that you have had the same experiences... and that is why you went to so much trouble to contact us. When you knew how short a time we stayed at that place, you wanted to know *why*... you wanted to know if it was because we had suffered the same. I am right, am I not?"

"Yes, more or less."

"There is something more though, isn't there? I sense there is. What more is there?"

"Difficult to say..."

"Try."

"Well, I have been having dreadful nightmares since I moved in... nightmares and strange dreams. There are times when I'm not sure if I'm awake or asleep, dreaming or not. In fact, *this* could be another dream."

"Yes, that started happening to me, but we left before it became too bad."

"Did your husband share your experiences?"

"No, or at least he *said* not. I have often wondered why he was so sympathetic though, and why he agreed to move so quickly."

"You haven't asked him?"

"We never speak of it. He is afraid it will disturb my mind."

"Ah, did he think you were going mad then?"

"If he did, he never said so, and at least was kind enough to indulge me. You have only yourself to indulge, and self-indulgence never ends well."

"That is not in my nature…" As I spoke, it occurred to me that I am the most self-indulgent man ever to live, and I struggled to suppress a smile. "Did *you* ever think you might be going mad? I know I have doubted myself much recently."

"Of course I did… but if I can question my sanity, then I cannot be mad, can I?"

"I have come to the same conclusion," said I.

"So, we are neither of us mad… and now you know my thoughts about that place, what explanation do *you* offer?"

"That's just it, I don't have one. I wish I did." I finished my wine and poured another glass; I was tempted to take the cigarette which my companion offered but managed to resist… I haven't smoked for many years and don't wish to reacquire that particular habit. "I am a sceptic… it is my nature to believe nothing until it is proved beyond all doubt, and that is why I cannot accept your theory about ghosts, whether you meant it literally or figuratively."

"I understand that, but it leaves you with nothing. Wouldn't it be better to accept any idea, however improbable? At least you would have something to hold to until another theory presents itself…"

"I am sure your suggestion is well-meant, but no, I cannot."

"Then I am lucky because, unlike you, I am happy to admit of any possibility, and it is no matter to me, because I have *faith* and I *believe*."

"Ah, you choose the assurance… the *comfort* of a religion? Well, that is a thing I cannot accept, I simply *cannot*."

"That is patronising…" She shrugged and reached for her drink, "but I shall let it go. There are many men of science who toil long and hard to explain away the mysteries of the world but who are still content to believe in a god. The difference between them and you is that their minds are open to anything… and even though they know they will not live to prove the existence of a god, of *their* god, perhaps, they are confident nevertheless of its being, one way or another. Maybe, one day, long after you are gone, or perhaps *tomorrow*, a man in a laboratory will capture a god in a jar?"

"Well, I must admit, that might be a start…" I wanted to ask how anyone might prove that the thing in jar *was* a god, but I thought it might have made me look like a cheap, confrontational pedant, and so left the question unasked.

"Better late than never, I suppose," she said with a feeble smile. "Tell me, do you think you are in *danger*?"

"What sort of danger?"

Likho

"*Any* sort of danger... physical, psychological... *spiritual*."

"Ah. I see."

"You do?"

"No, not exactly, but I shall try. First, ghosts, if they exist, cannot possibly do harm. Second, the old man – the one whom no one believes exists – *he* cannot possibly do me harm... and third... third... no, I don't think there is a *third*. I don't see how anything in that place can do me any harm, except maybe the stairs... and, perhaps, the possibility that I could be sent mad by a combination of bad dreams and fatigue... mental and physical. Beyond that, I see nothing to fear."

"I suppose I know the answer before I ask the question, but do you really refuse to accept the possibility of *spiritual* harm?"

"Yes, of course." I thought for a moment, emptied my glass and then went on "but I will listen to whatever you might care to say on the subject... my mind may be closed but my ears are not."

"Well, the way to open a mind is through open ears, I suppose." She lit another cigarette, poured some more wine and then sat back again with a contemplative look on her face. "It is rather difficult, is it not? I'm not sure how to go on... perhaps I should just say what I believe and then it is up to you...

"Good and evil, heaven and hell, gods and devils... I believe in these things, I believe they are as real as we are, and I believe the possibility of eternal damnation to be a very real danger. It is not one I wish to face... and I hope to lead a good enough life to be spared such a fate when I die. There, that is what I believe, and believe it with absolute, unconditional sincerity. Evil is not always obvious, you know? It hides behind all sorts of masks in order to trap us... and we must be able to see it when it presents itself because that is the only way we can keep it from us..."

"Doesn't your god *deliver us from evil?*"

"*Please*... don't be flippant... and *no*, he doesn't. God doesn't *save* us... he shows us how to save ourselves. But we are not *compelled* to learn, we are free to do as we please. Just don't expect to save your soul with deathbed regrets... there's no last chance, no final fork in the road leading down a flower-strewn lane to redemption... and anyway, that flower-strewn lane to redemption might not be what you think... though evil is ultimately ugly, it must be beautiful at first...

"Now, I will speak plainly again...when I lived in your apartment, I had a strong feeling of the presence of evil... and though you may call it what you will, it doesn't change *what* it is. There is something wrong there; something bad... and it has some connection with those dead children... and I believe it has the power to do real harm. I mean *real* harm... physical, mental, and spiritual. Whatever it is, I am certain it caused the deaths of those children by some means, and since then it has worked through them... that place is hiding something evil, and it has very likely been there always. Can you imagine it? Some malevolent spirit, something *demonic* has been in that house for centuries, though how and why I don't begin to guess. How many has it tormented, or driven mad... or killed? I *know* it was going to kill me, and now, whatever it is, it is after you. You look at me with an expression of sympathy, just as you might look at someone who is dying... or irretrievably mad."

"Do I? Sorry, my face often acts without thinking; it is forever getting me into trouble. I am sorry for you because I *do* understand how it is... the distress and frustration of not knowing what is real or imagined, or of how to explain the experiences one is having without being thought mad, or intoxicated...

"I don't know how or why you saw and heard what you say you did, and I can't explain any of the things which have happened to me since I moved to that apartment. You have your theory, and that is good if it helps you... and in *that* respect I am a little jealous because I have no theory at all. In my mind is one mighty conflict... I cannot accept what cannot be proved to be real, yet am experiencing things which cannot be proved to be real but which I am nevertheless experiencing and therefore *must* be real, even though I know they cannot be... so it is very likely that even if not now mad, I *shall* be soon... so perhaps it is *I* who deserve sympathy?"

"You are quite right..." said she, with a nod of her head, "and I *am* sorry for you, though not for that... I am sorry for you because I believe something bad is happening to you, and your naivety is sustaining it. I don't know you; I have no reason to involve myself, I am not here from any sense of obligation. But I *do* feel a responsibility... and I don't think my conscience will let me rest if I do nothing, and *that* is why I am here. If, however, you choose not to hear, well then, what can I do?"

"You can do *nothing*," I assured her, "and you should consider your conscience duly discharged – at least as far as *I* am concerned, that is."

"You think it that easy?" She looked annoyed.

"Well, isn't it?"

"Consciences, sir, are not so easily *discharged*, as you put it..." she paused a moment and then went on, "I will say one last thing, and then I leave you to yourself and your own judgment... and wherever that might lead. If you want an end to this, you must leave that place.

Will you leave it? Leave it today... now, this minute? Don't go back... stay tonight in an hotel, find another apartment, send for your things... but don't go back there. Not even for a second."

"To ask a man to flee his home is a serious matter."

"Well, sir, this matter *is* serious, don't doubt it."

"I don't doubt your sincerity."

"It is not my sincerity you need have faith in... tell me, do you fear dying?"

"No."

"Do you fear for your soul?"

"No... I fear only that I might have one."

"Really? Why?"

"Simple... if man has a soul... a thing that is separate from the corporeal body, well then, that might survive physical death, and that means death is not the end, and if it is not then everything I know and believe is wrong."

"Would that be so bad?"

"To exchange the finite for the infinite? Yes, I think so. I would rather be certain of only one thing than uncertain of everything."

"What *do* you fear then?"

"Only that I should go mad... and thus not be in control of myself. Madness *does* frighten me... madness in *me*, that is."

"I think that is the least of your problems."

"Really? Tell me, then, what do you think is going to happen to me?"

"I cannot say... but *something* will, and it will not be good."

Likho

"After all, then, we come back to that and nothing more."

"Yes, if you will not listen or trust me, then no, there is nothing more. I shall pray for you, of course, though it will do no good…"

"Oh, I wouldn't go troubling any gods on my account… I'm sure they have many more important matters to worry about. But I am being flippant again… I must say that when that boy brought me here earlier, I had no idea what I was in for, and now I am no wiser."

"*What boy?*" The woman looked startled.

"The boy whom you sent to deliver your note… the one who brought me here."

"I didn't send a boy… I sent a taxi… the driver was to deliver my message and then bring you if you would come. I sent no boy… I think you are joking, are you not? I must say it is in extremely poor taste…"

"I assure you, madam, I am serious. I was brought here by a scruffy boy of about twelve years old…"

"Oh, no, no, no… that is not possible… *not possible*…" She reached for a cigarette with one hand and her drink with the other. "You are lying…"

"I assure you, madam, that I am not… and I find your accusation offensive. I was brought here by a boy of about twelve, as I said, and if you do not believe it then come with me and speak to the wife of the concierge… she must have seen him since it was to her whom he gave your note."

"No, no… that cannot be right." Her hands were trembling, and the only colour remaining on her face was in the dark blue shadows around her eyes. It would not be overstating matters to say she looked frightened to death and was very likely so because of what I had said.

"Why should you be bothered who delivered your message? It is obvious that the man you charged with it decided to keep your money and delegate the task to another... I see only reasonable explanations and no cause for such distress."

"You think there is nothing odd? Nothing slightly out of the ordinary?"

"Oh, you think I was led by the ghost of a murdered boy, perhaps? Well, I did think his appearance a little old fashioned... though if he was a ghost then from his dress, I would say he lived a century ago and certainly no later. But whatever he might have been, he was not the spirit of a child dead thirty years or so... and of *that*, I *am* sure."

"How easy you think this all to be... but please excuse me," she said, "I shall be back directly." With that she rose from her seat and walked slowly away in the direction of the ladies' cloakroom.

As I watched her cross the room, a sudden feeling of fatigue descended on me; I sat back in my chair and closed my eyes for a moment...

Now, just how long that moment lasted, I know not; when I opened them again it was dark outside, the snow was falling heavily once more and there was no one to be seen in the square. On the table in front of me sat an empty glass and next to it an empty wine bottle. As for company at that table, there was none, and no evidence that there ever had been any. No empty glass, no ashtray... our lady had gone and all trace of her had been removed.

"Excuse me," I called to a passing waiter, "what happened to the lady who was here?"

"Lady? I saw no lady sir."

"She was here; sitting here with me... a young lady, very pale, smoked a lot... you must have seen her?"

Likho

"No, sir, I have seen no such person. Maybe it was earlier, before I arrived?"

"What time did you get here? Have you not been here all afternoon?"

"No, sir… I started about one hour ago. You have been sitting there alone."

"No, that is impossible… unless I've been sleeping?"

"Ah, well, sir, that might explain it… perhaps you have been sleeping." The waiter looked at the wine bottle and my empty glass in a way which I interpreted as a suggestion that I was drunk, and that my lady friend must have been an imaginary one.

"It is quite possible that I have been sleeping, but only momentarily, and I was most certainly awake when I came here, and when I came here it was for the purpose of meeting a lady… that lady was here, we talked for some time, and now she would appear to be gone."

"Well, sir, I can think only that perhaps she found her prospects to be… well, disappointing?" He smiled in a rather suggestive manner and turned to go.

"What are you implying? How dare you, sir? How dare you?" I stood up, although a little shakily, my voice raised in indignation. "What an insult … who do you think you are?"

The impudent waiter shrugged and walked away. I picked up my coat and without another word stormed out of the café and into the deserted snow-covered square by the old south barbican.

Speechless and in a state of furious confusion I walked quickly across to the gateway, passed between its round towers, beneath its ancient arch, its rusting portcullis and then on into the gloom of the passage beyond, lit still by torches which added the luxury of a little warmth on a cold winter's night. A few paces more and I was in the narrow alleys of the old town where scarcely a light showed anywhere, and the frozen cobbles had been forsaken for firesides hours ago by all with the sense to do so. I, on the other hand, was without any sense at all, my only thought being to go back to that café and launch a violent assault on that waiter. But I kept going on and not back, and after ten minutes more found myself at a small bar in another empty snow-covered square...

My temper had subsided somewhat, but that only left confusion to run wild and as I sat down at a table, my mind was a mess of thoughts. What had happened to me today? Had I been to meet the woman who had lived in my apartment? I thought I had... but perhaps it had all been in my imagination? Ah, but I had my invitation, did I not? I had the note she had sent... and I had put it in my coat pocket on my way to meet her. Will you be surprised to know that it was no longer there? It should have been... I remembered putting it there. What had happened to it? And what had happened to me?

I had received a note, I had followed a boy to a café where I had met a young woman, we had shared a bottle of wine and then she had excused herself for a moment, disappearing without a trace. Had she been real? It was all so vivid in my mind that I could not believe it to have been no more than another dream...

And what about the business of the boy? That was another very odd thing. The woman had insisted she sent no boy. Do you see why I might be confused? Indeed, do you see why I might begin again to doubt my sanity?

11. SHADOWS, AND SHADOWS…

Tuesday 20th
The one-eyed woman is back…

For the last five days, wherever I go, *she* is there, lurking in the shadows… and though barely perceptible, she *is* there… I know it, I can *feel* it. All right, I know that doesn't square with my ideas, but I'll admit it here, to my only confessor, this journal.

I see her no more clearly now than I did when she first appeared in my apartment, drawn from the darkness by moonlight, clouds, and a tired mind. If that were all, I shouldn't care; but it is not… because, you see, though the apparition has not grown in substance, the sense of menace which comes with it grows more threatening by the day, and it makes me want to run fast and far from some unknown danger. Maybe I should?

But wait a minute… am I now to let fear govern me? Am I to be fearful of the dark? Of imagined demons unseen in lightless corners, and, like a child, terrorised by the thought of ghosts hiding in wardrobes or monsters under beds…?

It is absurd. Dark is an absence of light. That is all. And the only dangers which darkness hides are physical… there are no bat-winged devils waiting to push us to death and damnation down an ill-lit staircase, and any perils which befall us are due to our own recklessness.

No. All I see are shadows, and shadows are not to be feared by a rational man. A shadow has no life of its own; a shadow does not *think*, it bears no malice towards anyone, and whilst it might mask a murder now and then, it is never a willing accomplice.

But alas, none of this is making her go away...

When I can't see her, I can *sense* her, and even when I can neither see nor sense her, I know still that she's there somewhere, and that if I look hard enough, I'll find her – a shadow in a shadowy corner.

Of course, she doesn't always hide... no, sometimes she likes to make my life easier and appear in plain view, although she's never so obliging as to remain... no sooner do I see her than she's gone again, just as it was the first time I saw her in my apartment, which, strangely, is the only place she isn't appearing at present. Perhaps she finds the lighting unflattering?

There is something about her that is distinctly unwholesome; I can't describe it but if I believed in such things, I might say it was *evil*. I wonder if anyone else sees her? It is not a question easily broached to a stranger. No doubt that ridiculous psychiatrist would tell me not to worry, because whether real, a nightmare or whatever she is, what harm can a little old woman do anyone?

Anyway, I have just returned from my morning walk and, as has become usual, I have had sight of the old one-eyed woman. Now, you might think it odd that I should remain in a place if I find her already arrived, and I agree that that would indeed be odd. The difficulty is that I don't seem to be able to see her, however hard I try, until I am seated. By then I feel obliged to remain despite the old woman. It is silly, I know, because I could easily make my excuses and leave, and I don't know why I don't. But never mind that because today I *did* see her as soon as I entered a café and so, without stopping to think, I turned and went out again. There is another café about twenty yards along the street and I walked quickly to it, wondering all the time if I was being followed but not feeling brave enough to look back. I reached the café and went in, confident that the old woman could not be there because she had not overtaken me on the way, and so it was with a feeling of satisfaction that I sat down, having outwitted my tormentor. Never taking my eyes from the window, I removed my coat and placed my order without looking at the waiter, determined as I was to catch the one-eyed woman if she should come by. After ten minutes I had not seen her and so allowed myself a smile as I savoured my little win, though it was a victory soon forgotten...

Relaxing a little and turning back into the room my attention was drawn to a dark shadow in an ill-lit alcove. I looked away quickly and with a growing sense of unease stared out of the window again. I wanted to be sure it was her but was afraid it might be, and of what that might mean. I stared out into the street, at the building opposite, at its doorcase with a heavy ornate architrave which was supported on either side by larger-than-life caryatids. One of the figures, the one nearest me, was standing on a rustically carved plinth and at his feet were smaller figures who seemed to be trying to escape the giant; as my eye moved up to his head, I saw the face of a cyclops looking back at me. I'd never noticed it before and the sight of him gave me a fright, causing me to spill some coffee on the tablecloth where it began to spread in a large brown circle as it soaked into the white linen. I placed the cup on the saucer as quietly as I could and then with a napkin dried my hand before pointlessly trying to mop up the spilt drink.

The presence of the sculpture could be no more than a coincidence, but it was a disturbing one nevertheless and made me more certain that if I were to look around, I would see the one-eyed woman; I knew I was going to look anyway, despite an increasing fear, because seeing her there would be better than never knowing. Slowly but cautiously, I turned, compelled by curiosity, to see the one-eyed old woman half concealed in the shadows…

Her face was a pale blur, but I could see her long grey hair and black dress and though there was a haze of cigarette smoke between us, I was certain I could smell her. Turning away again I sat staring at the table and the coffee stain on the cloth whilst with a shaking hand I groped in a pocket for some coins, dropped them next to the empty cup and then made for the door.

I was several paces along the street when I became aware that someone was calling out to get my attention. Looking around I saw the waiter from the café holding my coat. In my hurry to leave, I had left it behind. Surprised by my own negligence and delighted to have it restored to me, I reached for my wallet to find a banknote to reward the young man for his kind act, the execution of which had caused him nearly to slip on the icy pavement.

"Oh dear…" I said, "how could I forget you?"

"I beg your pardon sir?"

"Ah, sorry… I was talking to my coat."

"I see." He probably didn't, but it was kind of him to say so.

"Tell me," I asked, "do you know that woman in there? The old one? With only one eye?" The waiter turned and peered in at the window.

"No, sir, I don't think…" he spoke hesitantly, still looking inside, then turned to me saying "sorry, what woman? I don't see anyone…"

No doubt nonplussed, he returned to his tables, and I stood for a moment holding my coat. It means a lot to me,

Likho

my coat... together we survived a vicious assault by sword-wielding statues, and it would have been a most unfitting end for it to be forgotten in a cheap café. I put it on, pulled the fur collar up close around my neck and then went on my way down the street.

"Seeing things which are not there is bad enough," I said aloud to myself, "but now I'm talking to a coat." Nothing to worry about, I suppose. The time to worry will be when *it* starts talking to *me*...

I had no plan at that moment other than to walk. Without noticing much on the way, I found myself at the embankment and leaning lazily on the wall. The river was running high but slow; in a day or two it would be frozen solid, and ice was already forming on both banks. The water ate away at its thin edges, breaking off small pieces which it carried down to the bridge. I watched them go for a while, quietly betting on which would hit it and which would pass straight through but after a while I grew bored. It was cold, I was feeling hungry, and besides which, I had noticed a dark figure standing in the shadows of one of the sculptures on the fourth pier. I wasn't close enough to be certain, but it looked like an old woman in black with a cloak of long grey hair, and I suspected that a closer view would reveal her to have only one eye...

As I ate my lunch I began to ponder on my state of mind. I believe there is a school of thought which says that if you think you are mad then you are probably not, as the mad do not question their sanity. Now, that was a reassuring idea because I thought I was going mad. If, however, I am not mad, or going mad, then how do I account for all the things I have been seeing, or *think* I have been seeing? I cannot. There is no rational explanation.

Darton

Things in the shadows, things seen in dreams... these are not things to worry about... at least not until they step out of the shadows, out of the dreams and into one's conscious waking hours. Then what? Where do they go next, once they are accustomed to the daylight?

A curious thing happened later, or rather, *didn't* happen. I went out for supper as usual, expecting to see my one-eyed woman spying on me from an ill-lit corner. Well, I know not why, but she didn't arrive. There was no sign of her. Could she have gone to the wrong place? Or maybe I was in the wrong place? I don't think that is how it works. Her absence unnerved me just as much as her presence would have done, and I kept looking uneasily about the room whilst picking at my food with a fork, pushing it around the plate and eating little of it. This didn't go unnoticed by the waiter who came to enquire if there was a problem.

"Yes," replied I "indeed there is. The one-eyed woman is not here."

"The one-eyed woman?"

"Yes. She is not here. She *should* be, but she is *not*. *That*, sir, is the problem."

"Sir is expecting her?"

"Sir was." I looked about the room again. "*You* haven't seen her, I suppose?"

"I couldn't say sir."

"It's simple enough... either you have seen her, or you have not."

"Well, I have no recollection of seeing such a person sir, if that helps?"

"It does, and then again it doesn't."

"Well, sir, does your friend have a reservation?"

Likho

"How should I know? I don't take the bookings for your restaurant."

"No, indeed sir," the waiter was beginning to get irritated; I didn't care. "Nevertheless, sir, if you could tell me madam's name then I could check for you."

"I don't know her name... come to think of it, I'm not even sure if she *has* one."

"That will make it difficult, I think, sir... our patrons generally have names. That is how we identify them when they make reservations. It's something of a convention, I believe."

"Oh dear, this is all very inconvenient, *very* inconvenient indeed." I shook my head and tried to appear very inconvenienced whilst feeling nothing of the sort.

"I see..." the waiter said with a nod of his head.

"You see? I doubt that."

"Fair enough. I *think* I see, but even if I don't see *well*, I see at least *twice* as well as a one-eyed woman..." The waiter did his best to suppress a laugh but failed. "Is there something else I can get for you, other than a one-eyed woman?"

"I can't think of anything," I said thoughtfully, stroking my chin and looking at the menu for no reason. "No. I can see nothing here... or anywhere else." I glanced around one last time, settled my bill and walked out into the street, leaving the staff of the café to whisper amongst themselves about the strange man who'd just left... presumably in search of old women with one eye, though for whatever reason he sought such a creature no one could think. Perhaps they imagined me to be an itinerant retailer of monocles?

It crossed my mind to go looking for my missing shadow, but where to start? I walked around for a while and then went into a bar; might she be there? She wasn't. A café near the town hall? No, no sign of my one-eyed woman. In truth I knew that I could have searched every bar and café in the town and still not found her because she is not to be found. She always finds me; that is how it works.

The night was freezing. The sky was clear, and the temperature had plummeted. The snow which had fallen during the day had melted during the few minutes that the sun had managed to shine on it, and then refrozen in a thick sheet of ice which made the paths treacherous. A freezing fog was descending on the town and visibility was becoming poor. I decided to go home. To walk on the pavements was dangerous so I was compelled to keep to the roads which were mostly free of ice. There was no traffic, there was no one about other than me and the only sound was that of my footsteps. The hazy light from the streetlamps was fog-bound in bluish-yellow spheres which couldn't reach into the doorways and deep recesses of the ancient buildings which confined the streets of the old town. It must have been close to midnight, though I wasn't sure on which side of it we were, and the night was such that even the slowest-witted dog wouldn't stray out of doors, so it was with some surprise that I thought I heard steps other than the echo of my own. I stopped but all was quiet, at least until I set off again when the sound of someone walking quickly came from somewhere ahead on the right. I could see no one through the fog, but then a dark figure dashed out and crossed the street in front of me, mounting the pavement and running on out of sight... someone in a great hurry to get home, someone careless of the dangers of icy pavements.

I walked on and as I entered my street, I saw the shadow once more. It came to a halt just ahead, as if waiting

Likho

for me to catch up, and, as I approached, it set off again, only this time it ran across the street and back again several times before eventually vanishing into the thickening fog which had become so dense that one could almost grab handfuls of it. The footsteps died away, and I was all alone again, the only living soul out of doors on that freezing winter's night… well, alone except for someone standing in a doorway opposite mine. A small movement drew my attention and as I peered hard into the darkness, I was certain I could make out the form of a person, possibly one with very long grey hair. I stood still for a moment, then began to move cautiously towards the figure, and the closer I got, the clearer it became. It was the old woman. I could see her blurred white face, and her single good eye catching the light from somewhere and sparkling in the darkness. Stepping on to the pavement I was only four or five feet away. Then, without thinking, I leapt into the doorway and on to her, determined to catch hold of her… at last to have the chance to interrogate my shady persecutor…

The old woman was not there, and I fell to the ground in an undignified heap, confused, and bruised. Somehow, she had slipped away…

She was there, then she was gone, and nothing remained but a faint foetid and sickly smell; I'd smelt it before when she'd been in my rooms… the stench of a decomposing corpse with a base scent of sweet flowers. It sticks in the throat and nostrils; you can taste it and it stays with you for hours however much you try to overcome it. So, if she *had* been there, then where had she gone? And how? Did she simply melt into the shadows? Or had she been drawn from them only by my imagination?

When I leapt at the black apparition I had fallen on my left knee and as I stood up and straightened my leg, it began to throb painfully; I didn't think it serious, but as I walked across the street, I felt obliged to limp to ease the discomfort. I climbed the few steps to the door of my building and let myself in to the lobby, which was deserted and silent, just as it should have been at that hour of the night. With my poor aching knee, I mounted the stairs to the second floor where to my surprise and annoyance my neighbour's door was open. I had hoped to avoid him, but the invitation was irresistible. In I went and there he was, in his chair as usual. He looked up when he heard me enter and his old lips stretched into a forced and half-hearted smile.

"It's rather late to be calling on neighbours…" The insincere smile turned into a twisted sneer and the tone of his voice was cold and unfriendly.

"I am very aware of that, thank you, and I wouldn't have bothered but your door was open, and I felt compelled to come here on a matter of some importance." I spoke coldly in response to his unfriendliness. I had one question for him, and it was as good a moment then as any other to ask it.

"You sound like a cheap nineteenth century novel. What do you want that is of such importance?"

"Who is that woman? The old woman with one eye? Who is she?"

"I have no idea who you mean. What old woman with one eye?"

"Ah, you know very well… I saw you with her… I have seen you with her twice, and on the second occasion you looked at me… so you know I saw you with her. You know who she is. Now I wish to know too. Who is she?"

Likho

"Why do you persist with this? I have told you before. I do not go out of this room… and I tell you again now that I don't know what you are talking about."

"You are a liar, sir, a *liar. I* know it. *You* know it. I have no interest in your private affairs, but this concerns me because that woman is becoming a source of annoyance, and I wish to know who she is. In fact, I demand to know…"

"Demand? Oh, that's good…" He began to laugh at me. "He *demands* to know…" With his face turned to the ceiling he laughed even harder, his eyes screwed tightly closed and his old body shaking in his chair as he gripped its arms. I was furious and the more he laughed the angrier I became. I took a step towards him. I wanted to hit him, and I felt my fists clenching in readiness, but I resisted the urge and only shouted at him to shut up instead. Seeing no point in remaining there I turned towards the door and as I passed through it the old man fell silent. I looked back at him.

"I can't tell you who she is, this woman you think you see," the old man spoke breathlessly as he recovered from his fit of laughter, "but I can give you some advice…" I made no response but remained motionless just beyond the doorway, "don't try to find out."

I turned to go and, as I went, he began laughing again. An urge to strike the man came upon me but, managing to suppress it, I left him alone in his foul and squalid room, pulling the door shut behind me with as much force as I could manage… an uncharacteristically intemperate act, but one which relieved me of some pent-up aggression, and made my feelings clear at the same time. As dust fell from the top of the frame, the sound of the door slamming echoed up through the building, returning several times from dark, unseen corners, and bringing with it the curses of disturbed sleepers in their beds; for once, I didn't care.

Stepping forward, I stood against one of the serpentine columns of the loggia, my left arm wrapped around it and my hand resting between its scaly coils. The landing, the stairwell, the lobby below and the floors above were all silent. The gas lamps burned unsteadily and the flickering light which they cast across the floors crept cautiously forth and back as if in some ritual mating dance with the shadows; my unblinking eyes followed as they moved together in close embrace, and, as I watched, slowly I fell under the spell of this entrancing tango…

I cannot say how long I remained there, but I was brought back to life all at once by the foulest odour. Recoiling in shock, I stepped back a pace, falling against the wall behind where I stopped a moment to recover; then, my composure restored, I moved nervously forward to the unguarded edge of the landing and the place where I'd stood so carelessly, only inches from a fall to certain death on the floor of the lobby below. Suddenly overcome with vertigo, I held fast to the column again – *so* fast that my fingernails broke as they tried to dig into the stone.

The stench of putrefaction filled the air. With a handkerchief pressed against my nose and mouth, I remained motionless, staring down into the darkness…

At the foot of the lower stair, a thin shadowy figure stood just beyond the reach of the lamps, though just near enough that the dull yellow light was able to give it vague definition on its left side; it was that which enabled me to see it. At first, I had had only a sense of it being there, but as I stared harder and harder, it came into focus. Then, lest I doubted my senses, it turned slightly towards the wall, and one of its eyes caught the light. *One* of its eyes? What am I saying? It was too dark to see, but I *knew* it all the same – it *had* only one eye…

As I watched, my visitor began to move. She floated towards the stairs and then started on a slow and menacing ascent to the first floor. After a few minutes she reached the landing beneath me and moved out of sight, but I stayed where I was and watched the bottom of the next flight, my eyes fixed on the spot at which she would come back into view. Fear urged me to run but I was paralysed by curiosity… my desire – a desire for which I can give no account – my desire to see her suppressed the instinct to flee fast and far. Anyway, as I have asked myself in the cold light of day, what would be the point in running? The child who hides beneath the blankets from a ghost has yet to realise that mere bedclothes are no obstacle to a thing which has no solid or tangible form; I, on the other hand, know only too well that there is nowhere to run from a terror which can be everywhere, because it exists only in your mind.

As I waited for the woman to reappear below, my attention was drawn by a sound from the right, halfway up the stairs. There she was, the shadow the light cannot reach, climbing ever closer. I stepped back and retreated into a recess by my door; it was possible to see the top of the stairs, and I was able to watch her as she came up.

Without thinking, I pressed myself hard against the wall to keep out of sight.

Sweat was streaming out of me and drenching my shirt; the wet linen was clinging to me like a skin, and I was freezing cold; but, as much as I wanted to shiver, I dared not make the slightest movement. My heart was beating so violently I was afraid my ribs would break, and the sound of cracking bones would guide that thing to my hiding place.

Minutes went by and with the passing of each second, I expected the shadow with one eye to appear in front of me. Nothing seemed to be happening though and so with curiosity overcoming fear once more, I peered out to have a look, an action I regretted even before I'd done it. She was there, waiting just out of sight and only about three feet away.

I pushed back against the wall in a last desperate effort not to be seen, though I knew it was pointless. She was close enough for me to see her face. It was a grey-white ill-defined thing; the black hole of its eye socket was the only distinct feature, but it was blurred and seemed to be moving about in a strange dance. There was no nose that I could see, and below the absent nose there was no mouth either.

The woman, if it were one, suddenly stood directly before me. Her face was at the level of mine, and I watched in terror as a dark line appeared on it, just below where her nose should have been... it was as if an invisible hand were drawing it on with a charcoal stick. It was a mouth. Something had drawn a mouth on her... a mouth which she opened slowly into a wide lipless grin, a grinning mouth from which she began to exhale foul breath, breath which carried the stink of faeces and sour milk. The stench was so bad it made my stomach heave and I had to work hard to stop retching, swallowing down the vomit which had risen into my mouth. She stood, motionless, staring at me with her one eye set deep in its black socket.

There was something else in that black hole. I wish I could say it was a vision of hell and damnation, something apocalyptic and thus easy to explain. It wasn't though. It was far worse than that... it was *nothing*, a deep everlasting

Likho

nothing, a black empty nothing where everything which has ever existed or has yet to exist has ceased to be, and where souls are condemned to remain even beyond the end of time. Does that make any sense? A place from where a hell would look like a heaven. Imagine being condemned to that? That was what I saw, and I have no better words to describe it.

The woman, or shadow or whatever it was suddenly moved away. Before I could blink, she was standing outside my neighbour's apartment, and I watched as the old man's door opened... I watched her pass through it, and then watched as it closed silently behind her.

My hands shook so much that I struggled to unlock my own door, though I did it somehow, and once inside I stood leaning against it for a moment before slipping slowly to the floor. When at last I sat on the cold tiles I realised that I had soiled myself. I began to cry but I was too confused to understand why just then. Later, I supposed it was self-pity... my own pathetic tears for me, a poor sad wretch for whom no one else would ever shed any. I couldn't remember ever crying before, so I had a lifetime's tears to shed... tears which the deaths of my parents had not caused to flow, tears which *nothing* had ever caused to flow. No man's misery had ever moved me enough, no child's suffering, nothing... nothing had ever induced me to shed a single tear. After all, what good did tears do for a man's misery or a child's suffering? What trouble can be solved by crying? Tears don't feed the starving and the thirsty can't drink them. Tears don't cure sickness or mend broken bones, and an ocean of them can't bring the dead back to life, or reverse time...

12. THE ISLE OF THE DEAD[12]

Wednesday 21st
I remained all night by the door, huddled up in a tight ball and with my coat pulled close to keep me warm. I think I must have cried myself to sleep…

When I awoke, my body ached from head to foot, and it was with much difficulty that I managed to stand. My knee was causing some considerable pain, and an unpleasant smell reminded me that fear had caused me to soil myself. For all that, I manged to limp to the kitchen where, in a highly nervous state, I poured a large glass of brandy. My hand shook uncontrollably as I raised it to my mouth, spilling some of it on the way; despite that, I managed somehow to drink a mouthful… and then another, then a third and a fourth, and then to refill the glass and empty it once more.

By midday I was drunk. I had bathed and dressed but a bottle of wine was never far from my side throughout the morning. The concierge's wife failed to present herself, and her daily chores remained undone; she brought nothing for my lunch, and only the dead, grey ashes of yesterday's fires lay in every hearth. Consequently, it was cold, *icy* cold, but the brandy and wine had done their job, and I didn't feel too bad. My hands had stopped shaking, and when I looked in the mirror, all traces of the night's traumas were gone… or so I thought, but then, I was drunk and beginning to feel more confident. Drink had given me an appetite which demanded some lunch and so, wrapped in my faithful great coat with its fur collar, I set forth rather grandly in search of a quiet café. My knee was still causing some discomfort and so for assistance I took with me an antique silver-topped cane which had once belonged to a grandfather I had never known. It was a splendid old thing which I had rescued from my parents' house – not for reasons of sentiment, but simply because I liked it; it might have belonged to a grandfather, but it was no precious heirloom as far as I was concerned. I thought I looked like a fine gentleman indeed with my long coat and cane... the only thing missing was a monocle, but that might have been excessively theatrical.

I passed no one on my way out, nor heard a sound that might indicate anyone in the building was alive and as I crossed the silent lobby, I felt like the only living resident on the Isle of the Dead...

Out on the street I turned left and set off in the direction of the old museum quarter. It was not too far, maybe a mile, and just to the south of the university. Some of the town's major museums are in parts of the old ducal palace, a large and rambling collection of mediaeval buildings which were begun in the early tenth century, extended, remodelled, burned down, restored, rebuilt and remodelled again until the middle of the seventeenth century, by which time they had reached their present form. By the way, those phases of development are not exhaustive or necessarily in the right order, apart from the first and last, obviously. From what I recall of our history, the final noble resident of those splendid buildings lost his head in the closing years of the seventeenth century after several years of anti-imperial machinations. I don't remember his name, or that of the sedition-weary emperor whose patience he finally exhausted... I was never much good with names, but I imagine he had a long and impressive string of titles; his nemesis, for the record, was someone-or-other the sixth or seventh *dei gratia rex imperator*. But never mind them; they're dead and gone and no concern of ours. Of course, if I see any statues of them, I shall take care not even to think of inviting them for supper…

The streets were quiet; I supposed that was due to the freezing weather and treacherous pavements which, again, I found it wise to avoid. There was such little traffic that the chances of being hit by a car were small, though the trams were a different matter as they rattled past, unhindered by anything but the deepest snow and relentlessly ploughing through the streets conveying cold and miserable passengers across the town, a town which they could barely see through misted windows and rivers of condensation…

Thirty minutes after leaving home I was in an ancient narrow street which ran between the old buildings of the ducal residence. On one side were the old imperial stables and riding school, and on the other a range of buildings which now house the royal armoury and ancient regalia. There is a large square at the end which was once a courtyard but is now home to some particularly good cafés, and it was there that I was intending to eat. Despite my coat I was freezing and in urgent need of a drink to warm me, and with that thought I went first into a bar where I stood at the counter and drank several glasses of brandy in order to restore the feeling to my fingers and toes which were hurting from the cold.

I stayed there for nearly an hour listening to the conversations of the other patrons and watching the waiters at their work. My mind wondered casually through numerous subjects but at last settled upon the one I had been trying to avoid all day… my encounter with the one-eyed woman. As I thought about her my hands began to shake again and I had to order another drink in the hope of steadying my nerves; needless to say, it did the trick very nicely.

What *is* she, my one-eyed woman? Is she only a construct of shadows? Shadows don't have eyes; shadows don't stink like rotting corpses. Is she a corpse? Corpses don't walk... well, not beyond the bounds of mediaeval cautionary tales... '*Such as you are, so once were we, and such as we are so shall you be*' or something like that. God, I hope I don't end up like her... But what is she? Ghost? Demon? Such things do not exist... but I *have* seen her, *ergo*, she *must* exist. There is no magic, nothing supernatural about her... she is just a foul-smelling leprous old woman. Ah... have I stumbled on the answer? Is she an old leper? It is possible, *definitely* possible. I rather like the idea. It explains much... her face, the smell, the old man's denial. She is an old leper, and he is ashamed or embarrassed... all very simple. I ordered another drink and quietly congratulated myself on having solved a mystery... well, I should say *almost* solved.

If the woman *is* an old leper, she is no danger to me or anyone. But what is her relationship to my neighbour? Wife? Sister? Mistress? Why doesn't he just say so? I could understand that he might want to keep a sick and leprous old wife from the world, but he must know I'll find out somehow. Obviously, he doesn't trust me... and why should he? After all, he doesn't know me well. Is there still such ignorant prejudice against lepers? Actually, I don't really know very much about it.

By the middle of the afternoon, I had not had my lunch but such interest as I had had in in eating had gone. I didn't have time to be distracted by food; I was too busy with the mystery of my neighbour and his eyeless, nose-less and noisome companion. If she does have leprosy, then

Likho

why has it been left untreated? Maybe it is something else... I remember once reading that cases of syphilis are sometimes mistaken for leprosy... perhaps the old woman has syphilis? That would give the man more cause to hide her away and deny her existence. That would explain his shame and embarrassment.

I took myself and my theorizing to another café where I continued to speculate on the mystery of the old woman and my neighbour. If she is in the final stage of syphilis, then it is quite probable she is mad. Why does he keep her at home? Wouldn't an old woman in that condition be better off in a hospital? The old man is plainly not able to care for a sick wife, whether suffering from leprosy, syphilis or anything else.

Afternoon gave way to evening, and I, to another drink. I had moved to the university quarter by that time and found myself sitting in a quiet bar and looking across the narrow street at the neoclassical wall of the medical school. Adorned with countless statues of great physicians from antiquity, the building was deserted, its windows dark, and all the knowledge contained in its vast library was inaccessible – everything I could possibly want to know about leprosy and syphilis, and no doubt centuries of accumulated wisdom on madness too, all safely locked up for the night. Oh well, it was probably all written in ancient Greek anyway...

Much as I had hypothesized and postulated all day, and despite my confidence that I have begun to unravel my neighbour's intriguing web, I didn't think there was much point in considering it any further. It is nothing more than speculation, and unlikely ever to be anything else, unless the old man should be willing to confirm my suspicions. But a theory which cannot be proved is no good to me and the thing that annoys me most is that since it is my theory then it is down to me to prove the case, and to do that, I shall have to tackle the old man once more...

With that in mind I left the café and walked out into the freezing evening. A heavy fog had come down upon us again, and again I was the only man on the street, or so it seemed. Everything was lost in a fine icy mist. Café windows were fuzzy squares of yellowish light, and those inside were no more than blurred and ill-defined figures projected on to semi-opaque glass screens. On the other side of the old coal market, trams rolled by and, through the thick wet cloud, the sound of their warning bells and the squeal of steel wheels on steel rails cried out danger and death to those in peril on the street... and as my imagination took flight, it became the sound of a single bell ringing out from a buoy anchored over a razor-sharp reef, and the screech of rocks cutting through the hull of some storm-driven ship; then, with all hands lost to the sea, half-muffled, the bell tolled for the dead. It was mournful, melancholy and quite perfect for my mood... *the tolling of the bells, iron bells... what a world of solemn thought their monody compels...* the words of the poem came into my head, a poem learned years ago, recited once and forgotten since. Who wrote it?[13] I don't recall but it doesn't matter because whoever composed such self-indulgent, absinthe-induced rhyme is certain to be long dead...

Crossing the deserted marketplace, I found myself on one of the wider streets which lead up to the old town hall. I walked slowly because the pavement was icy, because I had no destination in mind, and because I didn't want to go home. I didn't want to go home because... well, because it was a place I didn't want to be.

Likho

All my efforts to make a solid from a shadow have failed. Of course, that doesn't mean the old woman doesn't exist, and I know I can *never* prove she doesn't; but until I can prove that she *does,* I find myself caught atop a very spiky philosophical fence thanks to my overwhelming need for her *not* to exist, *quod non est probandum…*

It comes down to a simple conflict between what I know to be possible, and what I have seen. I accept that there are things which we know exist but cannot be seen, but those things do not *require an opposing force or condition* in order to exist… that is to say, things which do not exist but *can* be seen…

There is an old problem-solving principle which states that *among competing hypotheses, the one with the fewest assumptions should be selected.* Well, my preferred hypothesis is based *only* on assumptions, and assumptions make poor foundations, I think. Then there is that other train of thinking… *when you have eliminated the impossible, whatever remains, however improbable, must be the truth.* I can't quite remember where that one comes from either. What can I say? Eliminating the impossible leaves me with my hypothesis based on the fewest assumptions… or does it? Yes, it does… all very confusing… it's enough to drive a fellow mad, and it is beginning to do just that.

Perhaps madness isn't such a bad prospect? If that's where I'm heading, well, I don't mind so much. I'm not enjoying the journey much though…

Anyway, on I walked, going nowhere particular. I passed only a few people, all so well wrapped up against the cold that only their eyes were visible. No one spoke; no one exchanged polite greetings, and I have an idea that we were insulated against each other as much as the weather. It suited me, I had my reasons; I wondered what theirs were.

Darton

At last I went into a café for my supper but I wasn't hungry; I drank much and ate little, and after eating little I went to another café and drank more. By around midnight I was tired, a little the worse for drink and no longer troubled by the prospect of lepers, syphilitics or much else. I was ready for a fight if there were to be one and happy to start it if necessary. By the time I had picked my way across frozen streets and reached the door of my building I was set for an argument and determined to have one. That old man was going to answer my questions whether he liked it or not…

I let myself in and climbed the stairs quietly. His door was open as usual, and he seated in his chair.

"Good evening" he said, "I see you have progressed from speaking like a cheap nineteenth century novel to dressing like one."

"What are you talking about? Actually, I don't care. I'm not here for amusement… mine or yours."

"Then why are you here? I can think of no other reason."

"I am here because I want answers."

"Then ask your questions, sir."

"Who is the old woman with one eye? Don't deny knowing her. I saw her last night… she came in here, into this apartment. I watched her open the door and enter. Who is she?"

"This again."

"Yes, this again. Who is she? Why is she following me around the town? Who is she?"

"I have told you before. I cannot say."

"Cannot or will not?"

Likho

"One or the other... it doesn't matter to you. Whichever it is leaves you in the same position. I cannot tell you anything about her."

"I do not believe you, sir."

"Please yourself. I can tell you nothing. Why do you not listen to me? I told you last night to forget about it..."

"And yet I do not... and shall not until you tell me what I want to know. From what you say I infer that you *know* but for some reason are *unable* to speak. Am I right?" The old man made no reply and simply stared with an unfixed gaze and an expressionless face. I repeated my question and again he said nothing. "I am staying here until you tell me."

"You are welcome to remain as long as you wish, though you will find me poor company" he said at last.

"I've never found you otherwise..." I paced across the room and back again. "Look, I am not unreasonable, am I? Is it unreasonable to want to know who that woman is? I think she is following me with some purpose... a purpose which, by the way, I believe will prove disadvantageous to me. Am I being unreasonable? *Am I?*"

"I cannot tell you."

"Wouldn't you be curious in my position?"

"I can tell you nothing."

"Are you afraid of something? Are you frightened of *her*?"

"I can tell you nothing."

"That's it, isn't it? You're afraid of her... why? How? Maybe she knows something about you? I am right, am I not?"

"I cannot tell you."

"Yes, you can. Tell me, she won't know."

"I cannot tell you."

Darton

I began to grow increasingly mad. I wanted to hit him... not particularly to hurt him but more to vent my growing frustration. My hand tightened around my cane, and I began slowly to raise it. He watched but said nothing; he didn't seem the least troubled by the threat. I held the stick above my head for a second and then brought it down, slicing through the air to strike the table next to him. It struck with a loud crack which reverberated around the room, but the old man never flinched in the face of what would probably have been a fatal blow had it been aimed at his head. I intended only to scare him a little, but I had failed even to do that.

"I cannot tell you." He looked at me with the same lazy expression he had maintained throughout. It made me even angrier.

"Tell me" I said through gritted teeth.

"I cannot."

"Tell me."

"Shout all you like. Shout until your head explodes for all I care... I cannot tell you what you want to know." He shrugged and smiled. The smile grew wider and then he began to laugh.

"Tell me who she is..."

He laughed so hard he began to shake in his shabby old chair.

"Shut up shut up shut up shut up..." I shouted at him. "Just shut up..." He didn't. He laughed louder and more violently.

Overwhelmed by frustration and rage, I dropped my cane and grabbed the old man by the throat.

"I'm not afraid of *you*" he said defiantly, exposing his rotten teeth in a wide grin.

Likho

"Tell me who that woman is…" I tightened my grip a little. He began laughing again. "Tell me… or I swear I *will* kill you." The threat only made him laugh even harder. My thumbs pressed on his larynx, but he made no attempt to free himself or to push me away. I tightened my grip again – his eyes began to bulge, flakes of skin fell from his wrinkled old neck, and, for a moment, I thought he might crumble to dust in my hands, like a desiccated old mummy. As his face reddened, his only reaction was a defiant stare. Perhaps he didn't think me serious? If he *did* think his death was imminent, he showed no fear, no sign of suffering. But I *wanted* him to suffer, I wanted him to die in agony, screaming for mercy… mercy which I would not grant, because I despised him so much for what he made me do.

And so, with all the hate I could muster, I choked the last of his miserable life out of him, stopping his breath and his mocking laughter forever. A final shudder went through his body, and with a last spasm of his fingers, his life passed out of him.

I let him go and his head fell back in his chair; his mouth dropped open, his black tongue hanging out of it. My fingers had left blue-black bruises on his throat, and as I backed away in horror, his dead bloodshot eyes followed me…

13. SCAFFOLD OR ASYLUM?

Out on the landing, leaning against the wall, panicking and breathing hard, I couldn't quite believe what had just happened. The lamps flickered and then went out, leaving me standing in darkness... such perfect and well-timed cover for a murderer. A faint light from the floor below set some vague shadows dancing across the wall, and a feeble glow in my imagination gave me some small hope that this was no more than another nightmare from which I would soon be drawn by the sound of birdsong into a sun lit morning...

I knew, though, that it was no dream, because the cold sweat which soaked my shirt told me I was very much awake, and in some serious trouble.

I have killed my old neighbour.

I have killed him...

He is dead, sat in his chair, just as I saw in my dream; this time, though, it's all too real. The thought of it all made me feel sick. For a moment, as I stood there, I thought I was going to faint, and I had to steady myself against the wall again until the nausea passed.

I had left the door of the old man's apartment ajar, and a thin shaft of light escaped from within, running across the floor and beyond, where it was devoured by the darkness. It will swallow me too, if I let it.

But wait... *was* the old man dead? Perhaps he wasn't. Perhaps I hadn't killed him... maybe he is only unconscious? Maybe he might be revived? These thoughts piled into my head, one on top of the other. *Hope* is a strange thing — that most persistent of feelings which seems never to know when it is beaten...

It was, then, with faint hope in my head and a dreadful sinking feeling in my stomach, that I resolved to make a last check. I knew, just as you do, that it was pointless, and I'd rather not have done so, but I knew also that I had to all the same. So, making no sound I crossed the small vestibule and stood in the doorway of the old man's sitting room. I don't know why I was so careful to be quiet since there were no ears to hear but mine...

The old man was there, just as I had left him moments earlier, and just as I remembered him in my dream. He was dead. His open eyes bulged from their purple-ringed sockets, his blackened tongue hung from his gaping, blue-lipped mouth, and on his throat were the black and blue bruises left by the hands of his killer. In my dream the identity of his murderer was unknown, but now the crime was solved, the criminal revealed...

Approaching cautiously and with a shaking hand I lifted my cane and prodded him in the ribs, reluctant as I was to lay another hand on him. He made no movement, there was no sign of life. He was dead, and it was I who had killed him. Stepping away from the corpse, I backed towards the door, foolishly afraid to turn away from him lest he rise and come after me... well, it would be no more or less strange than many of the things which have been happening recently. On reaching the small lobby I turned, dashed out to the landing and pulled the door shut behind me.

Why did I go back in? Why did I have to know if he might be still alive? What a fool I was... I should never have gone back in. I could have closed the old man's door and walked away, taking with me only the thought that he *might* be alive and that I had *not* killed him. Why did I have to know? *Why?*

With that thought screaming around in my head, I turned towards my apartment, reaching into the pocket of my coat as I went and fumbling for my key. There it was, ice-cold to the touch though reassuring all the same, but as my fingers closed on it, the air froze around me, and the faint and silvery sound of children laughing came from somewhere behind me. There were two of them... they began whispering to each other, and though I tried to make out what they were saying, their language sounded foreign to me; maybe it was an invented and secret language of their own? I wanted to see them, but I dared not turn my head because I feared I would see no one.

They moved close, closer still, and as the temperature dropped further and further still, I felt them directly at my back, pressing against me, as if trying to push me forwards. I was rigid with terror, though, and unmovable; they pressed harder and harder, but, much as I *wanted* to move, I remained firmly fixed to the spot. Then, having failed to shift me, they gave up and simply passed *through* me. How can I describe it? I'm not sure I have the words, but I'll do my best...

At first, there was a shock – like the blast from an explosion – which winded me; then, as I struggled to breathe, I felt them move *inside me*... squeezing and pushing, displacing anything in the way. I felt sick, soaked in sweat, and a panic came upon me such that I wanted to run in every direction at once. I couldn't run, though, as I was paralysed by fear. My chest tightened, and it felt as if my heart was being crushed... the icy hands of those children were clasped around it, their small fingers digging into it, gripping so hard that it strained to beat. I cried out in pain until, unable to bear it any longer, I fell to the floor...

I suppose I must have fainted. When I came to, all was quiet. Slowly, very slowly, I got to my feet and leaned against the wall, still breathless. For a moment, my memory was blank; I stood, confused and disorientated. My eyes adjusted to the darkness, and I could just make out the door to my apartment; pulling the key from my pocket, I took a step forward. Then, suddenly, the silence was broken once more by laughter; this time it came from inside that empty apartment next to mine. It was loud at first, then faded as if moving deeper inside. My heart started racing again, and my hand shook so much that I dropped the key as I tried to insert it in the lock. Panic-stricken once more, I fell to my knees, and with no light by which to see, I searched blindly with my hands on the cold floor; there seemed to be a thin film of icy water on the tiles, and the tips of my fingers moved over it like a figure skater on a frozen pond, though without such grace and purpose. The few seconds it took to find it seemed like hours but find it I did and with a speed of which I thought myself incapable, I jumped to my feet, unlocked the door and flew inside to the sanctuary of my home.

A bottle of whisky in my study helped calm my nerves and I had soon consumed nearly quarter of it as I sat at my desk with my mind racing through the events of the day minute by minute, reliving every miserable second. After half an hour or so and feeling more composed, I sat with my hands folded on the writing block before me, and for no reason I can think of, staring at the painting on the wall above. It is a portrait of a fine gentleman in military uniform, adorned with a blue moiré sash with the insignia of some chivalric order proudly displayed on his large chest, and a proud expression on his face. I don't know who he was... one of my ancestors, I suppose. The picture came from my parents' house, along with much else in my apartment. It is well-executed, and therefore, I imagine, a good likeness; it is unsigned, so the name of the artist is unknown, but I doubt it was anyone of great renown. I have studied him often – behind his pride, I see a deep sadness in his eyes, and I cannot help but wonder why. Was it the loss of a wife or lover? Perhaps a child? Perhaps a secret regret? A murder, maybe?

Have *you* ever murdered anyone? What did you do? Run? Confess? And if not, have you thought about it? Do you think it possible to get away with murder? I suppose that as long as murder is not suspected, it might be possible. Do you think there might be people living freely amongst us who have committed a murder so perfect that it has never been detected? We can never know, unless, of course, they confess.

Staring up at my grand ancestor, my thoughts returned to *my* crime, and I began to work coldly through the options available... coldly, clinically and *criminally*...

First, can I get away with it? When the body is discovered, as it is sure to be, there will be no doubt that murder has been done... so who will be suspected? I am certain to be... after all, I have already drawn attention to myself, even though no crime had been committed at that time. The old one-eyed woman, wife or not, will find the old man dead and alert the authorities so it is just a matter of time before the police come knocking, and if I am arrested, tried and found guilty then I shall go to the guillotine...

I will face execution for certain unless, of course, I am judged to be mad. What of that argument? I was not in my right mind. I was not in control of myself... I killed him during a brief fit of madness. Is that my best defence? Plead not guilty due to insanity? But then I risk being locked away in some dreadful asylum for the criminally insane for the rest of my days. That is not a fate to be wished for, and possibly one worse than death.

Scaffold or asylum? Well, I should prefer *neither*...

Might it be better for me if I go to the police and confess? Who knows?

Maybe the best thing is to do nothing and plead ignorance of the whole business. After all, no one saw me. No one saw me come home, no one saw me enter the old man's apartment and no one saw me leave it. With no witnesses there is nothing, no evidence, circumstantial or direct to connect me with his death. If I can refute all allegations confidently then there is no more to be said about it. But wait... am I sure I wasn't seen? How can I be? Just because I saw no one it doesn't follow that no one saw me.

As poured another glass of whisky, another possibility came to mind... I dreamed of this murder a few weeks ago or had a premonition or whatever it was... so what if I were to go to the police and repeat what I told them then? I tell them I have found the murdered body of my old neighbour. As with the boy who cried wolf, they will refuse to believe it and send me away thinking only that I am perhaps a bit mad. What am I worried about?

I wonder what will become of the old man's corpse? Perhaps it will remain where it is, decomposing, discovered by nothing more than blow flies and maggots which will pick his bones clean; then, one day some poor unsuspecting soul will find his skeleton... a skeleton with no obvious injury and nothing remaining to betray a murderer. What could be better?

But what of the concierge and his wife, and what of the one-eyed woman? What is to be done about them? Other than murdering them too there is nothing to be done, and the body count is already one too high. Actually, each of us will be suspects, will we not? But if I go and report my discovery of the crime, that might just serve to deflect attention from myself, if the police decide to investigate...

That was it, and thus it was that, with my mind made up, I went bravely, and very possibly, stupidly forth, into the cold dark night to cry murder, pretending to be driven half mad by my discovery of the crime. It was late, well beyond midnight, but it didn't seem prudent to wait until morning because the police might be more inclined to send someone to investigate if the hour were more agreeable...

With my coat billowing behind me as I dashed along the street I must have looked like an overly theatrical vampire in search of a victim, crossing and re-crossing the street as I did to avoid the worst of the ice on the pavements. The thought made me laugh, but I was soon at the door of the police station, and suddenly nothing seemed very funny at all. I climbed the few steps and went into the reception room. The lamps in the back room were dim and one man sat alone at a desk nearby.

"Excuse me" I said, leaning on the counter and unravelling my scarf which I clutched nervously in a shaking hand. The man looked at me, put down a document he had been studying and got up. "I am sorry to disturb you, especially at such a late hour but it is important that I speak to someone."

"*Important*? Or urgent?" The man replied rather sullenly.

Darton

"Does it matter?" *Here we go again*, I thought.

"Of course it does. What is important might not be urgent, whilst what is urgent is can sometimes be important... although what you consider to be important or urgent might, in fact, not merit either classification in the opinion of others." He sighed at me as if I were a schoolboy beyond all hope of understanding.

"Well, then, it's very urgent... I must report a murder."

"*Must* you?" He was irritated and made no effort to hide the fact.

"I must, yes, really, I must."

"Right... murder, eh?" He shrugged rather indifferently. "Planned, in the process of being done or done already, sir?"

"I beg your pardon?" It was my turn to be irritated. "Must we go through this again?"

"Through *what again*, sir?"

"Oh, never mind... what do you want to know?"

"At what stage is this murder, sir?"

"Oh, yes. Well, it has been done."

"Murder... done already, eh? A man is dead then?"

"Have you known a murder where a man *wasn't* dead?"

"Good question, sir, very good question... I don't *think* so, no. Still, never mind that. So, from what you say, may I infer that the victim of this murder is now dead?"

"You may. He is dead... very dead, I'm afraid."

"Afraid? Afraid of what sir? Not going to harm you if he's dead, is he now?"

"No, I mean that I am afraid he is dead... he is dead, *I regret to say*... I do not fear him because he is dead. Then again..."

Likho

"Ah, well that's a very sensible attitude to have, if I may say so sir? Anyway, if the fellow is dead then it isn't really urgent, is it?"

"It isn't?"

"Well, no… I mean to say, he's not going anywhere, is he? I expect he'll still be dead in the morning. Not going to get up and walk away in the night is he sir?"

"It's funny you should say that."

"Is it?"

"Yes. It is. You see the last time he was murdered, he did just that… well, not exactly that… I mean, he didn't get up and walk away, but he did come back to life the next day, or evening… actually I'm not sure… but anyway, he had definitely been resurrected by late the following evening…"

"Really? Resurrected, was he?" The policeman looked at me as if I were mad, and I suppose I can't blame him for that. "Murdered and came back to life, eh? And just how did he do that then, sir?"

"No idea whatsoever." I shrugged and then added "Sir."

"I see."

"I doubt it but never mind. I wish only to impress upon you the point that if you delay your investigation, you might find that he isn't dead… that he's come back to life somehow. Do you see what I mean?"

"I do indeed sir, but consider, then, if that should be the case, we will have no murder to investigate, will we? If he *is* dead then he'll be dead in the morning; if not, well we won't have wasted our time and annoyed the superintendent by getting him out of bed in the middle of the night for nothing. Do you see what *I* mean, sir?"

"Am I to understand that you will do nothing until the morning?"

"That would certainly be *my* preference, sir."

"What of the murderer? Don't you think you should get out there and look for him, or her?"

"Well, how long ago was this crime committed sir?"

"I don't know. I discovered the body only recently."

"Then it could have happened hours ago?"

"Well, yes, I suppose so…"

"Do you have reason to suppose that the perpetrator could be waiting nearby then, just to be apprehended?"

"Well, no…" It wasn't going quite as I had expected. I didn't want them to come in the morning. It would be too soon. I didn't want them to come for at least five years… I began to worry. "Look, I think I should speak with a senior officer, a detective perhaps? I should give my statement whilst it is all still fresh in my mind, shouldn't I?"

"Memory not too good, is it? You think you might forget something over the next…" he looked at his watch, "seven or eight hours?"

"I might. I think it would be best if I could speak to an inspector or someone… do you have one?"

"I do. He won't be happy to be disturbed at this hour though."

"Is he not on duty then?"

"Oh yes, but he won't be pleased to be troubled."

"Well, do you think I am thrilled at having to be here in the middle of the night?"

"I don't think, sir, I am a policeman." He spoke with no hint of irony at all.

Likho

"I am aware of that. Look, perhaps you could just get him out here, I can give my statement and then it's done…"

"He won't like it sir, but if you insist…"

"Yes, I think I do."

"Right. Take a seat." With that he disappeared into the shadows and left me alone. I sat down and put my head in my hands… I was exhausted and desperately afraid I wouldn't be able to keep my nerve, such as it was. There was a clock on the wall which ticked loudly though irregularly as it varied the length of each second, and with my mind concentrating involuntarily on that sound I could no longer accurately judge the passing of time… so I was uncertain if it was ten or twenty minutes later when the policeman came back to the counter and beckoned me over.

"The inspector will be with you directly sir. He's not happy…"

"Not happy at all…" a voice said from behind me. I looked around and saw the man I had spoken to before. He recognized me at once. "Oh, it's you again. You were here before, weren't you? Some question about… anyway, you had better not be wasting my time again, especially not at this time of the night. Please sit down." He pointed to the chair I had just vacated. "Now, if I remember correctly, didn't you come here recently to ask if you'd previously been here to report a murder? It was you, wasn't it?"

"Possibly."

"What do you mean? You did or you didn't… which is it?"

"Hard to say… you see I thought I'd been here to report a murder… my old neighbour was murdered, but you told me no such person existed. You were most insistent that no murder could have been done. Now, bear with me a while... I thought it was all real, but the next night my neighbour was alive. He hadn't been murdered at all, just as you said he couldn't have been, although he *did* exist, even though you said he didn't... am I making sense? Well, anyway, the next day, at least I think it was the next day, I came back here to tell you that there had been no murder, but you said I'd never been here in the first place, so I supposed that the first visit to report the murder must have been part of a dream. Have you got all that so far?"

"Excuse me for asking, but are you a bit mad?" The inspector tapped the side of his head with a forefinger.

"Mad?"

"Yes, mad."

"Possibly," said I with serious face, all the time wanting to laugh. "Why?"

"Never mind. Please go on."

"Well, you'll never believe it, but he has been murdered *again*. I came in late this evening... that is to say, earlier this evening, or rather *last* evening, since it is now tomorrow... no, that's not right either, never mind... the thing is, I found him dead in his apartment, just like the last time. Strangled, I'd say, same as before..." I went on with my account. He listened attentively and looked thoroughly bored all the while. When I had finished, he said nothing for a minute or two, then he stood and walked over to the counter and spoke quietly with the other policeman. That man then walked away, and the inspector came back to me.

"Is there anything else you wish to add to your story, sir?"

"My story? It is not a *story*... it's a statement... *story* implies fiction, does it not?"

"Do you have anything else you wish to say... to add to your statement? Fact or otherwise."

Likho

"I don't think you believe me, do you?"

"Does it matter if I believe you? The important thing is what you believe, don't you think?"

"What a strange thing to say... what are you suggesting?"

"I suggest nothing, sir."

"Well, you sound as if you think I am lying, or mad, and that I am making all of this up... you are only humouring me."

"I think you sound sincere, sir, I think you believe what you say to be true."

"But you don't believe me, do you? If you don't, or if you think I am raving, then please just say so, because so far you have been only patronising."

"Well, that was not my intention." The inspector sat down again and leaned towards me, a rather pitiful expression on his face. "Look, sir, this is all very curious, and also rather difficult... you see, I can tell you for certain that no one has occupied that apartment for the last sixty years... we keep our eyes peeled and our ears to the ground, you see, we like to know what's what and who's where... that sort of thing, you know." He tapped the side of his nose with a forefinger.

"You are wrong..." I said, a little aggressively, "there was a man living there, an elderly gentleman. I have seen him many times, I have spoken with him, and now he has been murdered again, maybe for the *second* time..." I couldn't help but laugh. Suddenly it was going exactly as I had hoped. I had only to be careful not to make such a fuss that the inspector felt obliged to accompany me home to see for himself.

"I'm sorry, sir, but you are wrong, or mistaken, perhaps. You cannot possibly have seen what you claim. Are you certain you weren't dreaming again?"

"Quite certain."

"You have been drinking though, I can smell it."

"Yes, but I have not been to sleep yet, not since I woke this morning, so I cannot have dreamed anything. I saw that old man dead in his chair not an hour ago, well an hour and a half... two hours, perhaps three." The inspector shook his head and then stood up again; he walked back to the counter and spoke with the other policeman who had returned a minute or so before and was waiting quietly but trying to attract his attention. He passed a folder to the inspector who then browsed briefly through the pages within before returning to me and sitting down again.

"These are our records relating to that apartment," he pointed at the tatty, faded brown file and taking a sheet of paper from within. "Now, sir, the last occupant, well, how shall I put it? He *left* sixty years ago, and, as I said, it has been vacant since. This is a picture of him..."

"That's him..." I exclaimed in genuine surprise, "*that is him...*" There he was... his wrinkled old face staring out from a faded old sepia photograph. His eyes were wide, and his mouth tightly closed and slightly twisted, sneeringly contemptuous of the camera, or its operator, and, perhaps, of anyone who might ever look on it. It was an expression I knew well, and as I stared at it, his eyes seemed to grow bigger and wider, and, I was certain, his thin cracked lips began to move...

Still holding the photograph, I covered my eyes with both hands to block out the light which was suddenly causing a sickening throbbing in my head. For a moment or two I sat in silence, afraid to move or even to speak lest I should vomit.

Slowly, the nausea subsided, and I sat back against the wall, comforted by the feeling of something solid behind me. With trembling hands, I returned the dog-eared picture to the inspector. "You say this was taken sixty years ago?"

"I imagine it is older than that," he replied, "but I couldn't say by how much."

"No, no… it cannot be. It is not possible…"

"It is." With that, he opened the file again and removed another page which he held close to his chest while he spoke. "I have another photograph which you should see."

I snatched it angrily from the man. It was my old neighbour again… he was sitting in his chair, his head slumped back, eyes bulging, mouth open and tongue hanging out… and on his throat were the marks made by the hands which had strangled him… just as I had left him earlier, and just as someone else had left him sixty years before…

14. SANCTUARY

Saturday 31st
Darkness, silence, nothing… I don't know how to describe it but, for a while, I was somewhere between life and death. In that time, you might have counted seven days; had I been capable I might have counted seven seconds, seven years or seven millennia. On awakening it felt like it was the blink of an eye… only it was a blink which lasted a week, an imperceptible involuntary action which began in a place seven days previously and ended in another a week later. There was nothing in between, *nothing*, not even a memory of nothing. I can only think of it as like having been dead.

Perhaps Death offers free samples? Now, there's a thought… *roll up, roll up, come on, don't be shy… worried about dying, sir? Not sure if it's right for you, madam? Why not try it? See if you like it? Step inside, nothing to pay now…*

But enough of this silliness…

Now, you may recall that I murdered my neighbour? Well, the police inspector showed me a photograph of the old boy…there was no doubt that it was him, the man I knew as the occupant of the apartment at the top of my stairs, and he was sitting, just as I had always known him to, in an old armchair in his squalid room… and he was dead. Dead, just as I had left him earlier that evening. The photograph had not been taken that evening though, but at some time some sixty years previously. And that means only one thing – *I didn't kill him*. Actually, it means *two* things, because the first leads to a second… and the second thing is that I *am* mad after all. There, now isn't that a relief?

Darton

You will not be surprised to know that I was carried off to hospital which, of course, I don't remember. I'm told I offered some resistance, and indeed so reluctant was I to go that I had to be heavily sedated; and, lest I expressed a desire to leave, as it were, I was kept in that state for seven days. When I did become conscious again, I was anxious to know what had happened. Well, wouldn't *you* be?

Despite the loss of seven days of my life, I felt well-rested, if not weak from hunger and lack of exercise, and I think I can say that the man who woke up was not the raving lunatic who had been admitted to the asylum a week before.

Now, Time had advanced nicely without me, and I had no choice but to accept it; much harder to accept, however, was being confined in the place in which I found myself...

For centuries, the old asylum has been a place feared, avoided and spoken of only in whispers, even by the less ignorant of the people. You are unlikely to encounter man or woman, rich or poor, who will admit even to knowing anyone who has been sent here, and a mother would be less ashamed to have a son wrongly executed for murder than have it known he had been committed to this place. To the unenlightened mind, the hospital is not some lifeless stone thing but rather a living creature, its body imbued with all the worst qualities and crimes of its inmates. Generation after generation has believed insanity seeps out through the walls, infecting anyone who passes too closely, whilst its windows are eyes which might mesmerise and ensnare anyone foolish enough to look at them. It does make one wonder who is the crazier... those within or without? Like all children, I was terrified at the very idea of the place, imagining unimaginable tortures being inflicted

Likho

upon mad patients by madder doctors. The mere mention of the old asylum could be relied upon always to guarantee a child's good behaviour... and send the mildly manic cowering in a corner.

On how things were done centuries ago, I can only speculate; but there is no evidence of any mediaeval medicine being practiced on shaven-headed screaming lunatics as far as I have seen. Given the choice, I would have declined to come, but here I am and with nothing to do but make the best of it.

I have a private room which is a little bare but nevertheless comfortable, though its old window is high up, too high for me to look out of it, and it still has bars on the outside to remind me that this place has been as much a prison as a hospital through most of its history. Indeed, at first, I was unsure of my status... patient or prisoner?

"You are free to leave whenever you wish," a nurse informed me, "as long as the doctors believe you to be well enough."

"Ah, then I may *not* leave whenever I wish?"

"Yes, I said so."

"You said I was free to go if I was *believed to be well enough*. That is not the same thing at all."

"The same or not, it is no matter... it doesn't change your situation."

"It does if I wish to go but the doctor does not think me well enough."

"*Do* you wish to leave?"

"I'm not sure."

"Not sure? The question is simple enough... there are only two options... *yes*, or *no*."

"Sorry, is that a question?"

"No. It is an invitation to clarify your answer to the question."

"I see. It wasn't clear."

"No, it wasn't. Do you wish to clarify it? That *is* a question."

"I meant that what you said wasn't clear. Never mind, my answer is the same… I am not sure if I wish to go. I am not qualified to say if I am well enough to leave, and I like to make decisions only when in possession of all the relevant facts. As I lack expert advice on my situation, I am not able to decide if I wish to go or not."

"Well, if it were up to me, I'd say you were as sane as I am… a man who knows what he doesn't know is a sensible man indeed, and one who will *admit* to it is wiser than most."

Wednesday 4th

I have been here for two weeks. I haven't felt like writing every day, and besides which, there has been little of note worth recording…

I have been resting in my room and enjoying the solitude, disturbed only by indifferent meals and the occasional visits of a nurse. There is a library to which I have access; the subject range is extremely limited, but then I suppose one must be careful what one allows patients to read in such a place as this. Books on horticulture or religion seem to be our lot; the former are well-thumbed whilst the latter are dust-covered and undisturbed. I chose a history of garden design; I have no interest in the subject, but it seems the lesser of the two evils…

My reading has been interrupted occasionally by consultations with a doctor; our first was conducted in his office to which I was escorted through the empty passages of the old building by a rather sinister orderly…

Likho

"Most of the people here are too mad to be allowed to go anywhere alone, far too mad, if you know what I mean?" The man grinned and winked at me before chuckling to himself. Bald, unshaven, scar-faced and with the look of a mediaeval headsman, he might have been a character direct from the *Grand-Guignol*, and no doubt appears regularly in the nightmares of many a patient confined within these walls; he's yet to show his face in mine, but it's only a matter of time.

The doctor is a friendly enough fellow, although I thought him perhaps a bit too young, which is a ridiculous judgment to make since there *must* be young psychiatrists… I'm sure they're not all kept hidden away from the world until their sixtieth birthdays. Anyway, I sat down in front of his desk and waited for him to speak.

"You must be missing your family and friends?" He asked as he relaxed back into his big leather chair.

"No."

"No?"

"No. I have none."

"No family, no friends?"

"No. I had parents, but they are dead; I had only a passing acquaintance with them as I was sent away to school. I knew their names but little more. As for friends… well, I have never had much use for them."

"No wife?"

"No, I have never had much need for one of those either."

"I see." The doctor looked thoughtful for a moment. "Ordinarily that and your previous remark about friends would launch us on to a lengthy series of discussions on relationships, and an assortment of complexes… but I think we can spare ourselves that for now... unless you would like to talk about any of those things?"

"No, I wouldn't."

"Good, and nor do I. Now, tell me, did you have no friends at all when you were a child? At school, for example?"

"No. From what I saw, friends appeared to be troublesome and not worth the bother."

"Really? Why?"

"I am surprised you need to ask... the boys who had friends were fighting half of the time, or showing off and trying to outdo or humiliate each other... I suppose it's that primitive instinct to prove dominance, subjugate competing males and win breeding rights. Whatever it was, I couldn't be bothered with it. It has always seemed to me that friends are no more than people with whom to fall out... simple, really... have you never observed that?"

"You must have been very lonely?"

"No, not a bit. Being without friends and being lonely are not inseparable concepts; the second is not an inevitable consequence of the first."

"Indeed." The doctor looked thoughtful for a moment, scribbled a note and then went on. "You never felt any need for a friend? For any sort of companion? Someone with whom to share jokes, games, secrets... happiness, sadness... someone with whom to talk?"

"No." There was a pause, as if I were expected to go on but I had given all the answer I had to give and so said nothing more.

"You don't think that friends can enrich your life?"

"How might they do that?"

"By bringing something different or new into it."

Likho

"All I ever saw was people bringing trouble into each other's lives, either in expectation of help or just for mischief. Who needs the troubles of another when we each of us have enough of our own?"

"Well, you have a point, though most people would tell you that in the end it is worth the risk, that the benefits far outweigh the troubles."

"And that is their business, and very likely your problem."

"Whose problem are you?"

"You think I am a problem?"

"Do you think you are?"

"No. I think people *have* problems but are not in themselves problems."

"I think you are right." The doctor sat forward and leaned on his desk. "And that brings us back to your problems. Convenient, eh?"

"Very. Well done."

"You think I am manipulating our conversation?"

"Aren't you?"

"Of course I am. How else do you think I work?"

"Does it matter what I think?"

"If I said it didn't then I probably shouldn't be a psychiatrist, and that reminds me that I am not the patient here."

"That may be so, but we are both in the asylum."

"Yes, and I'm sure you'll be free long before I..." He sat back in his chair again. "So, let's concentrate on your release rather than mine. We were talking about friends and your decision to have none. Was it a conscious thing, or a gradual process?

"Well, I don't recall making a decision, but by the age of nine or ten that was how I thought.

"Really? Then you had friends before that?"

"No. I didn't like any of the other children at my school... and, more to the point, they didn't like me much, from what I recall. They thought I was a privileged spoilt child because I didn't mix with them, but you have to consider that I was brought up alone and in the isolation of a nursery, away from other children... I remained aloof because that was the only way of being that I knew. How could I be different? And out of ignorance *they* mistook aloofness for snobbishness."

"What did you think of *them*? What opinion did you have of them? Did you hate them?"

"No, of course not. Why should I? I didn't know them, or why they thought as they did. Besides, I had nothing with which to compare them. How can one feel anything about people one doesn't know? I felt nothing, no like or dislike, or hatred, nothing. I didn't judge them. I try not to judge people."

"Judging is not the same as having an opinion. Surely you had an opinion about them?"

"No. I base my opinions only on what I know, on facts. If I am ignorant of some or all facts then I do not form an opinion, or a consequent judgment. It is unfair to do so, don't you think?"

"Yes, I do, though I find it hard to believe anyone could restrain his thoughts so rigorously."

"You think I am disingenuous then?"

"No, quite ingenuous, in fact. I believe you; I believe you to be sincere and honest."

"Thank you."

"Thank me if you must, but I have never been convinced that sincerity and honesty do a man much good in this world. Hypocrisy and mendacity seem to me to be far more beneficial, even for a man who would be sincere and honest."

"You are very cynical, I think."

"I am a psychiatrist. It is my job to be cynical... besides, how can I get into a man's mind if I accept everything he says without question? I must test him, observe his behaviour... all those little subconscious actions which give away the true state of a mind."

"Which speak louder? Words or actions?"

"They are complementary."

"In every case?"

"I believe so, yes."

"Well where *you* test the man, *I* leave it to him to prove his case... you seek to convince yourself; I wait to be convinced."

"Then you see yourself as passive?"

"I'm not sure what you mean."

"Neither am I... well, let's see," the doctor paused for a moment and chewed the end of his pencil. "You exist alone in the world, regardless and despite it. You don't seek to influence anything, and you don't allow anything to influence you, unless it has your considered approval... is that about right?"

"You put it very well, yes. Until I am sure of a thing, I form no opinion and make no judgment."

"Yes, you said something similar just now... so, if I introduce you to two men and I tell you one is a cold-blooded murderer and the other is life-saving doctor just stopping off on his way to sainthood, whose company would you prefer?"

"Neither or both, I would not choose one above the other. I have only your word for it that they are what you say... and if a man is good or bad it is no matter to me until he does me good or harm; if he does neither and there is no provable evidence regarding his character, then I could not reasonably have an opinion of him, good or bad."

"Faultless logic." The doctor sat forward and leaned on his desk again. "And that, sir, is part of your problem."

"Not judging men or doubting their honesty is a problem?"

"Well, let's put it this way... how can you believe or trust a man if you do not first mistrust him and question his integrity?"

"I don't think I quite understand. Is that what you believe?"

"It is simple. All things must be tested. If a man says a thing, then it must be questioned in order to prove it false or to remove doubt. Subjected to testing, all that is true survives; all that is *not, does* not."

"We are of similar mind... except that you start from a position of mistrust... guilty until proven innocent?"

"Guilty *unless* proven innocent..." the doctor said with a shake of his head. "Some *are* guilty."

"We are lucky that you didn't choose the law for your profession."

"An amusing thought. But anyway, you think as I do... if a man makes a statement, then he is obliged to prove it true, is he not? Logic, science, the same rules apply to everything."

"You are not a religious man then?" Even now, I'm not sure why I asked that. "Logic and science don't permit god to exist, do they?"

"As far as I am concerned, religion has been good only for causing arguments... and wars, and death, and destruction" replied the doctor, "and until science proves the existence of god, there is no place for him here...

indeed, here, Logic *is* god, and Logic says *thou shalt have no other gods before me...*"

"Then your asylum is a truly godless place."

"Well, if a man is wise then he will always have an open mind, so let's say it is, just possibly, for the time being, merely *godforsaken*..."

With those profound words the doctor concluded our interview, and I was taken back to my room to muse on the subjects of trust and honesty... those things which were going to be my undoing if I couldn't learn to be more contemptuous of them.

Sunday 8th.

The doctor came to my room where he found me engrossed in a most absorbing chapter on the development of the knot garden and the parterre, and so very grateful for his interruption.

"Which do you prefer?" I asked, "the formal or the natural landscape?"

"The formal, of course, with nature tamed and trained by man."

"Ah, you think nature is disordered and must be subject to man's rules?"

"Only as a metaphor for the human mind. Nature may do as it pleases, and besides which it always wins in the end; nature always reclaims what man takes from it."

"Does that apply to us?"

"What do you mean?"

"Might nature return us to the wild?"

"That's a good question."

"Isn't it just? Do you think it's possible for human evolution to go into reverse? Could nature reclaim man and return him to a state of wildness?"

"Well, it doesn't work like that, does it? There would need to be some advantage for us. Gaining advantage is the only thing which drives evolution. That's not say that it doesn't undo changes… I suppose a good example is some aquatic creature evolving into a land-dwelling thing with legs, and then some of them going on to evolve into snakes, giving up the benefit of legs in exchange for a *better* advantage. Anyway, it would take hundreds of thousands of years…"

"Quite. One short lifetime is not enough to achieve anything worthwhile."

"It is if you consider that our only purpose is to reproduce and perpetuate our species… and on that basis we outlive our usefulness, do we not?"

"Then if all except procreation is pointless, and I do not intend to procreate, well, that makes my life worthless, wouldn't you say?"

"I cannot disagree with your logic, and on the basis of that, you might as well go and kill yourself. I wouldn't be a very good psychiatrist, though, if I counselled any of my patients to commit suicide."

"On the contrary, I think you would be a particularly good psychiatrist indeed. As things are it is your duty to dissuade… no, *prevent* the suicidal amongst us from killing ourselves, but to those who are sincere in their wish to die you are merely an inconvenience, are you not? A man determined to end his life will do it one way or another, so if he has proved himself serious then why stop him? Why commit him to hospital and insist that he is ill, that his mind is unbalanced? Why is it assumed a suicidal man is mentally ill? It is inhumane and cruel to prolong the life of a man who wishes to die."

Likho

"What of those who *are* mentally ill? Should they be free to kill themselves too?"

"If they *are* ill then I leave them to you. Do as you wish, cure them if you are able… lock them up if you are not."

"How do you know who is sincere and who is ill? How do you know if a man needs treatment or if we should send him in a taxi to the old town bridge?"

"Again, I leave that to you as one who is qualified to know these things. As for me, I do not know."

"And you? Do you wish to die?"

"That's the wrong question."

"Is it? Yes, all right… do you wish, or intend, to kill yourself?"

"No."

"What about dying? Do you wish for that?"

"Yes, of course. Who doesn't? Well, except for those misguided fools with designs on immortality. I do wish to die, but not just yet… I hope to have another thirty years or so, but when I am sufficiently diseased or worn out, I shall not resist the inevitable. Does that satisfy you? Am I sincere? Or do you think me a danger to myself?"

"I am quite satisfied that you are not inclined to suicide or self-harm… but what about everything else?"

"Everything else?"

"The reason you are here, the things which disturbed your mind so much that you were brought to us. I see no sign of the man who was admitted here three weeks ago. Is he gone, or waiting quietly somewhere and planning a return? Do you know him?"

"No, I don't. I think you know more about him than I do. Is that a good or bad thing?"

"Well, let's think about it. It is good that he has gone, and better still if he's gone for good, but not good that you don't know him. If you don't know him, how can you prevent his return?"

"Do you think he could come back? And why are we talking as if about someone else, a stranger?"

"He is a stranger to you though, isn't he?"

"Yes, I have said as much... so tell me, are you saying I have some sort of split personality?"

"No, not all."

"You make it sound as if I have..."

"Ah, sorry, no. *Psychosis*, maybe... but I would never presume to diagnose that without a much longer period of study."

"Oh. Well, that's something, I suppose. Then what do you think?"

"I'm not sure... that is to say I haven't known you long enough to come to a conclusion."

"But you have some initial thoughts?"

"Oh, of course."

"Might I know them?"

"Well, it is my opinion that you have suffered what is generally known as a *nervous collapse*. As for the causes, well, the recent move to your apartment is likely to be one. It was a cause of stress, possibly subconsciously, and even more serious for that. Your sleep was disturbed... the consequent fatigue and depression caused panic attacks, false beliefs and hallucinations. Rest and medication seem to be working well enough though."

"I am *not* mad then?"

"You might be the maddest madman ever to live for all I know, but at present you appear to be perfectly sane...

though just because a man is lucid and capable of reasoned debate doesn't mean he is not insane to some degree."

"Do you believe there is an *acceptable* degree?"

"Ah, that's rather subjective, wouldn't you say? You might, for example, believe that you are a tree; such an assertion by you would cause some to suppose you to be mad and think you should be shut up in a hospital… but others might say that a tree is a good thing and does no harm, so it is no matter. Indeed, if we all believed ourselves to be trees the world might be a better place…"

"Yes," I mused aloud, "I don't think I should mind being a tree…"

"Then again, you might choose to live at the top of the cathedral spire because you fear the river will flood… again, an irrational belief but nevertheless harmless."

"How, or *when*, do you judge a man's sanity to be a matter of concern?"

"Oh dear…" the doctor replied, suddenly looking uncomfortable, "I wish you hadn't asked that. In short – and I mean *very* short – if you retain an awareness of yourself, an understanding of right and wrong, and can feel affective empathy, then you're probably all right. To put it another way, if you are certain that you are mad, then it is certain that you are not…"

"And if I am certain I am *not* mad?" I asked.

"Ah, well, in that case I should have you in a straitjacket quicker than you can say *padded cell*…" With that reassuring reply, he left my room, grinning broadly and looking very pleased about something; I'm not sure what.

Tuesday 10th.

The doctor has been to see me again.

"You are looking very comfortable" he said as he pulled up a chair and sat down.

"Well, maybe this place isn't as bad as people think" I replied.

"That's the first time anyone has ever said that…" he said with a rather surprised look, "at least, the first in my experience… but wouldn't you prefer the comfort of your home?"

"I used to think so, but that place seems to have been the source of all my problems. Here I feel, well… *safe*, I suppose."

"Not *too* safe, I trust?"

"What? I don't underst…"

"Ah well," the doctor began, before I could finish the thought, "we don't want you to become too comfortable, do we? This *is* a sanctuary, but you cannot remain here forever; we must send you back to the world eventually…"

"Surely there are some here who will never leave?"

"Yes… although for them it is not a sanctuary but a *prison*, and many would go gladly, given the chance.

"The incurable criminally insane?"

"Yes." The shortness of the doctor's reply suggested that he didn't want to talk more about it.

"Chained to walls in padded cells? Laughing maniacally all day and howling at the moon all night? Beyond help and hope?" My interest was piqued.

"You paint a dismal picture, my friend, and not a very imaginative one," he replied, "I thought you might do better than that."

"Isn't it like that?" Said I, slightly ashamed.

"No," he replied, slowly shaking his head, "it is much, much worse… you should come on a Sunday afternoon when we open to the public."

Likho

"That sounds a bit mediaeval..." I couldn't imagine he was being serious and so thought I might as well go along with it.

"Yes, and not for those of a nervous disposition" he said, then added "or those prone to nightmares."

"Ah, then you think it's not for me?"

"It might be one day," the doctor mused, "who knows? But let's leave the damp, rat-infested cells, passages and torture chambers of our worst dreams for the future. Wouldn't you prefer just to go home?"

"I'm not sure." I was genuinely uncertain.

"You will do just as well there as here."

"You think that I am ready to go?"

"Not quite," the doctor replied, "and that makes it the best time to go. A man should always act before he is ready... he will take everyone else by surprise – but better still, he will surprise *himself*, and that, my friend, is a good thing.

"That is a strange idea, but I can see how you might come to it," said I, "and so how can I argue?"

"You can't... and, *en passant,* one more piece of advice – never agree so freely with anyone – you might be throwing away an opportunity for useful debate. Or a *really* satisfying argument."

"Yes, very profound," I observed with a forced smile, "I shall bear that in mind, especially when talking with psychologists."

"That's the spirit... and what about going home?"

"Do I have choice?"

"No, you don't," replied the doctor, "anyway, most men are delighted to get out of here. I know I would be. *Working* here is bad enough... I can't imagine being confined as a patient..."

"Is that a joke?"

"No."

"I wasn't sure," said I, "I find it difficult to know when you are being serious."

"Well, I'm being serious now," he replied with a smile, "you can go home in the morning."

Out he went once more, the door swung shut behind him and I was alone in my room again. It has come to feel like a refuge from what drove me here, though I accept it is a place for treatment rather than a place to hide, and the time for hiding is over. Problems are doggéd and athletic things – it doesn't matter how far or fast you run, they are ever nipping at your heels; no doors or walls are ever sturdy or thick enough to keep them out, and they hunt you down no matter where you go. Only *confrontation* is anathema to them.

I *don't* feel ready to go home but I am to be turned out of my sanctuary and, like the mediaeval fugitive, I must return to the world and whatever awaits me beyond these walls.

Despite all reasoning, I admit I am tempted to run away. Run away? That's not quite what I mean, but it'll do. I am not thinking about *permanent* exile, but the thought of a long holiday abroad is an appealing one. And I *don't* have to go home afterwards because I can do as I please. I can sell my apartment, and I can live wherever I choose. I *can* run away if I wish. I am being irrational, of course. There is nothing in that place to hurt me; the things which hurt me were in my own head; if they exist still, then where e'er go I, well, there go they…

Fear can be our best friend, but irrational fear is a most dangerous enemy. Fear should be embraced; irrational

Likho

fear must be overcome… and logic is the one thing which it cannot survive.

It is an incontrovertible fact that my old neighbour does not exist; therefore, anything which contradicts that statement cannot be true.

Time to go home…

15. Ex Paradiso Expulsus

Wednesday 11th.
With the sanctuary door closed behind me, I stood alone.

It is only three weeks ago that I was admitted to that place; it felt as if it had been years, and it felt as if it had been only yesterday. Strange how our minds confuse us over the passage of time...

Under a white sky, the snow-covered streets had drawn such little colour as there was under a freezing white blanket; the town looked like a corpse, watched over by skeletal trees, and on their bare bony branches sat the blackest crows, all in deepest mourning.

I made my way home on foot, along treacherous icy pavements where the least lapse of concentration could have put me back in hospital, though with a broken leg rather than a broken mind. Watching my step meant I didn't think much about where I was going beyond the next few yards, and it proved to be a good distraction... a dread of breaking one's neck on a patch of ice is guaranteed to focus the wits far more than any dread of dead neighbours or night terrors.

The morning was bitter, and twice I was compelled to seek respite from it in a café. I imagined the doctor would say I was just putting off going home, but my feet and hands were so cold they were beginning to throb, and thus my stops were in order to avoid frostbite rather than slow my progress. It cannot be denied that it gave me chance to think about things too, and by the time I finished a second cup of hot chocolate I was feeling quite relaxed. I was going home where everything would be as I had left it, only there would be no neighbour, murdered or not, no nightmares, nothing odd at all, and when I got there that's just how it was...

The fires were lit, and my lunch was laid out ready, though how the concierge's wife knew when I would be back, I do not know. Maybe she hadn't noticed I was away? It didn't matter. Before sitting down to eat, I wandered from room to room as if I were viewing the apartment for the first time, as if I were a prospective buyer. It is a nice apartment; I like it... spacious and quiet, plenty of corners to get away from myself. Of course, the place isn't quite as I'd first seen it because then it had been empty whereas now it is furnished with all my possessions. One of those is the portrait of my unknown ancestor on the wall above my desk... the grand military fellow who looks a little cheerless, if you recall? I stopped for a while to look at him and, I don't know, maybe it was the light, or the angle of viewing but I think he doesn't look quite so sad after all. Perhaps he never did.

I should have liked my homecoming better if it had been under a blue sky, but, alas, it was clouded, and has remained so all day, by clouds of the sort that bring steady torrential rain or heavy snow. In our case it is snow, and it began in the middle of the afternoon, falling on to already frozen streets and so making them even more hazardous for a man on foot. I went to the window and watched it for a while. It fell slowly and steadily, gently floating past, some flakes sticking to the frosty glass, others drifting by to settle on the sill, or falling further to the street below. Watching snow is very hypnotic... well, you will know that if you have ever done it, and consequently an hour or so went by until the dim daylight faded into darkness. The growing yellow glow of the streetlamps made the dark black sky above darker and blacker until it was no longer possible to see anything falling from it, so with nothing more to watch outside, I closed the curtains and returned to my chair by the fire, where I became just as mesmerised by the flames, each one as unique as a snowflake, and gone just as quickly. As I mused on the transience of snow and fire, I began to regret not having become a scientist… or a poet, though I have not the brain for the first or the heart for the second…

Another hour went by, and I began to think about going out for supper. It wasn't late but I had a mind to be early to bed with a book and some brandy for company, besides which I needed a good hot bath before I could go anywhere. As I relaxed in the steaming water my mind was free of the nightmares and hallucinations of the previous weeks, and when I emerged from it a while later the face which looked back at me from the bathroom mirror was fresh, rejuvenated and free of the haunted expression it has lately shown.

The fresh snow which I had watched falling earlier lay thick on the ground, undisturbed by foot or wheel, the weather having long since sent everyone home, and it looked as if I was the only man to have forsaken his fireplace. As I made my way along the street the cold air froze my face, and my fingers and toes too despite gloves and thick socks. It was far too cold to be out, but out and cold I was and determined to go on, though I didn't go far. I turned towards the river and then into a small street which runs parallel to the embankment where I knew there to be several cafés acceptable in all respects – other than the food, but that doesn't matter to me. My stay in hospital has done nothing for my interest in eating which remains a necessity and not a pleasure.

Darton

The restaurant of my choosing was quiet, the waiter was not overly attentive, the menu unfussy but the selection of wines excellent. I drank a half bottle of a full-bodied claret which was far too good an accompaniment to my meal but nonetheless enjoyable for that. I finished with a glass of port, declining any coffee in case it should prevent me from sleeping. Then, after paying my bill and leaving a generous tip, I put my coat on and went out into the street. The snow was falling more heavily, and I had to wrap a scarf around my face against the freezing wind which had blown up from somewhere whilst I had been in the café. With my head down I walked as quickly as the icy pavements allowed, reaching my building about half an hour later. I climbed the few steps to the door and let myself in to the dark lobby, crossed quietly to the stairs and then walked up slowly through the shadows to the second floor. As I reached it, I felt suddenly nervous and though I dared hardly look, my eyes turned towards that apartment in which I have twice imagined the murder of an old man…

The door was closed. I wanted to push at it to make certain, but the thought that it might open stopped me. Turning away, I crossed to my door, let myself in and went directly to the fireplace in the sitting room, shaking the snow from my coat as I went; where it fell, it quickly melted into droplets of water which caught the light and sparkled in a trail across the floor before soaking into the boards. I would be lying if I said it didn't remind me of the nights when those mysterious children were about, but I do not lie when I say that I no longer find it disturbing because I know that none of that could possibly have happened.

A while later and ready for bed, I went to my library to select a book; a volume of local history came first to hand so, with that and a glass of brandy in my other hand, I went to my bedroom. The fire burned steadily in the grate and a lamp glowed softly by the bed which was offering itself up for what I hoped would be a never-to-be-forgotten night of the best sleep ever. I eased myself between the sheets, eager not to spoil the fresh white linen, pulled the quilt across me and settled back on my pillows. Reaching for my drink I noticed that the book had fallen open at a page about the old imperial palace, and a plan showing part of the formal gardens which, regrettably, exist no more. What a strange coincidence? I had recently become knowledgeable on that subject. I smiled to myself as I studied the old drawings and tried to work out just where they had been sited; it was hard to judge, but on the following page another drawing showed that the parterres and ponds had disappeared under various extensions of the existing buildings, and the construction of the New Residence, just over three centuries ago, and although it be magnificent, it is a shame some other arrangement could not have been devised to include the old gardens.

As I waited for sleep, I began to imagine I was there on a warm sunny afternoon…

There was no one else there, it was perfect. The sky was clear and just the right shade of blue; birds and birdsong were carried on air heavy with the scent of flowers, butterflies of every colour flitted by, and bees hovered above the thousands of flowers which filled the beds of the parterres. Water gushed from ornate fountains, scattering the sunlight into rainbows, cooling the summer air and sending millions of droplets splashing on to the rippling surface of a pool. Finches with brightly coloured plumage dived in and out of the water, shaking it from their feathers and chirping merrily before flying away to sit in the shade of a tree. A peacock called from somewhere; another responded, then another, before one came into view away to the right strutting proudly across the gravel before stopping nearby to spread its tail feathers in a fine display with its hundred eyes shining blue in the blazing sun. Just beyond the peacock was a large round pond bound by a low stone wall on which I sat for a minute and watched as fish of all sizes and colours went lazily by, all swimming anticlockwise, whilst on the surface floated exotic ducks, some alone, some in pairs and some trailing ducklings in their wake; for reasons known only to them, *they* all went clockwise around a pair of dazzling white swans who drifted effortlessly over the water, going in no particular direction at all.

Now, I'm not stupid... I knew I had fallen asleep, I knew it was all a dream, but it was a change to be having such a nice one rather than the nightmares which still lingered in a dark corner of my memory and so, determined to make the most of it, I strolled on with not a care in the world, enjoying the tranquillity of my personal paradise which stretched as far as I could see in every direction, the spires and towers of the town only a mirage shimmering in the afternoon heat, unattainable somewhere beyond the horizon...

The parterres gave way to immaculate lawns which were planted with small groups of blue and white flowers, all in straight lines at regular spacing; a little further on, orange trees were heavy with blossom... the scent was overpowering, the scene enchanting.

A forest of fruit trees covered the next mile or so before giving way to groves of stone pines, pools of cool water by which dryads sat whilst naiads and goddesses bathed, and beyond them a group of people stood in the cool shade of some cypresses. I couldn't think who they might be or why they were in my dream and so walked on towards them, attracted by idle curiosity. There were four of them and they were standing by what appeared to be a plain stone tomb, and as I drew nearer, I could see that they were studying it. Three were young men carrying staves, semi-clad in robes from ancient times, one in white, one in blue and one wearing red, whilst on the right stood a woman draped in blue and yellow; there was something familiar about them, and I had an idea that there they were shepherds[14]. It occurred to me that such a scene was not complete without satyrs, fauns, garlanded nymphs and bacchantes and, this being Paradise, my wish was granted as a troupe appeared in the distance, all dancing to the music of Time[15].

The shepherds were so deep in contemplation they seemed not to notice my approach. The man in the middle was kneeling and following something with his forefinger on the monument whilst the others looked on. At last aware of me, the four turned with smiling but slightly sad faces, the kneeling man moved back a little and then all pointed at an inscription carved into the ancient stone which, though eroded over centuries, could be read still... *ET IN ARCADIA EGO.*

No one spoke. I stood a while and read the words over and over in my mind before finally saying them aloud...

"*Et in Arcadia ego*... I know this, I've seen this before. I've seen all of *you* before... I don't understand it though... what does it mean? Why are you here?"

"*Et in Arcadia ego*" said the shepherd standing on the left, pointing at the tomb.

"I understand *that*... but I don't understand *why* we are here."

"Haec est Arcadia," said the kneeling man.

This is Arcadia... my school days are long gone but, even though I was never very good at Latin, I was unaccountably able to understand them perfectly.

"It is our land... our home," the third shepherd said, smiling and with a sweeping gesture which took in the scene, and then specifically his companions. He placed an arm on the tomb, as if embracing it, and spoke again "and this... this is the way to Elysium." His hand rested gently on the stone as his friends nodded in agreement; then they turned their heads towards me.

"It is not for you," said the shepherdess with a sad shake of her head. Then she moved her arm, and slowly the finger which had been pointing at the inscription was directed at me. "There is no place for you here... you are never to be welcomed."

I was being shown Paradise, eternal home to these perfect and beautiful people, where even Death was welcome... but where I was *not* and never shall be. Imagine that – Death is more desirable company than I.

"I understand" I said, feeling very disturbed by what they said, "but why?"

"We may not say," the woman replied. She shook her head slowly whilst the others looked at the ground, as if they were a little embarrassed.

"Well, which way must I go? Can you tell me?"

The four glanced at each other and then turned their gaze to the stone once more, standing just as they had been when first I saw them, but instead of the tomb, their forefingers were aimed at a point somewhere behind me. None of them looked back but it was clear that I was to return whence I'd come, and whatever was there was not for them to see...

Likho

As I turned to go the sky began to darken… the colour drained from it, and what had been azure became pale grey, then darker and darker still as the clouds thickened and dimmed the sunlight. A rumble of thunder echoed around me and so, supposing it was going to rain, I started to walk quickly, certain I had a long way to go to find shelter from a storm. All at once, I realised that I didn't know where I was. Nothing of the groves and gardens through which I had walked remained and in their place were the dark and dismal alleys of a poor quarter of the town.

I had never been there before. I was lost. The streets were deserted, littered with rotting rubbish; mouldering vegetables and parts of animal carcasses were piled high in places, and crawling with greasy black rats. A wild-looking cat hissed at me from a shadowy windowsill, then leapt to the ground where it set about attacking the rats, scattering them in every direction; I felt one run over my feet, whilst another tried to climb my leg, only letting go after I had hit it several times with the back of my hand. I felt unclean and violated by the touch of those filthy creatures and, though I couldn't see them, I was certain they were all around me and waiting for their moment.

Most windows were in darkness, though some narrow, feeble shafts of light escaped through gaps in shutters and, here and there, I could just about see that some doors had been boarded over. Those hastily affixed planks were roughly marked with crosses, and the red paint dripping down the uneven timbers was the only colour anywhere to be seen, and the only clue as to what might have happened. Where houses were dark there was silence, but from those where a light still showed came all the imaginable sounds of human suffering and misery, though whether cries of grief and pain or pleas for mercy and death, I couldn't say.

Behind me, everything had faded into blackness, and so with no retreat there was nothing to do but go on. The snow and ice which had lain thick on the streets earlier in the day was gone but the pavements were wet and slimy, and just as treacherous. A distant flash of lightning lit up the inside of a black cloud in the distance, and the thunder which it set off came rolling furiously after it. I wanted to get home before the rain began but I dared not walk faster for fear of slipping on the stinking greasy cobbles. I knew none of the streets or where I was in relation to the centre of town, and with the sun obscured and being uncertain even of the time, I had no idea which way to go. With all confidence ebbing away I kept to the path on which I'd found myself, hoping it might lead me to a more familiar one. Ten minutes later, maybe twenty, maybe more, I reached a small square from which several small streets led away in all directions. With anger and frustration displacing such little calm and logic as remained in my mind, I stopped, desperate for a sign... a street name or something to give a clue as to where I was or in which direction I should go. There was nothing.

The pavements around the square were lined with trees but all were dead – the lucky ones had been killed by lightning strikes, splintered by a single bolt; others, not so fortunate, were diseased and rotten, and their trunks and boughs were scarred and twisted in pain, the evidence of a slow and miserable death. The houses were in a terrible state, some without roofs, others with collapsed walls and all in a worse condition than those I had just passed. Some were occupied still by the living, and dim flickering lights showed at windows where the sick and suffering were confined within, left to die in despair from whatever this plague was which had so quickly overwhelmed the town.

The wind blew through the broken buildings, gathering up the cries of the dying and carrying them out, around the square and away into the darkness of the surrounding streets, leaving their bodies mute and breathless to wait for death…

The silence which came after the wind lasted only momentarily before a piercing scream cut through the air. It came from somewhere on my left, and I turned just in time to see a woman in a ragged nightgown leap from an upper window. With arms spread wide, she fell to the ground; the echo of her cry outlived her, but for only a moment.

The wind whistled around again, gathering a fresh harvest of souls, and it was followed by thunder which rattled through the crumbling hovels where it shook a few more stones loose as it went, frightened a few stray dogs, and a baby somewhere which began to scream for its mother, a mother who might have been lying dead by its side, or perhaps a mother who had just leapt from a window…

Surrounded by ruin and death I could not, and *cannot*, think of any meaning to this nightmare. I wasn't even certain if it was *my* nightmare, though my presence in it suggested otherwise. An hour or so earlier I had been in sunlit gardens, I had been strolling in Paradise… then I had been turned out of it, banished forever, and sent into this noisome rookery to witness the horrors of a plague. Perhaps I was being warned to mend my ways? Should I then fall to my knees and beg for absolution from my sins? Should I promise to lead a good and righteous life for which I would be spared the hell I was being shown? Of course not. This was an earthly, palpable hell from which there had to be a way out.

As it grew darker still, a streetlamp sparked and flickered into life on the other side of the square. With no other light, instinctively I stumbled towards it. As I reached it, a second began to glow dimly. I walked onwards, and when I reached it, another slowly lit up. Seeing and hearing nothing else, I advanced along the narrow street from one lantern to the next. I had no idea where I was being led, but where else should I go? I assumed, *hoped*, that they were being lit for me, to lead me home, or to whatever awaited me next. The lamps did not burn bright and threw little light on to the houses which lined the way, but occasional lightning flashes showed doorways where I thought I could see dark hooded figures hiding, pressing themselves hard against the walls to avoid being seen. Their presence worried me, their purpose worried me more, but I had to keep going, to follow the lights which were glowing ahead of me. I reassured myself that I saw no one, that I saw only shadows, and that shadows can do a man no harm. Surrounded by so much fuel for the imagination, I knew only too well how easily it could be ignited...

The street was endless, cutting through parts of the town I thought I knew and others I didn't recognise. I saw the outlines of familiar buildings standing black against a blacker sky, and passed some which I thought were in other cities, other countries, buildings which couldn't be where I was seeing them, but which were there nonetheless. Then I was back amongst the decaying slums, following the dim lamps along a street of houses all leaning awkwardly against each other for support, bulging and bowing outwards, threatening to fall at any moment. Each painful creaking movement of the walls had twisted doors and fractured

Likho

windows or thrown tiles down from the roof. Fragments of shattered panes were strewn over the cobbles, and as each flash of lightning tore across the sky, its reflection was caught in the shards of glass which carried it away like a river cutting into the depths of the darkness.

Death was everywhere, assaulting every sense, the stench and taste of it growing ever stronger as a sickly stream of bloody vomit, excrement and bodily fluids oozed from rotting corpses, ran beneath doors and over the broken pavements to the gutters where fat black rats fed on it.

The sights and sounds were dreadful; the foul stinking air made me retch until my throat was raw and my stomach twisted in an excruciating knot. Struggling to breathe, I came to a gradual halt and leaned against the black and splintered trunk of a dead tree, too exhausted to take another step, and too terrified of where that step might lead. Confused and beginning to panic, I thought of turning back, of running as fast as I could, away from the darkening horrors ahead. But, as my imagination began to work on those yet unseen sights, a deafening crack of thunder split the air behind me, and the shockwave pushed me forward. As I stumbled, I started to turn, but my face was struck hard by a blast of ice-laden wind which came at me with such a scream that I dared not. There I was, then, *on a lonesome road,* walking on in fear and dread, and terrified of whatever fiends might be treading close at heel…[16]

My only hope of salvation came from those flickering streetlamps which I prayed were meant to guide me, and though I knew not where or why, it didn't matter because I remembered that this was all just another bad dream, and in dreams both good and bad, all roads lead us home, and safely to bed…

16. 'What In Me Is Dark Illumin...'[17]

Thursday 12th
Whilst such sunlight as managed to penetrate the clouds and reach my bedroom window lacked the strength to throw a shadow on the floor, it was more than welcome on such a gloomy winter morning, and to be commended heartily for its achievement in breaking through...

My day began in a twisted tangle of sheets which had attempted to enshroud me during the night. The remainder of the bedding was strewn about the room, and a disembowelled pillow amongst a scattering of feathers gave support to the idea that someone had suffered a fearful nightmare...

I can only speculate on the reason for the state of things because I thought I'd slept rather well. I remember only a happy dream in which I had been strolling through gardens and picturesque antique landscapes... I think there had even been some shepherds. I could remember them quite clearly because I have seen them before, many years ago, in a painting, in a gallery somewhere, though I don't recall which... I have visited so many, and they all merge into one after a while. Anyway, it isn't important. My recollections of the dream remain rather imprecise, but nothing worrying has come to mind so why I should have had such a fight with the bedclothes is set to stay a mystery. Giving it no more thought, I unravelled my winding sheets and got up – I'm not yet ready for such *grave* attire...

Sitting now at my desk, I am thinking about how I might occupy myself. I shall go out for a walk, of course; I do not intend to change my daily routine, but I do think that the day should have more purpose to it. Whilst talking with the doctor in the asylum, he suggested it might be good for me to do a little research into the strange case of my long-dead neighbour. It would be helpful therapy, said he, if I were able lay that ghost finally to rest... I assume his choice of words was intended to be amusing, though it was perhaps a little tactless. Anyway, I'm not certain I care anymore. The only problem is that I have little voice in my head nagging away, telling me that I need to know, that I shall not be content until I *do* know and, indeed, suggests that my sanity depends upon knowing.

Well, I don't know about laying ghosts to rest, but I think I have come at last to understand why it is best to let sleeping dogs lie...

Later.

Just as the clock in my sitting room struck ten, I put on my coat and went out.

No noise came from anywhere in the building. Past the closed doors of the neighbouring apartments I went, free of care, and then made a slow and stately descent of the stairs as if I were entering an imperial ball; it was not an effect I intended to achieve, it was only that I was in no hurry, and I had no wish to trip on my way down our dimly lit *grand escalier*. The thought amused me, brightening my mood still further, and when I reached the lobby, I was smiling quite unashamedly. Fortunately, there was no one there to see it, and *that* nearly made me laugh aloud, though I have no idea why.

Fresh snow lay on frozen snow, frozen snow lay on ice, and beneath the ice lay the pavement. I made slow progress but at length reached the first crossroads where I halted for a moment and considered which way to go...

Likho

straight ahead, left or right? Ahead was the river, whilst to the right the street led up to an ancient convent and nothing much else of interest; the land on that side belonged to the abbey and thus bars and cafés were not to be suffered for so shalt the good people be led into unclean and sinful lives, or something like that. All rather silly, I thought, especially as the nuns are known for making a very strong fortified wine; they, of course, declare it to be medicinal and, indeed, it is, if you seek a cure for sobriety. The good sisters claim to be a discalced order, but I suspect they just can't remember where they left their shoes. Never mind, not my business... *my* business led me away to where the street afforded a choice of bars, free of prohibition, and nuns.

Sitting in a quiet café I took up my usual sport of watching the passers-by... some hurrying, others not, but all going about their business and ignorant of being observed. All of mankind was out there... men and women, young and old, some alone, others in company, some poor, some rich and others in between. On they went, trudging through the snow, burdened with shopping and discontented spouses, ungrateful children and spiteful in-laws, demanding employers and resentful employees, jealous colleagues, complaining neighbours and treacherous friends, and all troubled by lack of money or excess of it. On they went, caring too much for the opinions but nothing for the feelings of others, each standing alone on the axis of the universe and lamenting his unenviable situation. Well, none of those things apply to me – how very lucky am I? Except, I suppose, for the possibility of a troublesome neighbour, albeit a long-dead one.

I haven't seen him since my return from the asylum. Has his door remained closed since the night I thought I'd killed him? There is every possibility that I didn't imagine any of it and that his corpse is rotting away in his chair, with his mouldering apartment decaying around him. Well, I can't help but wonder and it has crossed my mind to ask the concierge, but I haven't seen him or his wife either. Putting the whole matter from my mind, I finished my coffee and went for a walk through the snow, pausing a few times to peer in at shop windows and even venturing into one to browse through some books for half an hour. At last, an empty stomach drew me home for lunch which was laid out as usual, though with no sign of she who had set it there.

It began to snow heavily in the early afternoon; for a while I sat by the window and watched it fall but eventually tired of it and went to sit by the fire and read my book about the old palace gardens. It is a shame to think of what is lost to us, and yet we are lucky how much is left considering that it is only in recent decades that we have begun to appreciate what is old and to take care of it, though that doesn't seem to apply to people. Is it not an odd sort of world we have fashioned? A world where a century-old vase might be priceless, but a man of the same age is considered of no value at all...

Had our country retained its imperial status would we now have anything left from the Middle Ages? Or would our town have been rebuilt over and over as successive emperors sought to define their reigns by leaving a more splendid city than their fathers? I think it likely. We are lucky then that we have been a political backwater for the last few centuries and that the fortunes of our nobility diminished sufficiently to save its ancient palaces from being remodelled in that anodyne neoclassicism which blights so many other cities. Ours is a beautiful town adorned with the most enchanting architecture, and for those with an interest we have buildings from all periods up to the middle of the eighteenth century when wealth followed power away and abroad, leaving our city to stagnate but preserved for the years to follow.

In every street, every square, everywhere there is an architectural gem to gratify the viewer, though most are unnoticed by men too busy to look now but happy to know that there are things to look at one day when they have some spare time. *Spare time*? What is that? Is it all those minutes which time-saving devices store up for us that we may enjoy occasional time doing nothing? I have never cared much for the idea of saving time… it is one promoted mostly by men who wish to sell me something I don't need. I have observed people who have saved time… with nothing else to do, they sit about in bars forever watching the clock, looking thoroughly bored. I suppose one day someone will invent the ultimate chronometer – one that *saves* time for us by staring endlessly at itself, so *we* don't have to waste precious moments doing even that.

My, how very philosophical I have become since my recent time in the madhouse? But I am reminded that it was too much thinking that got me there in the first place, though I suppose a little thinking is not such a dangerous thing as long as it's not too deep… indeed, perhaps one should keep in mind that the deeper a thought, the further away it is from the light.

And so it was with little thought that I went out for supper, with even less thought that I chose a restaurant, and then abandoning reason altogether jabbed my finger at something on a menu which was later brought to my table where I ate it without further care. A good bottle of red wine, some brandy and coffee completed my meal and then with a full stomach and an empty head I stepped out into the night and sauntered merrily home.

Darton

Pure white snow was falling from the dark black sky and the yellow light of the streetlamps glowed through the flakes as they fell to the ground. The pavement was thick with ice beneath the snow making it madness to go too quickly, but I didn't mind because I was in no hurry. I wasn't reluctant to go home, I was just in no rush to get there. I wanted to enjoy the deserted streets, the snow and even the freezing air which made my face burn and my toes throb, reminding me that I was alive and awake. Half an hour later my numb fingers were turning the key in the street door, and moments after that I was standing at the top of the stairs outside my neighbour's apartment where, to my surprise, the door was ajar.

I stood silent and still, staring at it, and resisting whatever it was that was trying to draw me in. Whether it was something in the apartment, or something in my head, I can't say, but I was determined not to enter.

A voice called out from within, and it was very like the voice of my old neighbour. I remained still and said nothing. It called out again, and this time I was certain it was the old man, though he sounded cheerful and inviting which was not in the nature of the character I had thought to live there.

No, I said to myself, *I am not going in there because that man does not exist...*

With that thought, I turned towards my apartment, and with a cold and shaking hand, let myself in. I went directly to the sitting room, having much need for warmth and brandy, and, if I am to be honest, the need for brandy was by far the greatest...

The only light came from a gilded candelabrum on the mantlepiece, and the candles that burned in it were also the only source of heat, with no fire burning in the hearth.

Likho

The room was freezing, and my breath condensed before me as I stood in the doorway.

"Well, good evening…" came the voice of my old neighbour. It hit me like a blow to the stomach and I fell back against the door jamb in shock, feeling sick and overwhelmed with a fear such as I've never known and cannot describe.

I could just about see his grey hunched figure; he was sitting in *my* chair, by *my* fireplace and holding a glass of *my* brandy. All at once, anger overcame all my other feelings and I stepped towards him, furious and raging.

"What in the name of… how dare you…" I shouted, "what do you think you…"

"Now, now," he replied, with a broad and infuriating grin on his face, "there's no need to be rude. If that is how you treat your guests, then it is not surprising no one calls on you…"

"When, and *if*, I want guests, I shall invite them. *You* have not been invited, and never shall be, and I require that you leave at once."

"Oh dear, oh dear," the old man said, still grinning, "but you have only yourself to blame. We were expecting you to call on us, but you did not… and so, despite the inconvenience, we are compelled to call on you."

"Well, you should not have done," said I, angrily. "I chose not to call on you, and for many reasons. You, sir, should learn to take a hint… and now I should be obliged if you would leave."

"All in good time, my dear fellow, all in good time…" he said; as he spoke, he pulled a watch from his waistcoat pocket, opened the cover and squinted at it. "Oh, look at that, it's stopped – *time* has stopped…" He held it up in front of his face where it began to spin and sway back and forth on its chain, the glass catching the light from the candles; he looked like a cheap music hall act.

"Is this your latest trick? Hypnotism?" I said dismissively. "Oh well, I suppose it makes a change from returning from the dead... I think we have all grown weary of that one. Mind you, I have it on exceptionally good authority that you *are* dead, and that can mean only one thing – that you do not exist, except in my mind. I am imagining you. And now I am going to imagine you gone..." Turning my back to the old man, I left the room and walked to my bedroom, removing my coat as I went. In the minute it took me to get there, the temperature plummeted; I supposed it because the fires had gone out and couldn't think why the concierge's wife had not been up to attend to them as she usually did in the evening. Shivering, I pushed the door open...

The room was lit only by a single candle, but it made enough light to see my old neighbour sitting on the bed...

"No no no..." I shouted, closing my eyes tightly. "No..."

"*Yes yes yes...*" The old man's voice was little more than a whisper, but it struck me like an ear-splitting scream. I stood motionless, confused and disbelieving my own senses. *That man is not there...* I repeated the words over and over in my mind, my eyes shut still as I wished him away.

My wish was not granted. I opened my eyes only to see my aged neighbour sat on the bed, the quilt pulled over his bony legs, as he rested on the pillows. He looked at me with an odd expression... the look of a victorious but reluctant gladiator in the arena, commanded to kill his vanquished opponent or forfeit his own life. I remained motionless, speechless and I don't know what... with all my deceived senses causing so many responses, it was hard to isolate any one of them. After a few moments, vertigo prevailed, followed swiftly by nausea... I staggered to a chair by the cold, dark fireplace, sat down and closed my eyes again; the room was spinning, and closing my eyes only made it worse, but it was better than the sight of that vile old man lying back in my bed, even though I *knew* he could not be there...

How cruel is the mind that practises such a deception upon itself? Especially as it can end only in madness and self-destruction.

No sound came from anywhere, and I thought, nay, *hoped* that meant my neighbour had gone. At first, hard as I tried to open them, my eyes resisted and remained tightly shut; but then, as if a trap had been sprung, they opened, and I could see as plainly as ever that the old man was there still. A shiver ran down my spine and the nausea returned.

"You cannot wish us gone" whispered he, with a reproachful look, "it's too late for that now." It was as if he were able to read my mind; but then, why should he not be able to? It was only in my mind that he existed. Well, *that* was what I was trying to convince myself.

As I stared at him, I became aware of a movement in the shadows to the left, though I dared not turn to look, and sat still with my eyes fixed on the old man. I didn't need to look; I knew what it was – and I don't need to say what it was, because you know as well as I do. It was how I have encountered her so many times... just out of sight, in the half-light, there but not there, seen but not seen, between reality and imagination, presage of a nightmare.

She held her position; the old man looked at her, then turned back to me and smiled.

"Well, my friend, the end approaches us," he declared, sighing as he spoke and looking relieved, "or, more precisely, it approaches *me*. As for you, well, you are not so lucky. I *am* sorry for you, really, though not as sorry for you as I am happy for myself."

I said nothing. I sat in my chair, shivering from the cold or trembling from fear – I don't know which, but I sat there... asleep or awake, sentient or dreaming, again I don't know which, but I said nothing. What does one say to a dead man? A ghost? A thing that isn't there? And if it be not there, *why* speak to it at all? These thoughts and many more tumbled in and out of my mind for an age, and it was no matter anyway, there was no hurry because, as my visitor had said, Time had stopped.

It grew colder, and a frost started to form on the floor. It looked very pretty as it caught the flickering light of the candle, and, for some reason, I felt obliged to say so.

"Did you ever see anything like it?" I asked my old neighbour. Fine ice crystals were forming in the air and fluttering down to the carpet which had all but disappeared. "It is very lovely... almost hypnotic to watch."

The old man said nothing but turned to the shadow beside him; frost had formed on her, too, and it gave her outline a little more definition, though still it remained vague and gently shifting as I stared at her.

"Aren't you going to introduce your friend?" I asked, pointing at her with a shaking hand."

"My *friend*?" He said, looking a little puzzled.

"Yes. Your friend... or wife, or whoever she is," said I, pointing again, "there, her."

"My *wife*? Ah... if only she were" he said, beginning to laugh, "if only she were... at least wives die, or can be divorced, or murdered. A man can get rid of a wife. Easy to be rid of a wife. No man can kill *her* though. *She* can't be killed because she isn't alive. She isn't living, but then again,

Likho

she isn't dead either. She doesn't exist, yet there she is, you see her plainly... well, as plainly as she allows – she's a shadow, a thing that lives where light cannot reach... you can *see* her, you can *sense* her, but you can't *touch* her. Oh, but she can touch you though, and whenever she pleases. Have you ever been touched by a shadow?"

"What? What are you talking about? Who is she?"

"Oh, believe me, you don't want to know" he replied, wagging a finger at me.

"When I do not want to know, I do not ask." I said, raising my voice a little. "Who is she? Who is your... this... this *shadow*?"

"This *shadow*," he replied in a sibilant whisper, "is evil, a bringer of misfortune... she devours souls. Death can't touch her... even the gates of Hell are closed to her. Just imagine," he said, casting a sly glance at her, "just think for a moment what *that* means. She comes from somewhere unimaginable, somewhere it is *impossible* to imagine... a boundless, timeless emptiness into which even God himself cannot reach. She is *likho*.[18]"

"*Who*?" I replied, "*what*?" I had an idea that I'd heard of her, or *it*, before, but it was a long, long time ago, and no more than a fogged remembrance was just out of reach.

"When she has you – and she *will* have you soon enough – well, then you'll know, you'll understand, and you'll realise what a fool you have been. If only you had been open-minded? If only you'd seen the signs and heeded the warnings... you have had every chance, many more than I did, or those children downstairs. You refused to believe what you thought couldn't be real, though you should have done."

"I don't know what you are talking about."

"No, I believe you don't. You have been remarkably stupid for one so intelligent…"

"Not so stupid," I said, interrupting my unwelcome guest, "that I cannot recognise a stupid old man who is trying to drive me mad, though for what reason I do not know; maybe it is for your amusement? I was convinced that you do not exist, but now I am certain that you do… although as for *where* you exist, I cannot say… whether you exist in the world, or only in my mind, well, *that*, I cannot say… but whichever it be, you cannot harm me, or frighten me. You have no power over me, no control. It is I who has control… control over *you*, and *that* thing…" I sat back, relaxed, and enjoyed my moment of triumph.

"You are quite right, my friend, quite right. *I* have no power here, or anywhere else." The old man paused, looked again at the shadow beside him and then went on, "she took such power as I had long ago. And such power as you believe you have, well, you shall not have it long… and even if you have it still, it is too late. Look around you…"

The fire was blazing in the grate, though no warmth came from it, and every candle in the place was burning with a bright and steady flame. My neighbour had vanished, and the shadow woman, Likho, had melted back into a dark and grimy wall. The paper was peeling, the plaster was black with mould, and had fallen away in parts to reveal the laths behind. Above the door, the ceiling had come down, and large pieces of the cornice lay on rotting floorboards. The door was hanging by its upper hinge, the handle missing. Behind me, the curtains were faded and motheaten, and the window glass stained and cracked. The only furniture remaining was the chair on which I sat, and the bed, and what had been fine linen was now torn and soiled.

Likho

As I sat amongst the decaying remains of my bedroom, silently surveying the dereliction, the light faded, the fire went out, and my visitors returned.

"Are you trying to show me the past or the future?" I asked, contemptuously, "or is it another of your party tricks? I'm very impressed. How *do* you do it?"

"None of this is my doing..." said my neighbour, reclining in my bed, "it is *she* who is at work now." He pointed at the shape-shifting shadow beside him, Likho, who drifted in and out of focus, grew in height until she reached the ceiling and then returned to the roughly sketched form of a little old woman in a shroud. Her head swelled and shrank; it was featureless one minute whilst in the next, a nose appeared; then a large Cyclopean eye formed on her forehead and moved down her face to become a large gaping mouth. The apparition faded in and out of the darkness, and with each appearance, it was a few inches nearer to me. It was as mesmerising as it was frightening, and I couldn't help but stare at it...

"*She*..." I repeated before suddenly regaining control of myself, "she? Oh, I have had enough of this...this ridiculous and incredible rubbish," I shook my head at the old man and tried something of a sneer to express my contempt, "I have had enough of it. You," I shouted, "do not exist. You are dead."

"Yes, I *am* dead. You are right. But I *do* exist, and not only in your mind..." He grinned at me, proudly displaying all his broken teeth. "Death is not the end of existence, and nor is birth the beginning of it. We exist. The rest is mere detail, a matter only of *where*..."

"Very well, I shall indulge you for a moment... let us say you are dead, and you *are* a ghost... so how did you die? Come on... let's hear it." The voice which I heard speaking was mine, but I didn't feel as if I were in control of what it said; I had become two people... one of them curious, beginning to relax and enjoy himself, whilst the other was terrified and unable to move or speak. The brave and curious me asked the questions, and the petrified me had to listen to the answers, a captive audience.

My dead neighbour looked at me intensely for a moment, as if he were organising his thoughts, and then began to speak.

"You ask how I died but you know the answer to that already... the police inspector told you... he showed you a photograph of my corpse. What he did not know, and so could not tell you, is the identity of my murderer...

"He was a young man of about thirty years, I think, and he lived here, in these rooms, about two hundred years ago. He was struck down by consumption, if I remember his story correctly. He suffered horribly, alone and terrified. Delirious, shivering on sweat-soaked and bloodstained sheets, his desiccated lips gasping for water, with the last of his strength he prayed to be spared. First, he prayed to God. But God didn't answer – God does not answer that prayer. Then he prayed to Satan, and *that* prayer *was* answered..." He pointed vaguely at the shadowy Likho. "*She* came. Whether she came on her own, or whether she was sent, I cannot say, but in the end, I think it doesn't matter which... though perhaps Satan is an easier master?

"Here he lay, in this room, dying, and willing to offer his soul in exchange for a few more years of mortal life. It seems a man's soul is never so worthless to him as when vanity prevails, and Pride is the most dangerous of the Sins...

"He gave up his soul," the old man went on, leaning forward and gesticulating wildly with his left arm, pointing first at me and then to the heavens, like an evangelist in his pulpit, "but it was Likho who took it, and kept it, and left his body to die. He was compelled to lie in this bed, to listen as a priest administered the last rites before Death came to claim his empty, soulless body; compelled to feel that body wrapped in a cheap shroud, thrown into a rough coffin, and carried away without care or ceremony to be thrown into a common grave, covered in quicklime and left to rot. Only after months in the ground did Likho bring him back here… here to this bed and the stinking sheets on which he had died.

"Was it worth it? Did he cheat Death? Well, he *didn't,* and he *did*, though not in the way he had hoped. His body died, but his *soul* stayed in this world, a prisoner of Likho, and, as a punishment for his vanity, he was condemned to remain here in this apartment, never to stray out of it or see the light of day again, other than as allowed by her. It is a most excellent cautionary tale, I think, don't you?"

"Oh, indeed," I replied, sarcastically, "if only it were true… but you *do* tell a good story. How sad that you didn't put such ability to good use as a writer of cheap Gothic novellas when you were alive… but don't stop there – you have yet to tell how you became ensnared in the plot."

"Your attitude does you no credit, my friend…"

"It is not my intention that it should," said I, interrupting rudely, "and, besides which, your opinion is no matter because you do not exist. But do go on, if you are able?"

"You are interested?"

"Well, let us say only that, perhaps, curiosity has the advantage of me. Do go on."

Darton

"There's not much to tell," the old man began again, "you've seen the photograph... he came to my apartment and strangled me. I didn't know him, I'd never met him... he appeared one night, introduced himself and told his story." He paused for a moment, looking as if he were trying to remember. "I listened to him, disbelieving but politely... well, that is until he said he was going to kill me, and then sat there in a state of alarm as he explained, very calmly, why he must do so...

"Condemned to remain here, day after day, year after year for all the days and years to come, to remain here even when even days and years exist no more... imagine the weight of regret upon him? Of course, you cannot. He prayed for death, and harder than ever he'd prayed for life. But we cannot die in instalments... Death calls only once. Likho, on the other hand, was a frequent visitor... she knew his thoughts, and for his regrets she made him suffer. She took him out to see how the world was going on without him; she made him sit in all his favourite places, and when he could endure it no more and cried to return to this room, she fixed him to a spot and left him to suffer, sometimes for years, a briefly glimpsed ghost in a shadowy corner. Other times she tormented him here... she let him understand that she would free him to whatever fate awaited but only in return for another, though with no chance of encountering another, it was the cruellest of all tortures."

"Ah, but wait," said I, wagging a finger at him like a reproachful parent, "if that were so, then how did he come to you? Did this... this *Likho*... did she take pity on him at last?"

"*Pity?*" he exclaimed, "*Pity?* You *are* mad."

Likho

"Oh, I am certain of it," I replied, "or why would I be talking to you, a dead man? But never mind. Why did she let him go?"

"I don't know, but as she only exists to cause misery, I'd say her reason was a selfish one. Maybe she was tired of tormenting him?"

"Ah, yes…" said I, rather gleefully, "and she wanted to torment you instead. What a wonderful idea. Oh, I love her for that alone."

"You will regret your levity, sir, and sooner rather than later…"

"I doubt it. But go on… I am most anxious to hear how you were so cruelly murdered by a disembodied soul."

"You know what he did. You've seen it… you've seen me dead in my chair… strangled to death. You have seen the marks of his fingers on my neck, although as for *how* he was able to do it, I am no wiser now than I was then. And *how* he came to me, again, I cannot say other than *she* must have brought him. He was there in front of me, put his hands around my throat… gently at first but then gripping tighter, harder… my eyes lost focus slowly, everything went red, and then black. It was all over in a few seconds, and with no pain, with no sensation at all.

"Of course, when I opened my eyes again, I had no idea that I was dead. My strange neighbour stood there still… and then he smiled… he smiled and told me he was sorry. He asked for me to forgive him, and then he was gone. Can you believe it? He asked me to forgive him."

"And did you?"

"*No*, I did not," replied the old man, "because, just then, I didn't know *why* he wanted forgiveness. Later, when I understood what he'd done, and why, I prayed that he should burn in Hell." He paused for a moment and looked to be deep in thought. "To this day, I wonder if that prayer were answered... but even if it were, I could not have wished him to a worse hell than the one in which he was trapped here. But who knows? Maybe he found forgiveness in another?"

"So, unforgiven, he left you there, a corpse, to rot in your armchair?"

"Yes," replied my neighbour, "though the stench of that rotting corpse soon drew attention; it was removed to a pauper's grave and that was the end of the matter. There was a brief investigation, of course, but it came to nothing." The old man shrugged and sat back, and I supposed his story concluded.

"Your tale is almost as amusing as it is unbelievable, and that, sir, is where we shall leave it..."

"No, we shall not." His expression became more serious as he narrowed his eyes and raised a finger at me. "I am not finished, not yet, and we're just getting to the part where *you* come in."

"*I think not*," I shouted, "because this is the part where *you* go out."

"Oh, don't worry, my friend, I shall not keep you long... I wish to be gone even more than you wish me gone. I don't want to be here, and I *would* go now except that I want to explain why what is to happen must happen..."

"Do you have to? But, if it means you will leave me alone, then go on – but be brief, for both our sakes." I was tired of listening, but it seemed to be the easiest way to be rid of him. I yawned slowly and obviously, just to make my point.

"Well, my poor friend," he began again, "Likho will let me go... if she can have *you* in my place. It is quite simple. She wants *you*.... and you cannot imagine how much. She longs for a man such as you... a man of intelligence who chooses ignorance, a man who sees and hears and feels but refuses to believe. Oh, how she loves souls like yours... souls destined for Heaven. She works against God, she works even against Satan... she holds souls which are rightfully theirs in a purgatory of her own, and it is worse than the wildest imaginings of the most fanatical inquisitor or mediaeval artist. We are not pierced with hot irons, burning in sulphurous flames, or devoured by demons; we are not tortured in such ways. She torments our minds...

"It has only been sixty years but for every second of those I have been facing an eternity confined here... even when *here* exists no longer. That is what awaits us, well, *you*. When the world is reduced to atoms and the last star has gone you will be here... just think about that. Is it not the worst torment possible? Think about it. Trapped in the blackest nothing where even time can no longer exist... that is worse than any vision of hell which the mind of man might conjure up."

"Is that it?" I asked, yawning again, "because it's time I was in bed. I have had enough of you and your silly stories. I have no intention of dying... well, at least *not soon*, so you are excused... you may return to... to... well, to wherever it is that you *haunt*, and leave me alone. I shall not take your place; you cannot kill me... how can you harm me? You cannot."

"*She* will do it, or rather, she will compel *you* to do it... you, sir, you are going to end your own life. You are going to kill yourself..."

"No, I am not... I am most definitely not" I laughed at him and shook my head. "Nothing will make me do that. If you are relying on my suicide to earn you your freedom from... well, from whatever you think *she* is, then you are going to be extremely disappointed. You are stuck here, and I am free. Your joke has gone too far, sir. Consider it at an end."

"Oh, even if I were able, I wouldn't. As for you, well, you might still be alive, but you are as good as dead... and that makes me as good as free. Likho will see to it. Anyway, you have only yourself to blame."

"What? *Blame*? Blame for what?"

"For your own unfortunate fate, my friend, that is what."

"Oh, really? And just how, exactly, have I brought myself to this? Assuming, of course, any of it to be true."

"You won't believe me, even now?"

"Of course not. Why should I?"

"You told me yourself that you believe only what can be proved irrefutably. You have never wanted to accept that there might be things which have no rational, scientific, philosophical, or logical reasons to exist. If only you had... you might have had the good sense to leave, just like your predecessors in that apartment. The woman, well, she saw what you saw, heard what you heard, but she was prepared to believe it. It frightened her and she left... and that place stayed empty until you arrived. If only they had stayed, then I could have gone years ago. Likho would have been happy to take them and let me go. You would never have been here; yours would have been a different fate."

"Oh dear, what a shame. I must blame that poor woman and her husband then? What went wrong?" It crossed my mind to mention that I had met the woman in question but then rapidly recalling that day in more detail, it occurred to me that perhaps I had not met her at all.

Likho

"Those damned children, of course. What else? They frightened the woman so much that her husband took her away…"

"Ah, yes, the children, I'd forgotten about them. Do go on."

"Those children have been a curse on me since the day I killed them… oh, don't look at me like that… I had no choice. I was as desperate to get away as the man who killed me, and I thought an innocent child would be perfect, I thought *she'd* love that, I thought she'd be sure to accept the child and let me go. I was only going to kill the little girl, but her brother tried to stop me. I pushed him away and he slipped on the wet floor, knocked his head on something and was unconscious… when his sister was dead, I put him the bath with her… he fought a bit but he was dazed, concussed… it didn't take much to hold him under until he was dead too. Believe me, I took no pleasure from what I had done, but it was necessary, essential… I felt sorry for them, but I had to do it."

"There is no such thing as a *necessary* murder; and the murder of innocent children, the cold-blooded murder of children, can *never* be justified… and your motive, such a *selfish* reason, is even more dreadful. If what you say is true, sir, you are a monster, and you deserve to suffer for all time in Hell. And if, as you say, you are there already, well then, I should make it my purpose to ensure you remain there. But you're still here…" I said, scornfully, "so you'll understand why still I don't believe you…"

"That is explained easily enough. Likho doesn't want children," the old man shrugged. "*I didn't know*… I thought the sacrifice of an innocent child would be perfect, but she refused it. She is not interested in the uncorrupted innocence of the child… she wants the innocent adult who has *resisted* corruption. Men such as you are, and such as I was, believe it or not... those of us who somehow remain free of sin and who, like it or not, were and might yet be destined for Heaven..."

"And the children?"

"Ah, well, they remained here, they *chose* to remain here... they wanted to keep me here by making sure I couldn't find another soul to take my place, and until you arrived, they were doing well. Sadly, for them, you have not given yourself up... and you can think it a victory if you like, but it is a pyrrhic one."

"I think *nothing* of it..." I said, as insouciantly as possible, to support my want of thought. "But, one last thing, before you go... what of the concierge? Their father?"

"You know what happened, the police inspector told you. He was driven mad by grief and killed himself. Then he came back here... to take care of his children. There is an irony of sorts because *he* wants me gone. Without me the children have no reason to remain... so when Likho has you, we shall all be free, one way or another..."

"Well, in different circumstances, this would have been most entertaining. In our present circumstance, it is not. I cannot see the future, but I can promise that you will not feature in it... your time is done, you do not exist... you are not real today, and I will not allow you to exist tomorrow..."

I closed my eyes and sat back in the chair... I wanted to sleep but I couldn't. I wanted to sleep more than anything, even with the threat of the worst night terrors. But sleep lurked somewhere nearby, perhaps afraid to come for what it might bring, and though I tried to grasp it, it kept out of reach. At last, frustrated and almost crying, I gave up…

Opening my eyes, I was surprised to find I was in my sitting room, next to the fire, which was blazing as usual, and on the table next to me was a glass of wine. What relief… to wake from another nightmare, to wake at home, and safe.

There was one question, though, which I couldn't answer – at what point in the evening had the dream begun? Did I fall asleep on the way home? I think it unlikely. The entire evening must have been a dream. I must have dozed off in the afternoon… I had not been out, I had not had my dinner… but then, if I had not eaten, why did I not feel hungry? Oh well, it is not so important.

Sitting back and relaxing, thoughts of a holiday drifted across my mind, and I began to imagine sitting at a table beneath an old café awning in the piazza of some antique hilltop town, sipping on a cold drink whilst lazily watching the afternoon sun beating down on rose-red rooftiles, and a stray dog dozing in a shady doorway, untroubled by the sound of birdsong from the eves above… the picture was so real that it was a relief to feel a refreshing cool draught on my back, and as it brought me back to wakefulness, I shivered a little and moved closer to the hearth, took a sip of wine, then sat back and closed my eyes, hoping to return to some Arcadian paradise on a Calabrian hill.

The cold draught came again. I moved closer to the fire which was burning nicely though now seemed to be radiating little heat. I stretched out my arms and held my hands in front of the flames to warm them. The room was growing colder, I thought, chilled by that draught, which was coming from somewhere, and despite sitting almost in the fireplace I could not get warm.

After a few minutes more I could bear it no longer and, rather irritated, rose from my chair with the intention of finding the open window or door and the cause of my discomfort. Turning around as I stood, I saw it...

17. One-Eyed Likho

What had the old man called her? *Likho*? What did it matter? Some things don't need a name, and for some things, no name can ever convey the feelings which the sight of them causes…

That thing standing there in my sitting room, behind my chair by the fire was… it was what? I don't know… I don't know how to describe it… because, though it was there, it wasn't there. It was a shadow… a thing made from shadows, made in shadows… a thing with a form which seemed to change continuously though subtly… it was there but it wasn't there, I could see it… but I could see *through* it too… it was there… I could smell the nauseating stink with which it filled the room, the cold air which emanated from it, thick with the sweet stench of rotting flesh, it filled my nostrils, and the taste of it stung the back of my throat.

What is it? This *thing*? Despite the fear I felt, I stared hard and tried to make out its shifting features… it was a mummified corpse, or a skeleton with dead skin stretched over dry bones, stretched so tightly in places that it had split to expose an empty black nothing beneath. What is it? This *Likho*? What is she?

There was a limb, an arm, or something that was once an arm, hanging from her left shoulder; at the end of it hung a dead hand with dead fingers bare of skin, the yellowing bones worn to sharp points. If there was another arm, it was lost amongst the shape-shifting shadows.

Though I had seen this thing many times before, her face had always been ill-defined and inconstant… but now, as shafts of moonlight lit up the room, I saw it clearly for the first time...

If a man wanted to give death a face, he couldn't do better than describe the one at which I was looking. The mottled blue-white skin was taut and shiny in places, wrinkled and dull in others; where it was tight over the cheekbones and forehead, it looked like highly polished ivory; as the moonbeams moved across it, I could see decayed and desiccated flesh flaking off her like plaster dust floating down from an old ceiling. Where an eye should be there appeared to be a patch of leathery skin... and the upper edge was fixed with three nails which, still glowing as if red-hot from the forge, had been hammered into the bone, whilst the lower was roughly pinned with the sharpest of thorns which caused trickles of blood to run down her cheek. The other eye was lost deep in its socket from where it stared out at me, and whether it was the left or right, I couldn't say because it shifted its position with every change in the light...

From what I could make out, she was missing her nose, though maybe she had never had one? Or perhaps she has one only occasionally? Who can say? Anyway, its absence left what appeared to be a dark hole in the middle of her face, and below that was another which I took to be her mouth...

After what felt like hours but can only have been seconds, I managed to step back a pace. As I moved, the living-dead shadow followed... ragged shroud trailing behind her and billowing menacingly in front at the same time. The little capacity for rational thought which remained to me shouted aloud in my head *"this thing is a creation of your own imagining, without your mind, it does not exist."*

Likho

The sight and stench of the shadow-corpse drove me back another step, and as I retreated, it took another step towards me, maintaining the distance between us. Behind me was a window, to the right the door to my study, and to the left was my escape. I looked towards it thinking to make a dash from the room, from the apartment, from the building, but when I looked back at that thing, she was shaking her head at me, as if she had read my thoughts. Would she bar my escape if I tried to leave? I turned to the window and then back to her to see that instead of shaking her head she gave a nod, stretching her mouth into a wide grin at the same time. That was it then... I was to leave through the window, though it was an exit no man could survive. I was to kill myself, just as the old man said, and this thing was going to drive me to it.

It was odd but for a moment I felt quite calm and fearless even though in the presence of that one-eyed terror. I had no fear of dying. What's the point? Rather than fear the inevitable, is it not more sensible to embrace it and make it a friend? And if it should prove to be a good friend then hopefully it will not cause one too much pain...

Well, I didn't think smashing my body on to the street below would be painless, or necessarily quick, and besides which, if all this were true, death was not going to be the end for me. What if I did nothing? If I declined to leap to my death and chose to remain here? What could the old man do? Could the shadow-corpse do me physical harm? The old man had suggested as much. Perhaps it, or *she*, would just dog my steps until I was driven mad? I couldn't imagine ever becoming accepting of her constant company and with that in mind I decided on a path of brave, perhaps reckless, self-preservation...

Darton

"No," I said, quietly but firmly, "You want me to jump from this window? I shall not do it. Why should I?" Likho made no reply but remained standing, staring and emitting waves of cold and noxious air. "Don't you speak? Of course you don't… because you don't exist, you are an hallucination. Or something in a nightmare. You are just some shadow in a bad dream, nothing more, and when I wake up, you will be left behind in that dream, with only a hope that I might return to you in my next sleep… you exist only because I allow it."

Something a doctor had said about ghosts came to mind… it is necessary only to take control and deny their existence. Do that and they will disappear. Wise words, but it didn't seem to be working. I tried again…

"You do not exist," I shouted, pointing into the shadows, "you do not exist… you do not exist."

I stared at her, and she stared back, unmoving. She didn't dissolve into the ether but remained, unaffected by my abjuration, her eye fixed on me.

Could she know what I was thinking? If she exists only in my mind, then I cannot stop her. But if she exists beyond the bounds of that place, if she is *not* my creation, well, perhaps it's possible to obstruct her? I forced my thoughts to the weather, the room, the furniture, my books, I thought about as many irrelevancies as I could and piled them up in the front of my mind to form a barricade, and then, *without thinking,* I was through the door and in the passage. Seconds later I was racing down the stairs, taking them two or three at a time with my coat, which I had managed to grab on the way, trailing behind me. A few seconds more and I reached the lobby. The concierge stood near the door, leaning on his mop and surrounded by a pool of soapy water, just as I had seen him before on several occasions. Why was he there? It was the middle of the night. As I raced past him and slipped on the wet floor, I realised his probable purpose... it was to slow me, or stop me leaving, or maybe even to cause me to break my back as I fell. I had forgotten he had an interest in my death.

I picked myself up and, clutching my coat, moved quickly to the street door but taking a second to look back as I went, afraid though I was of what I might see. The concierge remained leaning on his mop, a look of surprise on his face, but behind him came no one. The one-eyed thing didn't appear to be following me... and that worried me more because if she was not in pursuit then where was she and what was she doing? I felt safer when she was in plain sight, awful as that sight was.

The pavement was frozen, a treacherous death-trap for those in haste and on which the incautious might slip, breaking a neck or skull. It crossed my mind that that thing hadn't followed because she didn't need to. All the conditions needed to bring about a fatal accident were in place, and she had nothing to do but wait. Undeterred, I stepped into the deserted street and walked quickly down the middle where the snow and ice had been cleared. As I increased the distance between me and my home, I began to feel more confident, certain I had outwitted and escaped my one-eyed tormentor. All I had to do was take care not to die or be killed in an accident, and as I turned from my street into another, I wondered what would happen if I were to live out my natural life and die of old age? Would the old man find someone else to take my place in his ridiculous adventures? The further I was from him the less believable all of it became, assuming I wasn't dreaming... and if I were, then none of it mattered, did it?

Darton

The town was fast asleep. No light showed anywhere... not even the streetlamps were lit, but it was a full moon, and with no clouds to obscure it, there was more than enough light to go by. With the snow reflecting the moonlight on to walls and windows, it was almost as bright as day. I walked on up the street, towards the cathedral where the spires stood against the deep blue-black sky and every frost-covered stone shimmered like the millions of stars which filled the heavens from one end to the other. I stopped for a moment to enjoy the sight; it was beautiful, it was there just for me, and I felt privileged to see it. I didn't really know why I was going towards the church because it would be locked up and offer no sanctuary before daybreak. *Was* that why I was going there? Seeking sanctuary like some mediaeval criminal on the run? I have never believed in *any* god, so why should one of them reward me with his protection now?

Still, the cathedral remained my immediate goal and so I went on up the street with nothing much more in mind than reaching the top of it until, just ahead on my left, something stepped out of a dark doorway and into the light. It was her, that one-eyed thing standing in the moonlight, a hard black shadow in the soft white snow, and only a few feet away from me again. My heart began to race, my feet stopped and as I lurched forward, I nearly fell over.

Instinct told me to run, but caution won, and I stayed still, staring at her, Likho, or whatever she was called, and then I understood that she didn't need to pursue me because she could appear wherever she wished... she could appear at will, and why not? Wouldn't you if you could? Of course, no living creature *could* do such a thing... and so, drawing some courage from the thought that no dead thing can hurt the living, I began to taunt her.

Likho

"I don't know why you are following me. You can't touch me, you can't hurt me... go away... go back to your old man, go to hell, go where you like, but you might as well leave me alone. You don't exist Likho... *you do not exist.*" With that I started off again up the street towards the cathedral. I thought she might follow but I looked back to see her standing still on the same spot. Turning away, I went on...

Then I saw her once more. There she was, emerging from the next doorway... then, just as suddenly, she was coming from a narrow passage on the other side of the street... I began to walk faster, no longer worried about slipping on the snow which had started falling from the cloudless sky, almost as if it were the stars themselves which were falling softly across the town. It made no difference because as fast as I went, she was ahead still, stepping out of the shadows again and again, there at the next doorway, and then on the right... back on the left, then across the street once more... as I walked on, she came from every doorway and dark recess on both sides... appearing, disappearing, but always there, wherever I looked.

In a matter of minutes, I was standing in the shadow of the great cathedral. The northwest transept rose in front of me, a vast wall of sculpted stones and stained glass. The moonlight turned the windows into vast sheets of silver and threw the masonry into deep relief. Gargoyles and grotesques sparkled where the light hit their frosted features; forked tongues, horns and wings were brought to life by the moon and glistening ice...

Whatever magic animated the stones, it gave them no voice. No sound came from anywhere, inside or out. As I stood before the locked iron-bound doors, my attention became fixed on the tympanum... and there sat Satan, receiving the souls of the damned, aided by demons and monsters whose gaping mouths devoured the screaming sinners cast down by a group of angels. I could not but think it ominous that I had arrived at that place, at that spot, at the doors of a sanctuary which was barred to me, looking up at that image of Hell which had been put up there many centuries ago to remind we poor wretches of our fate...

Behind me the street was empty. That cyclopean woman had disappeared. Maybe she had given up? It was a small hope and one which was crushed almost directly it came to mind when out from the deep shadows of the porch she came, shifting noiselessly across the frozen ground and slowly shaking her head at me, just as she had done back in my apartment. There she was, pointing one of her bony fingers at the building behind her as if to confirm my exclusion from the church, a real Devil's Advocate excommunicating me. I laughed at her. It was all just another scene in a bad dream, and I would wake up soon, wet with perspiration, shaking with residual fear but relieved to see the daylight breaking through the window to send all my ghosts back into the retreating night.

I laughed at her again, I shook *my* head at *her* and then took a step back...

"*Never shake thy gory locks at me...*" said I, quoting another dimly remembered line from a play[19], wagging a finger at her.

Stepping back again I turned to walk away and at that moment Likho raised her head and leant back, looking up at the towering wall behind her. High above, in every niche, on buttresses, parapets and finials, every grotesque came to life. Row after row of them... winged devils, griffins, harpies, basilisks or whatever they were all began moving. Some leaned out, stretching their long necks to

Likho

peer down at us; others unfurled their wings as if readying for flight, whilst those creatures not endowed by their sculptor with the means to fly ran up and down the cathedral wall, starting and stopping like large lizards in pursuit of prey. I watched them for a minute or two and tried to follow individual movements, but as soon as I fixed on one it would stop, and I would lose sight of it.

As I stared up at the menagerie on the cathedral wall something launched itself into the air, circled around and then returned to its roost, high above on a parapet. It might have been a large bird… perhaps that was all they were? Birds and bats, and nothing more sinister? Another creature took to the air but, alas, I could not say if it was a crow or a chimera as it wheeled silently around and returned to a ledge just below the great rose window.

Likho turned her eye back on me and at the same time she raised a hand and wagged a finger, mocking my gesture. I felt odd, something had changed… it had grown colder, the sky seemed to be darkening, and Likho suddenly seemed to be more menacing as she became more animated… more agitated, as if in readiness for action. Staring into the shadows, I could see her lidless eye more clearly, I could make out the pupil surrounded by a deep blood-red iris, and a jaundiced eyeball looked as if it had been pushed from within until it bulged from its socket. With one arm directing the grotesques on the cathedral and the other levelled at me she thrust her head forward, and the black opening I supposed to be her mouth twisted into a wide grin, exposing what looked like an irregular line of long, broken teeth which vibrated and emitted a thin metallic sound, like the approach of a train pulsing along the rails.

Darton

Something obscured the moon for a moment and when it cleared, Likho had jumped forwards and grown in height again so that her face was level with mine and only inches away.

"Time to go..." I think the words and voice were mine, but I was not conscious of speaking. My left leg began to feel warm and when I looked, I saw a wet patch spreading down my trousers and a stream of urine run over my shoe and on to the snow which melted around it. Fear had taken control, and it told me to run... it told me to run as fast as I could, and without any more thought I set off along the path, keeping hard to the left and in the shadow of the church which I hoped might yet help me.

I didn't look back as I went and soon the cathedral was behind me, though its shadow seemed to race on ahead and across the square at the west front as I made for the street which led down to the river. What compelled me to go that way I knew not, and I didn't stop to think about it... my only thought was to flee fast and far from that *thing* which surely must have been at my heels.

As I reached the far side of the great parvis, something swooped overhead. Feeling a rush of air, I looked up to see the black shadows of large birds above, circling like vultures. Maybe they were vultures? I couldn't tell... or they might have been winged grotesques from the cathedral, commanded by Likho to attack? One broke out of the formation, dropped rapidly and flew low as, with wings spread wide, it passed only inches above me before climbing to re-join the others. I moved close into the buildings for protection but that meant slowing down to avoid slipping on the ice. Another swooped down but it couldn't get near enough to do me harm without the risk of a collision with the wall. Frustrated, it flew off again, but others followed in its path as one after another came at me. I felt safe though, because they could only get at me if they landed, and I was sure to be faster on the ground than they. Still, not daring to look back I went on, at last breaking into a run as I neared the bottom of the street, and I was in sight of the river and the old town bridge when Likho leapt upon me...

A hand grabbed my left arm and closed tightly around it just above the elbow, and the bony fingers dug deep into the flesh causing such pain that I screamed aloud. I tried to free myself but couldn't get hold of the thing that held me... I could feel it but couldn't see it or seem able to touch it, and as I struggled to throw her off, I felt Likho's other arm around me...

Sharp fingernails sank deep into my chest and pierced my lungs as her grip tightened like a python... with every breath I exhaled it grew tighter, crushing my ribs and sending waves of pain pulsating through my weakening body. I don't know how I managed to keep going but, somehow, I did, and all the time trying escape the suffocating shadow which clung to me...

I couldn't free myself though, and the harder I tried, the faster she held.

As I reached the bottom of the street, I was suffering indescribable agony and though I wanted to stop running, those flying grotesques had started swooping down again as I ran on to the embankment and across the empty frozen road to the pavement. Driven mad by pain and fear I dashed one way then the other, turned again and raced towards the bridge, desperately trying to shake Likho off whilst she held harder to me. Reaching the bridge, I started across it but a fierce gale was blowing down the river and I struggled to stay upright. I was in a desperate panic, and terrified as I wrestled with the wind, with the thing on my back, and fought against agony and exhaustion. Determined as I was not to give up, I could go no further. I had nothing left in me except fear, and not even enough of that to keep me going.

The river flowed below and the sound of the icy water swirling around the piers of the bridge was the only thing I could hear until a voice in my head said *drown her*. It repeated the words over and over... *drown her drown her drown her drown her... drown Likho, drown her... you can be free if you drown her...* and so, as one last effort to throw her off failed and with nothing else to be done I leapt over the parapet into the freezing black waters...

As I fell, I thought I heard a scream, but there was no time to think about it before I hit the water and was momentarily stunned by the shock. I couldn't feel Likho and so looked around, hoping to catch sight of her flailing about in the river before being dragged under by the current but I could see her nowhere... nowhere... until I looked up. There she was, her shadowy figure standing on the bridge parapet and hugging one of the statues, watching me with her one eye whilst a smile stretched her face wide...

Hardly able to breathe and with my limbs paralyzed by the cold, I sank deeper, dragged down by the weight of my coat. As I went, swept away from the bridge, I started to laugh, drawing the water which would drown me into my lungs. They had done it, you see, they had beaten me... the old man and Likho, they had beaten me. I laughed as I drowned, and as I went, I saw two children, a boy and a younger girl carried up on a stronger current. They were laughing too, they were happy, laughing and waving at me, waving me off on my way, and then they were gone, carried towards the surface and the moonlight which filtered

Likho

through the water whilst I was pulled down, further down until I was in darkness as the light above faded from sight, and all sensations and fear faded with it until I could feel nothing, hear or see nothing, and my final thought before I could think nothing more, as I lost consciousness, was one of absolutely nothing...

Likho

18. 'A Sadder and a Wiser Man, He Rose the Morrow Morn'[20]

(An unspecified day).
I don't know how I got here. At first, I thought I was back in the asylum... but, slowly, I became aware that I was in my apartment once more, sitting by the fire; it had not been lit, though the room was freezing cold, and I was shivering uncontrollably. My clothes were soaking wet, and water was dripping from me on to the floor where it was forming a pool around the chair.

It's possible that I'd been asleep, but then I had no memory of waking up... I had no memory of anything. Had I been ill? I didn't know what day it was, or the hour of the day, or even if it *was* day.

The outer door opened and a moment later the concierge's wife came into the sitting room. She didn't speak but went to the window and opened the heavy curtain. I was momentarily dazzled by the bright sunlight and by the time my eyes adjusted to it I saw that she was opening the outer casement, although it was the middle of winter.

That done, she began to sweep out the fireplace, and though only inches from my feet, still she didn't speak. She must have seen me but went about her task as if I were not there and didn't even seem to have noticed the spreading pool of water in which she was kneeling. The outer door opened again, and the sound caused both of us to look around. It was her husband, and I was somewhat surprised to see him because I thought he was dead, and apart from that I'd never seen him anywhere but the lobby with his mop and bucket.

"What are they saying? Any news?" He stopped by the open window, looked out of it for a moment and then turned back to his wife.

"Not much... went off the old bridge into the river, just like you said" the woman replied, shaking her head. "And you? Have you heard anything else? Has anyone found him?"

"Not yet, but no one could survive the water at this time of the year. He'd freeze to death before he drowned... a man couldn't last more than a minute or two... he's dead, he must be." The man shook his head slowly and then added "What about the other one?"

"The other... oh, yes, he's gone at last, thank God." The woman stood up as she spoke. "I don't know whether I should be pleased or not..."

"Well," the concierge looked thoughtful for a moment, "now that they *have* gone, there's no more to do here."

I watched him all the time he stood there in the hope that he might acknowledge me, but he didn't; he seemed to be aware only of his wife. I did notice an odd thing though... his clothes were wet, dripping wet, and the drips were collecting in a pool about his feet...

"Come on, they're waiting for us..." With that he left the room, and his wife followed.

"You'd think they'd have found a body by now though..." she said as she went, wiping the grey breeze from her hands on to her apron as her voice faded into the distance. "He ought to have washed up somewhe..."

Cold silence moved in slowly to fill the void left by those people, and no other sound came from anywhere to disturb it, not even from outside. I wanted to get up and go after them, but I couldn't move. My legs and arms were so cold that they were paralysed. Why didn't that woman make up the fire? I screwed my eyes tightly shut and tried to think but no thoughts came, none except a few fragments of dreams which I couldn't quite see, even though I concentrated hard. There was only snow... snow and shadows... white and black, and I was moving through it somewhere. There were large black birds, I was running, and they were chasing me... then I was at the river, on the bridge... the water was fast and freezing... and then...then it ended, all fading into blackness.

A thought came to me, a horrible thought which made me feel as if I were falling through space... it was *I* about whom those people were talking. What did he say? '*No one could survive the water... he's dead, he must be...*' Did I go into the river? And if I *were* in the river, then what...? I didn't finish the question because I didn't want to think of the answer.

A familiar stench began to fill the room. I opened my eyes. All was just as it had been when I closed them, except... except the pool of water on the floor had spread a little further and I could see my reflection in it. I could see myself sitting in the chair, and behind me were dark shadows... and in the shadows was the form of an old woman with a white face... a bony white face, and it looked as if she had only one eye...

Likho

Notes

[1] Shakespeare, *Hamlet*
[2] Edgar Allan Poe, *The Raven*
[3] John, Ch11, v25-6
[4] Shakespeare, *Henry V*
[5] This is also the title of the first chapter of RL Stevenson's *The Strange Case of Dr Jekyll and Mr Hyde* - "Did you ever remark that door? It is connected in my mind with a very odd story".
[6] *The Stone Guest* by Pushkin, after Byron's poem *Don Juan;* also, an opera by Dargomyzhsky.
[7] A quote from Mozart's opera *Don Giovanni*.
[8] As 6 above.
[9] Another reference to Mozart's *Don Giovanni*.
[10] Der Mond (German) – the moon.
[11] Shakespeare, *Hamlet*.
[12] A painting by Arnold Böcklin (1827–1901); also, a symphonic poem by Rachmaninov.
[13] Edgar Allan Poe, *The Bells*.
[14] He is thinking of *Les Bergers d'Arcadie* by Poussin, Musée du Louvre, Paris.
[15] Reference to another work by Poussin, *Dance to the Music of Time*, The Wallace Collection, London.
[16] Coleridge, *The Rime of the Ancient Mariner* - "Like one that on a lonesome road…"
[17] Milton, *Paradise Lost*.
[18] *Likho* is a malevolent entity in Slavic folklore; often appearing in the form of an aged female, occasionally with only a single eye, it is an all-knowing bringer of misfortune.
[19] Shakespeare, *Macbeth*.
[20] Coleridge, *The Rime of the Ancient Mariner* - this is the last line of the poem.

Milton Keynes UK
Ingram Content Group UK Ltd.
UKHW020905201024
2272UKWH00059B/613

9 798321 399125